TELL THE WIND AND FIRE

TELL THE WIND AND FIRE

SARAH REES BRENNAN

CLARION BOOKS

Houghton Mifflin Harcourt

Boston New York

Clarion Books
3 Park Avenue
New York, New York 10016

Clarion Books is an imprint of Houghton Mifflin Harcourt Publishing Company.

www.hmhco.com

The text was set in Bembo.
Library of Congress Cataloging-in-Publication Data
Names: Brennan, Sarah Rees, author.
Title: Tell the wind and fire / Sarah Rees Brennan.
Description: Boston ; New York : Clarion Books, Houghton Mifflin Harcourt, [2016]
| Summary: In this near-future retelling of the Dickens classic A Tale of Two Cities, a
deadly revolution breaks out in a New York City divided by light and dark magic.

Identifiers: LCCN 2015024993 | ISBN 9780544318175 (hardback)

Subjects: | CYAC: Magic—Fiction. | Revolutions—Fiction. | Love—Fiction.
Fantasy. | New York (N.Y.)—Fiction. | BISAC: JUVENILE FICTION / Fantasy &
Magic. | JUVENILE FICTION / Social Issues / Prejudice & Racism. | JUVENILE
FICTION / Girls & Women. | JUVENILE FICTION / Love & Romance.
JUVENILE FICTION / Classics.

Classification: LCC PZ7.B751645 Tel 2016 | DDC [Fic]—dc23

LC record available at http://lccn.loc.gov/2015024993

Manufactured in the United States of America
DOC 10 9 8 7 6 5 4 3 2 1
4500580565

This work is
most respectfully dedicated to
C.D.

"Tell Wind and Fire where to stop . . . but don't tell me."
—Charles Dickens, *A Tale of Two Cities*

CHAPTER ONE

I T WAS THE BEST OF TIMES UNTIL IT WAS THE WORST of times.

We had never been allowed to go away for the weekend alone together before. So our holiday at Martha's Vineyard was a rare and special treat, sweet as only things that come seldom and do not last can be.

Those two days were long and sunshiny and warm. When I think about them now, I remember the pale amber of the sky at sunset, like light shining through honey. I remember the last time I was purely and uncomplicatedly happy, as I used to be when I was a child and my mother was alive.

Happiness is self-sabotage, a mean trick that your own mind plays on you. It makes you careless, makes you lose your grip, and once you lose your grip, you lose everything. You certainly aren't happy anymore.

I was very stupid. It was because I was happy that I made my first mistake.

In the weeks that followed, I made more.

Ethan and I lingered in the sun-drenched orchards too

long and missed the train we were supposed to catch, a direct train back home with plush seats and clear walls that Light magic pulsed through until the walls themselves looked like they were made of diamond. Staying an extra night was out of the question: Dad would have panicked, and it would have been all my fault. I was responsible for him. Taking care of him was my job and my penance.

We had to catch the last train home to Light New York. It was one of the commuter trains that wound through the sky on rails that shone like glittering threads, stopping at tiny stations on the way. This kind of train even stopped in the Dark cities. Ethan and I bought the tickets and stood on the platform, reassuring each other in voices that did not sound terribly assured.

"It might be fun," said Ethan.

I told myself he didn't know any better. Rich people think like that about slumming it, putting on other people's lives like a disguise at a party. It is fun only because they can cast off the mask at any time.

"Why would it be fun?" I asked.

Nevertheless, I felt my shoulders relax as the train came into view. The train was an older model, but magic made it a shining rope of Light in the night sky, like a crystal necklace suspended between the stars.

It was just a train like any other train. The buried had their own compartment and would not be allowed into ours.

We had reserved a private train car. Nobody, from the Dark or Light city, would have the chance to recognize me.

I made my next mistake. I promised myself everything was going to be all right.

Once you lose something, it tends to stay gone. This is especially true with chances.

The train streamed, sparkling, up to the platform. I saw a glimpse of the car carrying the buried ones with its black-screened windows, and then Ethan and I boarded the train. Moments later, we were in our own tiny room, tangled together on a bunk. The moonlight flooded into and ebbed away from our small window, tide-like, with the movement of the train.

We would be traveling all night.

I don't always sleep through the night. I tear myself out of sleep, heart pounding, sure something terrible is happening. I have trouble feeling secure. Except with Ethan.

I only sleep well when I sleep beside Ethan. I fell asleep in the flickering light, warm in his arms, warm as kissing and skin had made the tiny space between us. The train was rocking, gentle as a boat on a calm sea, and he was stroking my hair.

"I love you," he murmured to me, and I knew he would keep saying it even after I was asleep.

In the two years since my father and I had escaped Dark New York, I'd woken a hundred times to night terrors that vanished as soon as I opened my eyes. It was bitter irony that I didn't wake when the real danger was coming.

I didn't wake until they ripped Ethan out of my arms, and then I sat up in the bunk with my heart pounding and my eyes full of moonbeams to find the nightmare was real. Once the dazzle cleared from my vision, I saw six armed guards dragging my boyfriend out of our compartment and onto a platform. He was fighting, but they had already bound his hands with Light, a shimmering coil of magic around his wrists that he could not escape. They pressed him, struggling, onto his knees on the shadowed-dark stone, and in the cool moonlight I saw the flash of a blade.

I threw myself out of bed and hurled myself out onto the platform. In two bounds, I was in front of Ethan, grabbing the sword, my feet on cold stone and my hands full of cold steel.

All guards carry Light swords, blades tempered with Light magic, to prevent Dark magicians from messing with their minds, and the swords are precise and deadly, unstoppable, whether you are a Dark magician or someone born with no magic at all.

Most Light magicians are not taught to defend against guards' swords. They are meant to be used for our protection, used against our enemies. No normal Light magician would be trained to fight their own guards.

But I was.

Pain burned a line into each palm, but I hung on. My rings pressed against the Light-gleaming blade and blazed. My blood stained the blade, blotting out some of the light, but the guard gasped and found he could not move his weapon.

"Don't you dare touch him," I said. "I'm Lucie Manette, do you hear me? He's Ethan Stryker and I'm Lucie Manette. If you hurt him, you will pay for it in blood."

I knew it was a mistake as soon as I spoke. The guard's face showed not submission but angry confusion: he obviously recognized the names, but it was as if I'd said that we were the hero and the cute talking animal from a fairy tale. It didn't match up with any of his ideas, so it didn't convince him, and it wouldn't stop him.

It had been two years since anyone had doubted my word. It had been two years since I had dealt with anybody who wanted to hurt someone I loved, and I had forgotten how to bear it.

"He's a traitor," the guard said. "We have a warrant and a witness who swears he saw him passing vital security information to a fugitive member of the *sans-merci*. The fugitive was apprehended and killed, and the plans were found on her. The witness described this man with absolute accuracy. There is no possibility of error."

One of the guards wearing Light rings gestured, and Ethan's face was reproduced in light against the night sky, as if an artistic comet had traced his profile onto the darkness. His face shone for a moment, and then the magic faded and the lights went out.

"You know the penalty for treason. Move aside."

I understood now how the guard had felt, hearing words but not being able to make sense of them. I knew what happened to anyone accused of associating with the *sans-merci,* and I could not connect any of this to Ethan.

The *sans-merci* was the name the band of revolutionaries in the Dark city had given themselves. They had killed Light guards, risen up in fury, and even saved condemned criminals from the sword. The Light Guard had been given free rein by the Light Council when it came to the revolutionaries, and nobody could stand against the council.

Anyone suspected of being in league with the *sans-merci,* the Light Guard would not spare.

I did not know how to get through to them. There were not many Light guards in the actual Light cities. Guards were posted mainly in the Dark cities, to control the Dark magicians, and the rest patrolled the country to search for Dark magicians and take them to the Dark cities, where they belonged. Out here, these backwater guards did not even know a Stryker when they saw one. The guards were not used to answering to the Strykers or anyone else on the Light Council. "The council" was just a phrase that gave them power. These guards were used to being the ultimate authority.

I knew the penalty for treason. It was death: instant death,

death by the blade, death without a chance for mercy or escape.

I did not know how death could suddenly be so close to Ethan. I could not even associate him with the word. He had always been secure and protected, his whole charmed life. I had envied him and resented him and taken comfort in the fact that there was one person I loved who would be safe forever.

I didn't even dare look back at Ethan, at his shoulders bowed under cruel pressure or his hanging, vulnerable head. I kept my eyes locked with the guard's: the only thing stopping him from carrying out his orders was the complication of a barely dressed girl crazy enough to catch a sword in her hands.

The only thing standing between Ethan and death was me.

"I said, he's a Stryker," I insisted, making sure my voice rang out so everybody could hear. "He's Mark Stryker's nephew, Charles Stryker's son. You can't just execute him. The Strykers will bring a world of trouble down onto your head."

"If he's a Stryker"—I could hear that the guard didn't believe me; I didn't know how to *make* him believe me— "then he knows the law."

We all knew the law. I remembered how noble Ethan's Uncle Mark had sounded when he made the proclamation broadcast across the city, announcing new laws had been passed to stop the *sans-merci,* to give the Light guards the power to crush them.

The guards would use that power to kill Ethan, unless I stopped them.

"This is all a misunderstanding," I said forcefully. "Why take this unnecessary risk? Why not transport us both to the city? You can watch us every minute, keep us in restraints. Send word to Charles Stryker, and he will meet us at the station. He will explain everything. He will reward you."

Instantly I saw that I had made another mistake. I had not been this clumsy, once, but I had not been this desperate for two years. I was out of practice, and that meant Ethan was out of luck.

The guard's face — he was an ordinary guy, stubble and tired eyes, a totally normal man just doing his job and burning my life to the ground — closed like a door.

"The guards of the Light don't take bribes," he said, and his voice had the definitive sound of a door closing too. He gave a single brief nod, and I felt hands close around my arms.

"No," I said, desperate. I tried to twist away, out of their hold, even though I knew it was useless: once people begin using force, words will not stop them. "Wait — you have to listen to me! You can't do this!"

The only thing standing between Ethan and death was me, and I was not enough. Two guards dragged me back, kicking and fighting and saying useless things, a victim's chant of despair — *You can't do this,* when we all knew they could, *Stop,* when we all knew they wouldn't, and *Please, please, for the Light's sake, please,* when mercy was not an option.

"Lucie!" Ethan's voice cut through the sounds of my futile struggle. There were guards in my way, and I could not see him. "Lucie, I'm so sorry. I love you."

"No!" I screamed at him giving up, at the guards, at the whole uncaring world. "No. Stop!"

There was the long, slow scrape of a train-car door opening. I twisted in the guards' hold at the sound.

It was the car of the buried ones, the citizens of the Dark city, that had opened. Standing framed in the doorway was a doppelganger, his face shrouded by the doppelganger's dark hood, fastened with the enchanted collar.

He was a boy, I guessed, though it was hard to tell with the hood. He was tall, whipcord lean, and strong-looking, but something about him suggested that he was not full grown. He would be no help, I thought with a burst of frustration — he was a doppelganger, a creature made by Dark magic, with a face that wasn't his own and no soul. Nobody would listen to him.

I choked on my own hopelessness. The doppelganger was standing slouched to one side of the door, like a not-very-interested spectator.

"The lady's right," he said, and his voice was a drawl, as if he wasn't entirely sure why he was bothering to speak. "You'd better stop."

"Back inside, doppelganger," the guard with the sword, the leader, snapped. There was none of the hesitation there had been with me.

The leader nodded again, and one of the guards dropped my arm and advanced.

I saw the guard's walk turn purposeful and predatory as he came toward the doppelganger and uncoiled a whip from his belt.

"Don't!" The sound burst from me, without my permission.

At the same time, from the guard, came the order "He said inside, beast."

I heard the crack and saw the leap of the whip as it woke into light and transcribed a bright circle against the black sky. He struck at the shadow cast by the hood, aiming directly for the hidden face.

The doppelganger wheeled at the last moment, stepped out onto the train platform, and caught the lash on his arm, turning his wrist so the whip wrapped around it. He pulled, changing lightning into a leash, and yanked the stunned guard onto his knees.

Before the guard could scramble up or another guard could intervene, the doppelganger spoke again.

"I heard there was a witness who saw the accused

consorting with a member of the *sans-merci*," he said. "I just have one question."

Silence followed, the guards taken aback by his casual air as they had not been by my screaming.

I stopped straining against the remaining guard's hold and said, forcing my voice to match his, "What is it?"

"This terrible criminal your witness saw . . ."

The doppelganger threw his hood back.

The humming magic light of swords, my rings, and the train itself had transformed the platform into a brilliantly lit stage. The light was bright enough that I could see every detail of his face; it chased along his high cheekbones and the slightly crooked shape of his mouth, lending an icy sparkle to his dark eyes. His brown hair was cut very short, but I knew if it was longer it would curl. I knew the lopsided turn his mouth would take if he smiled. I knew the very line of his throat as it disappeared into the dark folds of his hood and the black edge of his heavy collar. I knew every detail of his beloved face.

Ethan was still on his knees, surrounded by guards. I could not see Ethan, and yet I could.

This was Ethan's face. This was Ethan's doppelganger — his exact physical double.

"How do you know," continued the doppelganger, "that it wasn't me?"

· · · ·

Another silence followed. We had a second chance, in this uncertain moment, to use words and change the world.

I had to get it right this time.

"An eyewitness sighting doesn't count if the person reported has a doppelganger," I said quickly. "Everybody knows that."

"Because it could have been me," the doppelganger agreed. "I mean, maybe it *was* him. Maybe he was out prowling the streets with his low political companions, and I was somewhere warm, having a lot more fun—possibly with this gorgeous thing."

He cast me a brief glance. The brown eyes I was used to seeing soften as they looked at me were flat and expressionless. His look made me feel colder and more exposed than the night wind did. I was deeply and horribly conscious that I was standing on this platform in nothing but a thin shift that hung open so my goose flesh was on display.

Very alluring. But this hideous charade had to be continued.

I tossed my long hair over my shoulder and sent the doppelganger a wink. "Maybe."

He spread his hands, as if to say "What can you do?" He was still slouching, which was fairly impressive when there was nothing in sight to slouch against. "Maybe he is guilty and I'm totally innocent." His mouth curved, as if he was amused by the very idea. "It only seemed fair to point out that you don't have all the information."

"Now you do," I stuck in. "It could have been either one of them, and if you kill the wrong one, it will be murder."

"Killing a beast isn't really murder," muttered the guard who had wielded the whip, spitting at the doppelganger's feet.

"You might not think so," I said, "but you'll be punished just the same."

I tested the grip of the guard still holding me. His fingers twitched, relaxed, and, under the steady pressure I was exerting, released. I walked forward, past the cluster of guards, to the doppelganger. He started when I approached him, oddly, as he had not flinched when the whip came down. I reached out, grabbed his hand, and towed him over to Ethan.

When the guards let me pass, I could almost believe we might get away with this.

"The only thing you can do is take us to the Light city," I said, sounding as certain and casual as I knew how. "All of us."

The guards parted and I could finally, finally see Ethan, my Ethan. They had knocked him onto his hands and knees, his broad shoulders were bare and his wavy, sleep-mussed head was still hanging, but he looked up as I stooped toward him. I gave him my free hand, and when his fingers closed around my shaking, sweat-slicked fingers, I felt steadier, my lost anchor regained, warmth and security a possibility once again.

Ethan got to his feet. A moment later, I had them both safe, keeping myself a step ahead, between them and the guards.

"Remember what I suggested earlier?" I asked. "Put us back in our compartment. Put a guard at the door if you like —I don't care. And call Charles Stryker. Let the Light Council sort out this misunderstanding."

They were off balance enough to do what I wanted, and uncertain enough now to listen to the name Stryker. When the guards ushered me, Ethan, and the doppelganger into the compartment that had been just mine and Ethan's, the leader was already looking worried.

Another guard said, as he shut the door in our faces, "I didn't know any of the Strykers had a doppelganger."

The door closed, and I sagged against it. I watched Ethan and the doppelganger retreat to opposite sides of the compartment.

"Funny thing," I remarked. "Neither did I."

I was furious, but there was something I had to do before questioning either one of them.

"Come here," I said, and advanced on the doppelganger. He took a step back and wound up sitting on the bunk, looking surprised and mildly irritated.

I held up my hands as if in surrender, though it was anything but. I held them so the doppelganger could see the Light magic rings glittering on all my fingers.

"I'm a trained Light medic," I told him. "Now let me see your wrist."

He gave me an unfriendly look, but he let me kneel down and snatch his hand again. I pushed back the worn fabric of his sleeve. The material tried to adhere to the burn, but I pulled it off despite the hiss of pain that slipped through the doppelganger's teeth. I had to loop my fingers around his wrist, over the burn, thumb and middle finger touching. I concentrated, coaxing to life the light hidden in every sparkling stone, letting it form a bright bracelet over his skin and mine. When I let go, I knew the light would wash the burn marks away. I was able to help, because he was not too badly hurt. My mother had been able to save people on the brink of death, but I was not a tenth as brilliant a magician as my mother. I could only do this.

I blinked away the remnants of Light in my vision, like dissolving stars, until all that was left was his intent gaze.

"There," I told him.

"Am I supposed to thank you?"

"No," I said. "I'm supposed to thank you. You saved his life and I love him, so I owe you more than I know how to repay. Thank you . . . what's your name?"

He hesitated. "Carwyn."

"Carwyn," I said, still kneeling, staring up into a familiar face with a strange name on my tongue. "Thank you. Buried how long, Carwyn?"

That was what citizens of the Dark city always asked each other when we met. That was what we called living in the Dark city: being buried.

He hesitated again, but when he spoke there was weight to his response, as if he had come to some decision. "Thirteen years, but I'm out now," said Carwyn. "Buried how long, Lucie?"

So that answered that: he had recognized me.

"Fifteen years," I said. "But that was two years ago. I'm out now."

"They're still talking about you in the Dark city," Carwyn said.

I picked up the dress that was on the floor and pulled it over my head as quickly but with as little fuss as I could manage, lacing up the front. Ethan grabbed a fresh shirt out of his bag.

He came and sat with me on one end of the bed, taking my hand again, and I curled into him, chin tucked against his shoulder and my hand pressed in a fist against his chest. As if I could protect him, as if I could keep his heart beating.

"I didn't know how to tell you, Lucie," said Ethan. "About him."

The train was in motion again. I leaned against Ethan,

but I did not look at him or at the stranger who wore his face. I looked out the window. The train was speeding along the slender bridge that the Light Council had built fifty years ago, toward the Light city of New York. I saw the tall, bright columns standing in clusters, the Chrysler Building with its prismatic triangle of lights at the top, blazing like a beacon, and Stryker Tower, a steel line studded with huge stones shimmering with Light power and crowned with a spike.

We were almost home, my new home full of Light, the home where I had learned how to be happy. I did not jump in front of blades there. I did not see blood or horror: I was not that person, not anymore. All I needed to do was keep my head down and my life could continue the way it was now, the way I had made it. I could be safe.

I remembered how I had felt on the train platform, knowing for the first time that someone could hurt Ethan.

I said, "So tell me now."

CHAPTER TWO

B OTH BOYS WERE SILENT. CARWYN JUST SAT ON the other end of the bed. I knew his eyes were the exact same as Ethan's, but they looked different to me, darker, almost black, with no depth in the color. I thought of the old saying that the eyes are the windows to the soul: no lights shone in Carwyn's windows. He was looking at me, but his gaze was almost challenging, and I did not know why.

Ethan was much easier to read. He looked horrified and guilty.

"You knew he existed," I said to Ethan. "When was he made? Why didn't you ever tell me? I told you . . ."

Everything, I wanted to say, but I hadn't told him everything. He still thought I was brave and good. I had told him more than I had told anyone else in the world though, and he had kept this huge secret from me.

I could have accepted it from anyone else, but I had been so sure that Ethan was open and honest, the one person in the world with no secrets and no shadows. I'd built my new life on that certainty.

"Lucie," said Ethan, "I didn't know how to tell you. I was ashamed. It's a crime to create them—I couldn't turn in my own father. And I was afraid you'd look at me differently, knowing I had one of . . . of them."

When someone young was dying, a Dark magic ritual could save them, but the ritual created an exact double. I had heard the horror stories, heard people say that the ritual gave Death itself a young, sweet face and let it walk among us.

Someone with a doppelganger was not just complicit in a crime. They carried a reminder of mortality on their shoulders, carried the shadows of doppelgangers on their souls. It was said that looking into a doppelganger's face would doom the original soul, that the doppelganger would hunt the original down so it could take their life and their happiness as well as their face. It was kinder to let someone die, people said, than create a doppelganger to save them.

I looked over at Carwyn, who was fiddling with his collar and looking supremely uninterested.

"Oh, don't mind me," said Carwyn. "Continue with your relationship drama. It is fascinating."

I rolled my eyes at him and turned to the boy I loved. "Ethan. Look at me."

He looked at me. I had always thought his eyes were different from anyone else's. I still believed it. Nobody else looked at me like that, light and warmth in their eyes because

I was there. There was gold in his brown eyes. There was light here, in Ethan, for me.

"I'm looking at you," I said. "And nothing's changed. Nothing will ever change, not for me. But I want the truth."

Ethan took a deep breath.

"My mother and I almost died when I was born," he said, and his voice was soft; apologetic, I thought—but, then, his voice was always soft when he spoke of his mother. "They were able to stabilize my mom, but they kept having to restart my heart, and it wasn't working. I was fading fast. My mother said they would have done anything to save me."

She died when Ethan was ten. She had been sick a long time, and being with her as she died had taught Ethan, I think, how to be gentle.

Ethan took my hand in his, fingers running lightly over not my rings but my knuckles, for the strength and comfort of skin on skin.

"So my father called in a Dark magician," he said.

It actually made me think better of Charles Stryker, that he had broken the law to save Ethan, done something that would ruin him if anyone learned of it. It made me think he might have loved his wife.

I thought better of Ethan's father for taking the risk, but it was such a terrible risk. I could not even let myself consider what would happen if this secret got out. I was so scared, I could barely breathe.

"They did the ritual, and I lived. But it created . . . Carwyn," said Ethan. He chanced a look at Carwyn, and I squeezed his hand. Ethan looked at me, appealing to me. "It was when I was a baby. It was years before I met you."

"If it was when you were a baby," I said, "Carwyn would've been a baby too. Nobody would raise a doppelganger baby. How could you collar or control one? And a baby couldn't escape or survive on his own. Your uncle would have twisted his neck and thrown him into the East River. How could he possibly have lived?"

"Quite a picture, isn't it?" Carwyn asked, looking out of the window. "Baby's First Collar. 'Who's an itty-bitty manifestation of ultimate darkness? Is it you? Is it you?'" He glanced over at us. We stared at him. He shrugged. "That was a rhetorical question."

I returned my gaze to Ethan, and he looked back at me.

"You said nobody would raise a doppelganger baby," he said slowly. "But someone did. My mother did. She insisted. She was so sick, and my dad thought that crossing her would kill her. Dad didn't tell my uncle. He sent my mother and . . . and the other child to live in the country. My mother would come up to be with me and my father—but she spent most of the first few years I was alive raising someone else. She didn't trust anyone else with him. She wanted to keep the child alive as long as she could."

Ethan's parents must have known it was only a matter of

time until Carwyn was discovered. All doppelgangers were Dark magicians, and nobody would believe Ethan had an identical twin who, coincidentally, could do Dark magic.

"When we were four, the Dark magician who made Carwyn told my uncle about the doppelganger and tried to blackmail him. Uncle Mark had the Dark magician killed, and he would have killed Carwyn if my mother hadn't told my father she would kill herself, too. My dad and my uncle sent the doppelganger off to the Dark city the same day, and my dad brought my mother back to me. I didn't even know about the doppelganger until my mother told me. She wanted me to know what my father had done. What he was capable of. And she wanted someone else to remember Carwyn." Ethan looked toward Carwyn. He had been carefully avoiding doing so, but now he met his eyes. "You should know that she loved you."

"You should know," Carwyn informed him, "that I don't care."

A doppelganger wouldn't. They didn't feel like other people did. I couldn't blame Carwyn for that, but from the expression on his face, Ethan could.

"She wanted to keep you."

"So what?" said Carwyn. "She didn't keep me. It doesn't matter to me what some dead woman wanted. She wasn't my mother."

"She was mine," Ethan said tightly. "Don't talk about her like that."

"Or what?" Carwyn asked. "Or the Golden Thread in the Dark, that sweet angel of mercy who now has her clothes back on, burns a little Light discipline into me? Oh, go on, sweetheart. It's nothing I haven't had before, and maybe with someone as pretty as you I'd enjoy it."

"Sorry to disappoint," I said. "I'm not going to hurt you. I told you, I owe you. I'll do whatever I can to help you."

"That goes for both of us," Ethan said, after a pause.

Carwyn raised an eyebrow. "I'm touched."

"Why did you do it?" Ethan asked suddenly. "Why save my life?"

Carwyn looked at me. I had to admit, I was curious to know the answer as well. It didn't seem like the kind of thing a doppelganger would do.

"It was a whim. It was that or buy the weird cheese-and-crackers package off the food cart."

I had honestly not expected a doppelganger to be sassy. I had never had a conversation with one before, and in stories they were mostly silent harbingers of death.

Ethan's expression suggested he would have *preferred* a silent harbinger of death.

I leaned forward a little, elbows on my knees, and asked, "What are you doing here?"

"I thought we covered that," Carwyn said. "Mommy and Daddy loved each other very much, so they did a dark ritual . . . ? Any of that ringing a bell?"

"I meant," I said, "where are you going on this train?"

"Same place you are," Carwyn said. "The Light city."

"What are you going to do when you get there?"

"Are you asking me out on a date?" asked Carwyn. "Because your boyfriend's right here. Awkward."

My plan was to help and support him in any way possible. If that meant ignoring ninety percent of everything he said, that was fine with me.

"Do you have a pass to get to the Light city?" I asked. "Do you have a permit to work? How long were you planning to stay?"

"I hadn't decided."

I noticed that the doppelganger did not answer either of my other questions. Ethan and I exchanged a look.

"You were going into the Light city without a pass?" Ethan said. "That's a crime."

"I guess we don't know each other that well yet," Carwyn observed. "It's possibly time to talk about some of my hobbies and interests. One of my hobbies is crime."

"So you're a criminal," said Ethan.

"My hobby is my job," said Carwyn. "My job is my hobby. It's a thing. Also, when we were introduced, you were about to be executed for a, you know, whatsit—oh yeah, a crime.

Are you upset because my thing is being somewhat successful at crime?"

Ethan leaned a little against the compartment wall, trying to ease me back with him. I didn't go, but I glanced at him and saw his eyes were thoughtfully narrowed. Ethan usually thinks the best of people; that doesn't mean he's dumb.

"You are pretty successful at crime," Ethan observed. "That's why you saved me, isn't it? You decided you wanted to go to the Light city, for whatever reason—"

Carwyn shrugged. "Just wanted to have a little fun. Sorry, do you need me to explain the concept of fun?"

Ethan shook his head. "You figured you'd come to the city and blackmail my dad. Then you saw me on the train platform. You saw a golden opportunity."

Carwyn grinned.

The city was getting closer and closer as we got to the end of the line, about to plunge into our last tunnel. I put my hand against the glass and looked out at the city, the buildings that made the gems in my rings briefly catch fire, the line of light that was Stryker Tower, so bright that it seemed like a colossal sword. The sun was coming up, and the dawn was embracing the buildings in swaths of rose and gold.

"I don't care why he did it," I said.

Both of the boys looked at me, Ethan's grip on my hand going a little loose.

"I mean it," I said. "I don't care. What I care about is

the result: what I care about is that we are all safe." I pressed Ethan's hand. "You're alive, and he made it so. I say we give him whatever he wants. Your father created him, so Carwyn is his responsibility. And Carwyn saved your life: your father owes him twice over. You have to take him home with you and make sure that Carwyn has everything he needs."

"I have many needs," Carwyn put in.

"You want me to reward him?" Ethan asked incredulously.

I lost my patience. Maybe it wasn't fair of me. Ethan wasn't used to life-and-death situations. I don't think he believed he would have died out there on that stone platform in the cold night. Not really.

"Yes," I said. "Yes, I want you to reward him for saving your life. I don't think that's unreasonable."

Carwyn, at this point, was smirking. "I like you. Can I put you on my list of demands?"

"And as for you, my little bonbon of darkness," I said, "I want you to shut up."

Ethan was stonily quiet. Carwyn, for a wonder, became almost quiet as well, aside from a murmured "Does anyone have a piece of paper? For, you know, my list?"

I spent the rest of the train ride putting on makeup and brushing my hair. I wasn't dressed for the media, not in a simple blue dress. It had been so long since I'd had to prepare for a performance, and I was not ready. But I could look better than I did now. I found a compact in my bag and stared into the mirror: pink, sticky eye shadow smudged on, hair shimmering gold. I looked tired from the night. I passed my fingertips under my eyes, letting my rings glow gently, and made the shadows disappear.

I snapped the compact shut and saw Carwyn giving me one of his flat looks, mouth curled in what looked a whole lot like contempt.

"You look beautiful," Ethan told me, which I didn't care about, and, "We can do this," which I did.

The train pulled into Penn Station with a creak and a rattle. I stood up from the bed without letting go of Ethan's hand, and I reached for Carwyn's and grabbed hold, pulling him to his feet as well.

"Come on," I said. "Let's get this done."

We went up the elevator into a maelstrom of reporters. One of the guards had told somebody, I thought, or someone had seen what almost happened to Ethan and recognized him. The station was packed.

Carwyn's hood was up—people did not take kindly to a doppelganger brazenly displaying a stolen face—but all it would take was a guard spilling the secret before he could be bribed into silence, or someone making a lucky guess about who the doppelganger next to us was.

Ethan's father was on the Light Council. Ethan's Uncle

Mark led it. There had been a Stryker on the council ever since it was formed.

They were the most powerful family in New York. But there were other powerful families, waiting for their chance to take the Strykers down. People were voted onto the council —nominated from only a small pool of the wealthiest and most influential Light magician families, but voted on. If the Strykers were implicated in a crime like creating a doppelganger, their power would be lost. All the protection they could offer Ethan, and me, would be lost.

We were in dangerous waters, the flashing light of every camera a threat. I was prepared to hold on to them both and push my way through, but I wasn't looking forward to it.

And then Ethan's uncle stepped out of the crowd.

It was the first time in my life I had ever been glad to see Mark Stryker. Not that he had ever been unpleasant to me. On the contrary, he had always been flawlessly, almost ceremoniously, polite. I knew how people acted when they were being recorded. Mark was like that all the time.

He was like that now, but we were in perfect accord. When he put a hand on Ethan's shoulder, loving and concerned for the space of three camera flashes, I sent him a perfectly distressed and grateful smile.

"My dear girl," he said in a loud voice, "I'm so relieved you're both safe."

His security detail swept unobtrusively after him, dark-clad and official-looking without being official enough to answer for anything they did. We were effectively cut off from the crowd of reporters.

"There's been some kind of terrible mix-up," I responded. "I'm so glad you're here to sort it out."

Mark Stryker raised his eyebrows, smile fixed in place like a picture on a wall. I'd never thought he looked like Ethan in more than the superficial way all the Strykers resembled each other: they practically had tall, dark, and photogenic trademarked.

Now that I had met Carwyn, I saw that Ethan looked more like his uncle than I would have dreamed. I saw now how different the same features could seem when they were illuminated by a different spirit. Same hawk-like nose, same high cheekbones, same thin mouth with the potential to be pitiless. Same dark eyes, which could look so flat.

Mark's frightening eyes locked on the sight of my hand linked with Carwyn's.

I knew that it would only call attention to the fact that he was with us, attention we did not need, creating questions we could not answer. But I was afraid of letting him go. I didn't want to lose him.

"A doppelganger," said Mark, with what seemed to be mild surprise and nothing more. The skin on the back of my neck crawled, as if stroked by a hand too cold to be human. "Here illegally?"

Oh God, I thought. He must be, and that meant he could legally be executed if he was caught. And thanks to us, he was well and truly caught.

"You shock me with that implication!" Carwyn said, and showed the inside of his wrist, where the date—September 12—burned with Light magic. A perfectly legal pass, inscribed by a Light magician official.

"But you said—" Ethan began.

"Be fair," Carwyn told him. "I just expressed my enthusiasm for crime in general. I didn't say I was committing a crime right that minute. I was given a pass to come and assist another legal Dark magician with the draining of the city's best and brightest."

"You must be very good," I remarked, almost involuntarily. He was young, and a doppelganger. To be sent to the Light city indicated enormous talent.

"That's what the ladies all tell me," Carwyn said.

Mark looked disgusted. "Who else saw . . . the creature?"

I knew what Mark meant: Who had seen his face? Carwyn had had his back to the train. I was certain the passengers had not seen him.

"Just these guards," I said honestly. I heard my voice shake, and Mark nodded as if confirming that it should. We both knew that I was signing the guards' death warrant.

But they had tried to kill Ethan. It was Ethan or them.

"Thank you," Mark told me. "I am certain a private

conference with these fine officers will clear everything up."

Some of his men, trained both to be subtle and to kill, depending on which was required, split from the protective unit around us and surrounded the Light guards from the train. I saw one of the guards' faces, pale in the stark light of the train station, as scared as I had been, and then they were lost in the crowd.

"In the meantime, I am afraid that you were recognized on the train, and it has caused some upheaval among our civic-minded Light citizens," Mark said. "There were rumors that the Golden Thread in the Dark had been taken off the train by the *sans-merci*. If you would be so kind as to spare some time to put the public's mind at rest . . ."

He smiled at me. I smiled back at him.

"Of course."

I grabbed Ethan's elbow. "Don't let Carwyn out of your sight!" I hissed.

Letting Carwyn disappear in the same way my mother had, the same way those guards would, was no way to repay him.

I left them both and went to Mark's side.

"Ladies and gentlemen!" called out Mark Stryker. "The Golden Thread in the Dark." Applause crackled, brief and abrupt as the clash of swords meeting. "As you can see, she is quite safe, and we intend to keep her so."

He took my hand and turned me to the crowd, a gesture

that read as protection unless you could feel his owner-tight grip. I blinked and added another sheen of distress to my face —wet eyes and parted lips.

"Thank you all so much for your concern for me," I called. I did not know what the story about the *sans-merci* was, and did not dare risk contradicting whatever people were saying. I kept it vague. "I was scared for a while back in the train, but I had Ethan with me"—people laughed a little, indulgent about young love—"and now I'm back with Mr. Stryker, so I know I'm safe."

I smiled up at Mark. He smiled down at me. We had perfected our smiles by then. This was easy.

Mark cleared his throat. "When the French scientist Louis de Breteuil discovered Light, he lit the world, changing and illuminating everything. Light replaced old and crude technologies with power that transformed a world. Nobody lives who remembers the world as it was, as a savage and lawless place where men used their limited resources to kill each other for those same resources. Light has saved us and spared us from such knowledge. Yet ever since Light has existed, it has had a shadow: the Dark, who use our blood in their spells, who benefit from our power and yet who think to rise up against us. The Dark are ungrateful and vicious, and they have forgotten the natural order. But I promise you, Light citizens, they have risen up in the past and failed. The Dark is always defeated. The Light cannot be quenched. Ever since the Garden, the serpent has existed. Ever since knowledge came into this world, evil came twined around it, and time and again evil has always been crushed. No matter what new measures we must introduce, our Light Council will remain dedicated to the protection of this city from dangerous insurgents. We will keep you safe."

The cadence of Mark's voice had changed from his earlier announcements, becoming low and persuasive. This was a very familiar speech, the essentials of which were so well known to me that they seemed like a prayer or a children's story. Since I knew it by heart, it seemed true.

Light magic commands all things on this earth. So long as the sun burns in the sky, we rule the world.

All we need is the sun . . . and to be drained. The use of Light builds up in our blood, begins to be painful. It feels like burning in our veins, in the same way muscles burn when overstrained, but it does not stop there. If a Light magician is not drained, the pain gets worse. Eventually the magician will burn away from the inside out, bones turning to ash, and blood to flame.

Long ago, people used to drain patients' blood with leeches to restore them to health, a barbaric ancient practice that did not work at all. Now the ancient lie has become truth. A practicing Light magician has to have their blood drained by a Dark magician. The more often we use magic, the more often we have to be drained. If we do not get drained regularly, we die.

They use our blood for power. But we need them in order to live.

That is why Dark magicians and all those whose families have produced Dark magicians live in Dark cities, rounded up and kept close to centers of Light, confined and controlled. We cannot afford to be without them.

We need them. That is the truth everybody knows and nobody speaks. That's why we resent them and fear them and tell stories describing how they are evil, how they deserve all they get and we deserve all that we have.

People always hate those they rely on.

I should know. As Mark spoke, I held his hand fast, leaned against him, smiled for the cameras in the circle of his protection, and I could not imagine hating anyone more.

"My nephew and his dear friend Lucie Manette have just been through a terrifying ordeal. They are in no condition to speak in public as yet. We will of course be releasing a statement in the very near future. We thank you for your consideration at this trying time," Mark said as the bodies pressed in and the lights flashed, hot and close and relentless.

Nobody challenged Mark Stryker. Nobody ever did.

We didn't have to speak. We were moving out under the glass dome, almost through to the escalators of Thirty-Fourth

Street, when we caught up with the others. Ethan had tight hold of Carwyn's elbow; I ran up and caught Carwyn's free hand, linking my fingers with his. I saw Mark strip off one glove, the supple leather crumpled in his fist, and touch Ethan's shoulder with a heavy ringed hand.

Then I saw Penelope, my father's best friend. She was running down the passage lined with small stores, past a bakery with a bright yellow sign. Her coat was flapping open and her rings were blazing, and I knew why she had come. I knew who she was there about.

"We had the television on," she said breathlessly, "and the news started talking about you and Ethan. There wasn't any warning, no way to prepare him, and he's having one of his spells again."

The one thing that could have torn me away from Ethan right then: my father.

"I have to go to him," I said. "I have to show him that I'm all right."

Mark Stryker did not look devastated to be parted from me. "Naturally you do. I'll send you and Dr. Pross in one of our cars."

"Thank you." I didn't spare him much of a smile. We were almost clear of the cameras.

I waited until we were out on the streets, people pushing impatiently past us. The purring and screeching of cars, the tap of men's business shoes, and the click of women's business heels formed an orchestra of city sounds that would screen what I had to say.

"Ethan, a word," I said, and dropped Carwyn's hand.

It felt like a betrayal, like letting him down, when he hadn't let Ethan down. I looked away from him, dark-hooded and silent on that bright busy street. I did not look at Mark. I looked to Ethan.

I dragged him a little away from Mark, Penelope, and the doppelganger.

"Go to your dad," Ethan said. "I'll sort everything out with Mark. Don't worry about me."

"I'm not worried," I said. "Because I know I can count on you to do the right thing and take care of Carwyn."

Ethan's eyebrows rose. "I'm pretty sure Carwyn can take care of himself."

"I'm pretty sure he can't," I said. "Because he's a doppelganger in the Light city, and that means he is in danger. He helped you when you were in danger. I have to go to my father, but you have to promise me that you will help him."

Ethan bit his lip. I looked back at Mark Stryker and saw how far he was standing from Carwyn. People on the street, those determinedly indifferent city people, were looking at Carwyn's hooded head.

I wanted to say, *I know what it's like to be buried, to be scheming in the Dark and scared of the Light. I know that saving someone else comes at a price.* But I didn't want

Ethan to think of the similarities between the doppelganger and me.

"Ethan," I said instead. "Please."

Ethan looked at me, his eyes amber in the city lights. "Lucie," he said, "I'll do my best. I promise. For you."

Penelope and her husband, Jarvis, lived in a vast brick building in midtown, not too far away from the theater district. Their apartment was a narrow snake of a living place, scarcely more than one large room divided into slivers. So, basically, it was a nice modern New York apartment and would have been nicer if they had not given their second bedroom to two people who had stumbled in from the Dark and stayed.

Dad and I had a curtain separating our bedroom into two rooms. Penelope and Jarvis had a Japanese screen between their bed and little Marie's.

I knew we should find a way to move out, but I didn't know how to voluntarily give up the comfort of having other people around, the small, simple happiness of coming home to find dinner waiting or the television on. Penelope and Jarvis had never mentioned wanting their home back, never even hinted; they always acted as if they wanted us to stay forever.

"I'm sorry that I had to drag you away," Penelope said as the car sped through the glittering streets.

"It's no problem," I said, and forced myself to smile. "Well, it's my problem. I can deal with it."

"You don't have to deal with it alone," Penelope told me. "Are you all right?"

"Never better," I said, and kept my hand against the Light panel in the car door, the square of magic that would brighten when the car stopped, waiting for it to release.

I owed Penelope and Jarvis better than this. When the car pulled up outside the building, I saw the lights blazing in every window in their apartment on the sixth floor. I pressed the panel before it had woken into full light, hurled myself out of the car before it had quite stopped, then ran up the stairs and through the door faster than Penelope could follow me. This was my responsibility and not hers.

Dad was sitting on the sofa, rocking back and forth. Light was cupped in his palms, building and building. The glitter of his rings had a sparking, restless quality, like electric wires gone wrong.

"Dad, I'm here. I'm so sorry I left you, but I'm all right. I'm absolutely all right."

Dad stared at me, his eyes vacant but for the glitter of magic.

"Dad," I said pleadingly.

Dad stared a little longer, then reached out and touched my hair, the shining golden length of it.

"It's like her hair," he said. "What is your name, sweetheart?"

"Lucie, Dad. It's Lucie."

"Oh," Dad said, slowly. He lifted a hand to my face, and the rings on that hand burned brighter, brighter, so he could see me. My eyes stung, but I wouldn't close them: I squinted and tried to keep my focus on him, past the harsh light and shimmering tears. Gold obscured my vision, the glitter of rings and the shine of magic on the walls, everything gold but my father's hair. That had gone silver back when they put him in the cage.

"You remember me, Dad."

"It was so very long ago," Dad muttered, and his other hand clutched my hair, like a child clutching a teddy bear. "Lucie! Lucie, you have to help me find her. I have to go to her and help her . . . heal her. She needs to be healed. She went to heal someone. I need to heal someone."

He'd had fits like this before, even while he was in his cage. I'd probably given him the idea. He wasn't a fraud like me. He was really good, and he really tried. He tried to heal people as if he were still a medic. He'd put his hand out through the bars of his cage to heal people; he'd run up and down the train healing people when we were making our way to the Light city. He'd collapsed in public over and over in the first few months, but he hadn't been like this for a year.

I'd thought he was better now.

It was my fault. I'd scared him, I'd reduced him to this state where he was fumbling after memories of a time when he'd been happy, when he'd thought he could help people and find my mother. We'd been idiots, once, fools in the dark together.

"She's dead, Dad," I said, and tried to keep my voice level. I helped him up from the sofa and kept his steps steady as we went into our room. I led him to his bed and made him lie down. His eyes closed as soon as his head touched the pillow, his body curled up in a trembling comma shape on the bed. I pulled the sheets over him and murmured, "She's dead, but we're alive. Don't you want to live?"

"It's been so long," Dad murmured back. "I don't know."

Good people are always ready to die for a good reason. It's only people like me who say, *Yes, I want to live. Yes, at any cost.* I had said yes for both of us, two years ago.

Dad's eyes opened, then fluttered shut, then repeated the gesture a few times before he settled. His eyelids looked as thin and fragile as yellowed old pages in a book whose story would soon be over. He muttered in his sleep, like an unhappy child, and I hung over him, knowing that his sleep might be disturbed.

I did not let myself cry for my father who was alive, or my mother who was dead. I had things to do besides cry: I had debts to pay.

I waited until I was sure my father was slumbering peacefully, then left to visit the Strykers.

CHAPTER THREE

I DIDN'T BEGIN THIS STORY RIGHT. PENELOPE TOLD ME that I should explain everything, because soon the world might be very different.

I don't see how I can explain the whole world, though. Am I meant to go back in the story to when there was one united New York, before any of the cities were divided in two? That happened before my father's father was born. It happened after the magic came.

When the power of Light and Dark was discovered, the world was transformed. There was no going back: the shine and shadow of magic swallowed the old world up.

That was when the world was torn between those who practice Light magic, born of sun and moon and stones, and those who practice Dark magic, which comes from life instead of light. Dark magic uses blood, and the dead.

No wonder the people who could do no magic were scared of Dark magicians, and not of Light. Besides, there were always more of the Light magicians—ten times more.

We were always stronger, and we were told that meant we were better.

The long-ago people who would become the first council of Light decided that those who practiced Dark magic were too dangerous to be allowed to live with the rest of us, even though we needed them close by.

The Light magicians, those among us who were first and best at accessing the new power, built walls around portions of our city. The Dark ones are kept in there, and with them all those who have ever had Dark magicians in their families, who might have Dark children.

They are not trapped. That's what they say, out in the Light cities.

I learned what they say in the Light cities when I was fifteen, but I was born in the Dark city of New York. Those of us who were born Dark or come to live in the Dark ask each other, "Buried how long?"

The Light cities are right, I guess. Buried is different from trapped. The trapped believe they can get out.

My dad was born in Light New York. He graduated from Columbia at the top of his class as a Light medic.

Dad was—and still is, sometimes, when he remembers —a dreamer. He believed in leading the whole Dark city into the light, in providing Light medical care for those within the Dark city, in doppelganger rights, and the acceptance and reintegration of the Dark back into the Light.

After he graduated, he applied for and was granted a pass into the Dark city, where he immediately got a job at Maimonides, the only big hospital we had.

That was where he met my mom. She was born in the Dark, like me, but she was a Light magician.

Unlike me, she never got her rings. She always had to hide that she was a Light magician, because her father was a Dark one. He had been discovered doing Dark magic in the Light city, and his life had only been spared because my grandmother stood between him and the crowd who would have killed him for being what he was. His whole family had been exiled to the Dark city, and my mother had been born there.

Families who produce both Dark magicians and Light magicians are very rare. We pretend it never happens; we all know that when it does happen and the council hears about it, the whole family disappears. We keep the Light and the Dark separated by walls, by beliefs, by blood. We pretend it is not true that sometimes people find each other through anything.

You can't get Light medic training in a Dark city, but my mother worked in the hospital anyway, did what Light magic she could do undetected. It's forbidden to do Light magic unless you're certified, unless you have the rings. I'll never have as much power as my mother, but I can do things she was never allowed to do. She could work miracles, but with rings she could have saved thousands of lives.

Light magic works better than Dark for healing, unless the situation is desperate, the patient on the very threshold of death. Then, only the Dark can fight back the last darkness.

My dad found out my mom was doing Light magic, but he didn't turn her or her family in. He taught her how to do more. He helped her do better. She was better than he was, he always said. She never wore the magic rings, but my father bought a necklace for her on the black market: one beautiful, fire-hearted diamond hanging from a silver chain. She never wore it outside the house, but sometimes at night we would close all the shutters, draw every curtain, and she would do magic that made that diamond blaze.

Mom and Dad considered themselves married, though Light magicians cannot legally marry people from Dark magician families. Mom pretended she lived next door with her parents and her sister and her sister's husband, not with us. On paper, I was the child of my father and a dead patient who'd had no Light or Dark magic in her veins. Mom and Dad would talk sometimes about getting fake papers for Mom, going to the Light city and getting her rings. Dad would get cards from his best friend from med school, Penelope, and she would always write "Hope to see you in the next year!" on them.

I never really believed we would leave. It would have meant leaving our whole family. I thought I would be buried all my life. I was used to Light magic being something my parents taught me behind blackout curtains, our family secret. I was a Light citizen from the day I was born, because any children of Dad's were qualified to be Light citizens. When he saw I was a Light magician too, he applied for certification for me and got me my rings, but I could stay because he was the chief surgeon in the hospital by then, and as far as the law was concerned he was my sole guardian. By the time I was fifteen, I had still never passed through the gates of the Dark city.

Light guards were posted at the gates, checking paperwork and making sure no unlicensed Dark citizens passed into the Light. The Dark city was ruled mainly by the Light guards, acting on behalf of the Light Council. Working directly under the Light guards were the most powerful Dark magicians. The magicians who made themselves useful to the Light were rewarded with blood, and blood to Dark magicians meant power. Everyone else in the dark, everyone weak, everyone powerless, walked in fear.

As a girl born buried, I knew never, ever to make eye contact with the Light guards, to walk the other way with my head bowed at the sight of anyone carrying a whip and wearing the snow-white uniform with its glittering insignia. We all knew stories, of friends of friends, of relatives, who had suffered at the hands of the guards and their interpretation of the Light laws.

Nothing bad had ever happened to me as a child. I was much loved, cautioned but always fiercely protected. The worst sights were kept from my eyes. Sometimes my parents seemed busy all the time, but I always had my Aunt Leila to look after me. She would take me with her on walks around the Dark city, under a shining clock enhanced by the guards' Light magic, distributing pamphlets condemning the laws of the Light Council under the guards' very noses. She was tall and stern and never afraid of anything, and I wanted to be just like her.

I think I would always, no matter what my life was, have been a scared child. I remember long nights in my child-hood, lying awake and feeling as if a heavy weight was press-ing on my chest, thinking about all the small things I had done wrong and all that I feared for the future. But I never feared what actually came to pass. My nightmares were not big enough to encompass all that. My parents told me that my imagination was too good, but it turned out that even my rac-ing, scared imagination was not good enough.

The Light can destroy the Dark. They say that in both cit-ies, but it sounds different in the Dark.

It was just the way life was. I listened to my mother and father and my aunt and my uncle discussing injustice, knew that Aunt Leila attended rallies about the Light Council's laws, but I did not think those laws would have any further effect on my life than they had already. I obeyed all the rules, and I thought that would keep me safe.

Until they took my mother away.

She used to go into the bad part of town and heal the people there who needed help and yet would not go to a hospital: people on dust, vagrants, criminals. Aunt Leila always said she was a fool for going, that she would get caught using Light magic or be suspected of different criminal activity. My father always begged her to be careful, and she always said she would be, and she was always back before morning.

Until one day when she was not. She never came back. We never saw her again.

My father hoped the Light Guard had merely taken her into custody. He went to get her back, and when he asked where she was, the Light guards said she had broken the council's laws and that he would not see her again. My father spat in a guard's face and insulted the whole Light Council: he said their laws were wrong and that they had murdered her. He marked himself a traitor.

He told the truth. He was punished for that courage, but people are always punished for courage.

My Aunt Leila and my Uncle Douglas took me in. We all knew that my mother was dead, that any Dark citizen could disappear and be lost forever with no excuse. Nobody cared if the buried died.

But Dad was a different matter: he was a prominent Light citizen in the Dark city. People would notice. They could not simply let him disappear, so they made him an example instead. They punished him in public.

I said before that Dark magicians use blood for their spells. What they did to my father is one way to get it—the most horrible way, which grants Dark magicians the most power, which gives them both blood and death.

The Light Guard imprisons the condemned in heavy black iron cages hung high in the trees in Green-Wood Cemetery. The victims are transfixed in place with long iron spikes, slowly dying, as the worst Dark magicians come drink their blood and drain away their life force.

The Dark magicians permitted to do this are those who collude with the Light guards, who are willing to betray their fellows for the Light Council's favor, for this rich reward.

They are only allowed to use criminals.

Which meant they were allowed to use my dad.

Dark magicians get power from all blood, but they draw the most power from the blood of Light magicians. My father, a powerful Light magician, was the richest possible prize for the Dark magicians who served the Light best.

People came from all over the Dark city to see people caged. The Light guards encouraged it: they thought witnessing the ultimate punishment was a deterrent to crime. I do not think people went to learn good behavior, though.

They went because of the endless morbid hunger people have for the pain of strangers. I had never gone there before—my gentle father would never have taken his child there in a thousand years—but I'd seen recordings, heard the cheering of the crowds drowning out the caged ones' screams. They watched the recordings in the Light city too, and they knew justice had been done.

When we heard that they had caged my father, I remember sitting in my aunt and uncle's kitchen. My mother was already gone, and now I lived completely in a nightmare. Everything that had been familiar and beloved was suddenly hideous to me: the boiling kettle shrieking with anguish, my aunt's eyes black as ink, the red tea towel a bloody flag. Uncle Douglas said heavily, "There is no way to save him."

But I found a way.

I should have said my Aunt Leila and I found a way.

The night my father had been sent to the cages, I was lying on the pullout sofa in Aunt Leila's office, staring dry eyed at a crack in the ceiling. I felt as if the crack might open into a great yawning abyss and swallow me up, erase all traces that our family had ever been. I wanted it to.

Aunt Leila came in, walking softly with bare feet on the worn carpet, and lay down beside me, not touching me but curled around me like a parenthesis closing around a word.

Aunt Leila was not often affectionate: this was a big deal for her. I turned slightly and looked at the locks of her very straight black hair crossing my hair like bars, and at the edge of her dark eye staring up at the ceiling crack.

"Do you remember the story of how they almost beat your grandfather to death when they found out he was practicing Dark magic in the Light city?" she asked.

I had heard the story hundreds of times, so of course I did, but Aunt Leila never said anything unnecessary. I knew this was important.

"That Grandma got in the way. She threw herself in front of him," I answered, my voice a thread, barely hanging on. "Yes."

"The mob caught him before he got to his house, and she saw him being beaten and went to run out into the road. Her family tried to stop her. They said, He broke the law, you mustn't, there's nothing you can do, think of your baby, stop, you can't do it, please stop. And she said . . ." Aunt Leila prompted.

"Tell the wind and fire where to stop," I answered. "But don't tell me."

"Would you stop?" Aunt Leila asked. "Or would you do what needs to be done?"

I wanted to cry, suddenly, as I had not been able to cry for days. But I didn't want to cry in front of Aunt Leila, who was the strongest person I knew. It was impossible to imagine Aunt Leila ever crying.

"I'd do anything," I said. "But I can't fight the cages, I can't get in the way of the . . . of the spikes. There's nothing I can do!"

"There's something you can do," Aunt Leila said. "It's just something different. You have your own weapons. The question is, are you willing to use them? Are you ready to do whatever needs to be done?"

Aunt Leila stopped looking at the dark jagged line in the ceiling when she said "weapons." She looked at me instead. She even touched me, in a light, thoughtful caress: not my skin, but my hair, and the stones in my rings.

Tell the wind and fire where to stop, but don't tell me.

"Look at you," Aunt Leila murmured. "I could put your face on a banner and march into the Light city. They won't even want to stop you."

The next day, I went down to Green-Wood Cemetery. I passed through the main gates, which had spiky towers and fretwork like lace made of stone and which resembled the entryway of some villain's fortress. Inside were rolling hills, gravestones like spires, even a lake and a pyramid. And past the bronze statues, hanging from pear trees and golden rain trees and dogwood trees, from branches that formed massive arches and leaves that were golden clusters, were the cages.

The cages cast coronas of darkness even by day. The smell of blood permeated the cemetery. Magicians stood underneath, absorbing power, catching the blood in vessels, reaching up to press their hands against the bars.

Inside the cages were the bleeding, moaning animals that pain had turned people into. I looked at the cages long enough to know which one held my father, and then I looked away.

In an ever-expanding ring around the cages were mourners. Not mourners for the dead in this cemetery, but mourners for the living trapped in their cages. Some of those who loved the caged were so racked with misery that they looked barely human, crouched around their pain, faces distended, screaming until their hoarse, cracked voices sounded like birds: they looked as bad as the contorted creatures in the cages.

The other people standing there were the audience, people who came out of curiosity, out of macabre interest in someone else's tragedy. Some of them were reading, or even making grocery lists, as they did so. This was only a stop for them, a diversion before they carried on undisturbed with their real lives. There were even a few women knitting.

They were bored. And there were thousands of people in the Dark and the Light cities who were just like me, who were a little saddened and a lot embarrassed by the ugly, epic tragedy of this place.

What I had to do was make everybody watch.

I was wearing a long white dress. White was not a

common color to wear, as it was seen as too plain next to all the colors we wore to contrast with the black of the doppelgangers' hoods. I stood out like a ghost among the living.

My Aunt Leila had brushed my hair until it shone like spun gold, and it floated behind me as I walked through the people and under the cages. I kept my face calm, so calm. I had to look right. I could not give anybody an excuse to look away.

I took a deep breath and lifted my hands over my golden head, concentrated, and pulled the light and power out of my rings. Lucent power spilled out of the gems, out of the gold circling my fingers. I reached up to the nearest cage, and I touched the fingertips of the wreck of a woman inside it, and I pushed my power through her, soothing her pain.

I didn't have enough magic to do any real good, not for someone hurting as badly as this caged woman was, not for more than a half a second.

But half a second was all I needed.

The woman's sobs eased for a moment. I moved on, touching everyone in every cage. It was exhausting. If you use too much magic, your body collapses so fast; I could feel the magic being tugged out of me as if I were giving blood, but I didn't let myself look tired any more than I let myself cry.

I moved through the blood-dark grass to my father's cage. I reached up and touched his hand.

He had not been in there long: his face showed human

pain, and not the dumb pain of an animal. But he had been there long enough.

He murmured, "Who are you?" as he touched my hair, a long ribbon of gold in his cold white hand.

"I'm Lucie Manette," I said, making my voice not loud but clear, so that it would carry across the graveyard and ring through the swaying leaves, the still waters, and the dead. "This is my father."

That was all I said that night. It was important to come in the evening, when there was the biggest crowd, as people went home from work and stopped to gawk at someone else's tragedy. The next night, I returned and did the exact same thing, and that time people had questions for me. I answered a few, and the night after that I answered a few more: that my father was a Light citizen, that he was a doctor dedicated to helping people, saving people, that all I wanted to do was help and save people too. That my father was my only family, that I had never had a mother.

Instead of explaining that he'd sought my mother, I said my father had been arrested because he was looking for a neighbor he pitied but whom I hardly knew. I said it whenever I was asked why my father had been arrested. I said it again and again. I called my mother a stranger. I denied my whole family. I never spoke their names. I never asked for justice for my mother. I never said that she had been taken by the Light for doing nothing but helping people. I never spoke of her murder or how our family had been devastated. I never even said her name. I let the Light get away with her murder. I let her be forgotten, I let her be lost. I lied and lied, and it never crossed my mind for a moment to do otherwise.

After every performance, I went home and slept, for thirteen hours, fourteen, eighteen. I slept like a dead thing.

Light citizens did not usually live in the Dark city and were almost never sent to the cages. Nobody was used to seeing a Light citizen in a cage, and they were even less used to seeing an innocent girl suffering, a girl golden with rings, an image of the Light city the way the Light people liked to think of themselves. The Light did not think people like them should suffer—only people who were different.

I looked like the symbol of what all Light magic should be. I looked right, and my image was captured on dozens of cameras. The Light Council could not get rid of me, not when the world was watching.

People started to say I was an angel. There were pictures of me all over the Dark city and the Light, pictures of a golden-haired child with a sweet, sad face and hands that were always bright. There were a thousand interviews. In the end, I talked to anyone who would ask me, talked and talked and never cried too much.

They called me the angel in the park, the angel of my father's house. They called me the Golden Thread in the Dark.

I said I just wanted to help people, to ease their suffering, but that was a lie. I didn't do it to help anyone but myself. I wasn't showing real compassion for strangers, I wasn't showing what I really felt. Real grief is ugly and uncomfortable. People look away from grief the same way they look away from severed limbs or gaping wounds. What they want is pain like death on a stage: beautiful, bloodless, presented for their entertainment.

My aunt and I came up with the plan, of what needed to be done, and I did it. I didn't care that nobody else could have done it, that nobody else had the privilege of being a Light citizen or the power of the rings. All I wanted was my father back, and I knew that I could make it happen.

My father told the truth and was punished. I told a lie and was richly rewarded.

There were riots in the streets of both cities protesting my father's arrest and my pain. People even called for the cages to be cut down.

I had become a symbol, and so the Light city decided to make me a symbol of the Light's kindness, of their mercy. I made the image and they used it, used me as proof that the right kind of people would not be victimized.

They let my father go. They gave us two passes to the Light city. I didn't stay to help anyone. I stood in front of all those cameras and never said a word about injustice, about

torture, about my mother. I said thank you instead. I turned
my back on the Dark and left.

I saved my father, but Ethan saved me.

When we came out of the Dark city, I found myself a
celebrity in Light New York. In the early days, I had photo-
graphers dogging my steps and disturbing my father. I had a
hundred interview requests a day. I also had a scholarship to
the Nightingale-Evremonde School, the most exclusive place
of education in the city.

I didn't want to go, but we didn't have a lot of options. So
I took the scholarship, the uniform, the charity . . . and, of
course, the note in every newspaper article about me that the
city had granted me this great benefit.

My father's friend Penelope Pross and her husband, Jarvis
Lorry, and even their little girl, Marie, had welcomed us into
their home when we came from the Dark city. I was so grateful. I hadn't known what we were going to do. My father's
body and mind were so broken, I did not know if I would
ever succeed in putting the pieces of him back together into
anybody I recognized.

They were so kind, but I missed my aunt and uncle so
much, I could barely stand it. Light New York was not my
home then, and I was sickened by the endless scintillating
wash of illumination from people's rings, since the shine of

rings used to only ever mean me or my father lighting our way home in the dark. I felt blinded by the brightness of people's clothes, the expensive array of colors worn—neon pink and virulent green and searing yellow, more vivid than any back in the Dark—and jewels, and the great stones set in the metal façade of Stryker Tower, which seemed as bright and as hard to look upon as the sun.

I felt every moment as if these strange lights were scalding me, as if I were always burning.

Every time I forgot, let myself breathe a little easier, I was caught unaware by a camera blazing at me going home, on the streets, on the steps of my new school.

A lot of people tried to be my friends at first, insistently asking about the Dark city, about how horrible my home had been, about the experiences of the last few weeks that I never wanted to relive.

Ethan never did. I noticed him, of course, because he was one of the Stryker boys: James Stryker and Ethan Stryker, each an only son of the Stryker brothers Mark and Charles, the leaders of the Light Council. Jim Stryker made a pass at me in the way many of the arrogant boys at Nightingale-Evremonde did, and he seemed enormously offended and not even slightly hurt when I turned him down cold.

I was offended that they were asking. They didn't know me, didn't want to know me. They only wanted to have the briefly famous and strange girl on their arm, to borrow some shine from the gold hair that had come out of the dark.

The gold hair seemed to be the one thing about me that was not changing, back then. I felt as if I was having an allergic reaction to this glittering city, when the truth is I was just growing up so fast, it felt like suffering: my face changing, chest swelling, my body as unfamiliar as the city, my nightmare-torn sleep disturbed by the shooting pains in my legs. Even if it had not been for my desperately hurt father and the savagely strange land, I would not have been looking for love.

At the end of one school day, I opened the door and went from a dim hallway to the scorching-bright flash of a camera: it made me stagger, but I didn't fall. Someone caught my arm and helped me stand up.

I blinked hard against the cruel light and looked into Ethan's kind, dark eyes.

"I've got you," he said.

I shook off his hand. "*I've* got me," I said, and hurried away through the city of blazing lights.

I didn't look back.

But I did notice him, then, as more than just one-half of the most richly shining duo of them all. He sometimes sat with Jim while Jim was holding court, but he was also involved in the Junior Council's charity work, and involved in the drama club for what seemed to be fun. I remembered the way he had caught me. His hands were bare of rings — he had no Light magic of his own — but they were steady and capable. He tutored a couple of the younger kids, but he didn't offer to tutor me, even though I was pathetically far behind the Light kids. Many other people had offered. Many, many other people.

Ethan gave me what no one else gave me: he gave me my space.

And that was why, one day at lunchtime, I walked over to his table and cleared my throat. But I wasn't the first one to speak.

"I'm sorry," said Ethan.

"I'm sorry?" I said.

"Nope, it's definitely me who should be sorry," Ethan told me. "I know that everyone watches you and tries to be close to you and that it bothers you. I know you've been through something that neither I nor anyone else here can imagine, and that you obviously don't want to talk about it—so I'm also very sorry that I'm talking about it. I tried to take a table that was pretty far away and not to look too much. Because you clearly don't need anyone else staring, even if you're beautiful. And it's not just about that: you're brave—you did something really amazing. Obviously I looked once or twice, and I wasn't as subtle as I thought I was being. So, I'm sorry."

He spoke as if he felt bad for upsetting me more than he felt anything for himself.

It was weird, having someone say something like that to me, and having it seem genuine. But it was almost nice, and there hadn't been a lot of nice things in my life, not for a long time. I liked that he had called me brave instead of good. Everyone called me good.

I knew neither was true, but it was still a nice change.

I cleared my throat again. "I was going to say that I know you tutor a couple of the younger kids, and I'm finding it really hard to catch up. I was wondering if you had a tutoring spot open."

"Oh," Ethan said. "Right." He rumpled his thick dark hair back with one hand, and I saw the tips of his ears go pink. "I can do that. I do have a price, however. I will require that you immediately self-induce amnesia about the last five minutes."

I held on to the back of the chair opposite his, and he was quiet. He gave me all the time and space I needed to decide.

I sat down opposite Ethan and said, "I can do that."

Ethan taught me how to catch up at school, taught me how to live in the Light city. He never took any payment. He never had a reason to do any of it, except that he had decided to care about me, and that he would keep caring about me no matter how I felt about him. When Penelope's husband, Jarvis, lost his security job, Ethan made sure his father gave Jarvis another one working in Stryker Tower itself and making plans for where best to deploy the Light guards throughout the Dark city. Ethan did it to make me happy: he did it because he knew I owed Penelope and Jarvis, and my debts were his.

I was a bad girlfriend. I don't say that because I felt guilty about it or like I owed Ethan. When you are broken and someone puts you back together, there isn't any way to repay that. I woke up screaming in Ethan's arms, lashed out to hurt him when I felt trapped or angry.

I didn't grow to love him because I was grateful. I loved him because he was the best and sweetest thing in my life, because being with him was always something I could look forward to, and because he made a new life for me and gave it to me as a gift, for no reason other than that he loved me back.

Anyone would love him, but I do not know if anyone could love him as much as I do.

I saved my father, and Ethan saved me. Maybe that is the only thing I have ever learned about love: love is when you save someone no matter what the cost.

Now that I knew Ethan had a doppelganger, I knew that someone had paid any price to save him once already.

I've heard the process of making a doppelganger explained like this: Human souls are made of light. It is what makes people able to feel, to love and pity each other, and if there is an excess of light, it is what enables people to do Light magic. If a soul is slipping into the dark, the dark will give the light back . . . if the light gives the darkness form.

One goes into the shadow of death, but two come back:

the real person, and the other, a creature made in the person's image, but out of darkness.

People are frightened by the idea of them, of something that looks human and is all darkness. Doppelgangers used to be slaughtered with less of a penalty than you received for killing a family pet, until thirteen years ago, when Charles Stryker, Ethan's father, changed the laws. Officially doppelgangers were human now, and it was murder to kill them. Still, we all know of doppelgangers murdered as soon as they were created, found in the Hudson River with their telltale faces destroyed, or beaten to death by people who hated them for their hoods alone.

The law says doppelgangers must wear hoods to hide their stolen faces, hoods fastened with collars that only someone with Light magic rings can take off. Nobody would ever change that law. Real people needed to be protected from the soulless.

My mother and father never believed any of it. They supported doppelganger rights, thought they should be able to vote and be allowed to live with faces open to the light.

Even in the Dark cities, doppelgangers were a little apart from us. There are very few doppelganger children; I never saw one. I saw their hooded figures on the street, ordered coffees from them, smiled reflexively at them in the grocery store and never knew whether under the shadow of their hood they were smiling back.

I was secretly afraid of them, though I would never have told my parents that. But at least I had seen a doppelganger before. Up until that day, I would have sworn that Ethan never had, not up close.

He was a golden boy in every sense of the word, untouched by darkness or suffering. I would have sworn that was true, and I would have been wrong.

There. That's it. That's everything I knew, back then. That is the world we lived in, with bright cities and dark twins.

That brings us up to that moment on the train, with the boy I loved and the stranger who had saved him.

Now you know everything, except the story of what happened next to all of us: Ethan of the Light city, Carwyn of the Dark, and me, who was born with a foot in each.

This is the tale of who I was able to save.

CHAPTER FOUR

T HE STRYKERS DID NOT ACTUALLY LIVE IN
Stryker Tower, because it was a place of business,
and it would be difficult to sleep in a building that
lit up everything within a three-block radius bright as day.
They lived in a different building, this one on the south side
of Central Park, with a carved stone entryway that reminded
me of a museum's and a doorman who had scared me at first.
I'd seen that doorman escort out people whose names Ethan's
cousin Jim had decided were no longer on the approved list.

This was such a bright place, a center for glittering luxury.
Death and doppelgangers and darkness were all things that I
had thought I'd left behind long ago.

Ethan had put me on the list and would never have taken
my name off. I had run through this echoing marble hall as if
I belonged here a hundred times, hand in hand with Ethan, in
from the park wearing a bikini top and shorts, bundled up in
a winter coat and laden with presents.

Everybody here thought of me as belonging to the Light,
as if growing up in the Dark had not affected me, as if the

shine of my rings had made me immune to my surroundings. But I knew who I had been in the Dark, and remembered those I loved in the darkness. I remembered it all even more vividly that day, when I had been so close to someone from the Dark like me. I felt out of place passing the doorman, as if he might stop me, read the darkness on my face, and have me thrown out into the street. I glanced up and saw my own golden head in the mirror-like surface of the ceiling as I went through to the elevator.

When I knocked on the door, Charles Stryker answered it: Ethan's father. Normally, it was the housekeeper or Ethan himself. Ethan's dad must have been in a state of some distress to actually open his own door.

Charles Stryker and his brother were alike, but Charles was older than Mark and he looked like the sketch before the oil painting: Charles's features a little more uncertain, blurred, the line of nose and jaw less decided and his eyes smaller, hairline humbly receding, while Mark's would never retreat.

I liked Ethan's dad more than his uncle, but I had never liked either of them much.

"Lucie," said Charles, who did like me, and he took hold of my wrists, his rings cool against my pulse points. He pressed a kiss as cold as the rings onto my cheek. "Very nice to see you, as always, especially after . . ."

Charles often abandoned sentences.

"Ethan will be so pleased."

"You know it," said Ethan, behind his father.

He clasped Charles's shoulder—he was always the one showing his dad affection rather than the other way around, and Charles always seemed puzzled but pleased by it—and his dad smiled at him, a smile weak as lousy tea, before he slipped away.

I stepped up to Ethan, arm around his neck, top lip pressed against his bottom lip, in my place, the perfect place. His body was solid against me, the curve of his neck pressed into the inside of my elbow, his breath warm against my cheek. The planes and curves and heat of his body all adding up to sanctuary.

Even when I felt like I didn't belong in the Light, I knew I belonged here.

"Hey," I murmured into the corner of his mouth, "where is he?"

Ethan flinched, making a tiny space between us where all the cold could rush in. I drew back, into the dark, silent hall.

"Ethan, where is Carwyn?"

"I did the best I could," said Ethan. "Uncle Mark was not pleased to meet him. Dad's in a lot of trouble right now, and I don't have any say because of the whole being-accused-of-treason thing."

I could not suppress a shudder. Treason. The weight of the accusation, the knowledge of all it could mean, forced the breath from my lungs. We needed to make a plan to deal with the accusation, to figure out who would make up such a wild and terrible lie, but first we needed to repay the one who had saved him from the accusation.

"Where is he?"

Ethan paused, then took a deep breath and answered. "He's in a hotel."

I took another step backwards. "Did you guys have him in the house a whole five minutes before you sent him away, for the second time in his life? Or did you not let him cross the sacred Stryker threshold at all?"

"Look, Lucie, he's got what he wanted. I made sure that Uncle Mark arranged somewhere nice for him to stay and gave him a lot of money. He can go out on the town now. There's even a pass sorted out for him—he can stay for a week."

"Oh, a whole week? That's so generous of you both. What about the pass he had that meant he could stay for real?"

Ethan looked frustrated. I knew the feeling.

"Uncle Mark would never let him live here. It would only be a matter of time before his face was seen. Besides, he doesn't want to stay. You heard what he said about crime. All he wanted was an adventure. Well, he's got one. With Uncle Mark's money, he can get all the booze and dust and girls he likes. What else did you expect me to do for him? What else do you want from me?"

"Not to leave him alone in a strange city," I said. "Your

dad is responsible for Carwyn, and Carwyn saved your life. That means Carwyn should be looked after!"

"We couldn't keep him here," said Ethan. "Jim doesn't even know he exists. Nobody can know he exists. I'm thinking about my dad here—"

"I'm not," I interrupted. "I'm thinking about Carwyn. You could have at least gone with him, if he couldn't stay here."

I understood that he couldn't have. Somebody would have been bound to get a photograph sooner or later. Charles Stryker would have been ruined; the whole council would have taken a hit. I understood all the practical concerns, but I understood as Ethan did not—as Ethan could not—what it was to be new and adrift in a sea of light. I understood what it was like to save someone, and pay and pay for it.

"Look, Lucie. Carwyn is a doppelganger. He didn't want company."

Ethan stood framed in the doorway of his apartment, limned with gold. A bright tapestry hung on the wall behind him, and he looked tired, annoyed that I kept trying to push darkness into his life. Ethan and I had fought before, but I had never felt this distant from him.

"Did you ask?" I said.

Ethan might not have understood me, but I didn't want to understand him, either. I did not give him a chance to answer before I spun on my heel and walked away. I left him standing in the doorway to brightness and retraced my steps, past the doorman and his list of chosen ones, under the shining ceiling, and outside, where, even in this city of Light, it was getting dark.

I knew where to go. The Strykers always sent business contacts—not friends, not family—to the same place. The James Hotel, which Jim claimed was named after him though it wasn't, was a tall glass building that reflected light but gave off very little of its own, like a discreetly expensive gemstone. It was easy to see amid the smaller buildings of SoHo as I walked from the subway station. I texted Penelope that I was out with Ethan and did not know when I would be home. My rings gave off the same muted light as the screen of my phone.

I didn't know what name the Strykers had registered Carwyn under, but when I asked for the associate Mark Stryker had checked in that day, they sent me up to the penthouse suite.

One of Mark Stryker's men was waiting outside the door. I didn't recognize the face, but after two years I knew how to recognize the demeanor. He must have been briefed, because he didn't interfere with me, so I didn't acknowledge him. I just went to the door and tapped on it.

"One minute," Carwyn said, voice muffled, and I wondered what he was hiding before he could open the door.

Once the door was open, it was clear that he hadn't been hiding anything. He'd just been finding pants.

The collar and the fabric of the doppelganger's hood attached to the collar had to be waterproof, I realized, because doppelgangers wore them even in the shower. Droplets hung from the leather and metal around his neck, turning it briefly into a choker with pendant jewels—until Carwyn, hood down and head half enveloped in a fluffy towel, vigorously resumed drying his hair and all the droplets fell.

"Oh, you again," he said. "Honestly, I'm disappointed. I hoped it was room service."

He took to scrunching up his hair with the towel one-handed so he could gesture, in a vague unenthusiastic manner, for me to come in. I walked in slowly. The floor was black wood, polished to shine like jet, and on all the walls were cubist paintings in gray and red. The light fixtures were metallic, shaped like boxes and spaceships. The light in one had run out, so I wandered over to it and tapped the shiny red dome with two fingers, rings clicking against the metal, and the light blinked back on.

When I looked up, Carwyn was watching me, but that lasted only an instant before he was drying his hair again. It was both less and more strange, seeing the replica of Ethan's body instead of Ethan's face. A body was more anonymous, not as easily recognizable, but Carwyn's was marked by the events of a life different from Ethan's. Carwyn was thinner, with the leanness of someone used to less and worse food, muscles less impressive but possibly more functional. He had a long scar up his abdomen, a nipple piercing, and none of the tan or the dusting of freckles from Ethan's days basking in the sun. It was reassuring to have dissimilarities to catalog, having it made clear they were different bodies rather than mirror images.

It was strange because I was the only one who knew Ethan's body, the intimate details of it, well enough to know what was different about this one.

"I'm sorry for what they did," I said.

Carwyn finished drying his hair and walked over, closer to me, to drop his towel in a damp heap on the bed. He retreated to a chair standing against the opposite wall, its carved wood painted black, and retrieved his shirt.

"What are you sorry for?"

"I'm sorry they took your pass and sent you away."

Carwyn snorted. "I know, right? I was so looking forward to playing a game of charades with good old Uncle Mark. I'm not their family. I didn't expect anything better than this."

"They owed you better than this," I said. "They already owed you support. You saved Ethan. They owed you thanks, and not shipping you off as if you were someone engaged in a business dispute with the company."

"So, what?" Carwyn asked. "You're here to thank me?"

"I already thanked you," I pointed out.

"You're here to express your appreciation by proposing a kinky doppelganger ménage à trois? In which case, I'm going to have to turn you down. I'm sad to say it, but Ethan gives me the impression he'd be about as exciting in the sack as an eggplant."

"You're wrong, but you're just going to have to trust me on that, because you're never finding out firsthand," I said. "He's mine and I don't share. You keep trying to make me angry or, failing that, uncomfortable."

Carwyn's eyes widened for a moment; startled, he looked more like Ethan. He walked across the room toward me again, stopping to sit on the bed, and shrugged and lowered his head as if conceding a point. Or, I realized a moment later, as if he was putting on his shoes.

"Doppelganger," he said. "Created pitiless and soulless to wander the earth tormenting mortals. Sort of my thing."

"You torment mortals with dumb sexual innuendo?"

"I'm also a teenage boy. You work with what you have."

I went to another painted-black chair on my side of the room. I removed the small cushion, which was covered in beads for maximum discomfort, and sat on the chair cross-legged.

"You can't torment me," I said. "Not unless you try a lot harder than you currently are. You did something good for me instead."

"Weren't you listening to Ethan back on the train? I did something self-serving and cynical that only coincidentally benefited you."

"Weren't you listening to me back on the train? You did something good for me: I don't really care what your reasons were. I haven't had so many good things happen to me that I'm going to quibble, and I don't care how much you try to insult me. Because I'm not going to listen."

I leaned my weight against my drawn-up legs, fingers laced in the ties of my shoes, and met Carwyn's gaze straight on. I couldn't tell if it was challenging or suspicious, hateful or simply curious, but it didn't matter what he thought of me, not really. It didn't matter what he felt about me, if he could feel anything at all: my mother would have said he could, and the whole Light city would have told me it was impossible. None of that mattered. What mattered was that I had come to this hotel to do whatever I could for him.

Carwyn was silent for a while. I stretched my legs out, and curled my fingers around the arms of the chair.

I started a little when Carwyn kicked the side of my shoe with his own. When I looked up, he was smiling a bit: a small and not entirely reassuring grin, nothing like Ethan's, but it looked genuine nonetheless.

"So," said Carwyn. "Charades?"

"Ethan said they gave you money," I told him. "And that you're set to stay here for a week and you have a pass. Is there anything else that you want? Is there anything else I can do for you?"

The doppelganger hesitated.

"Come on, Carwyn," I added. "I dare you not to be predictable."

"Well," said Carwyn, "I'm a growing avatar of darkness, and I've been waiting for room service a suspiciously long time. Like, two hours. I'm wondering what to do about it."

He didn't need to say any more. I'd seen doppelgangers in the Dark city not being served in shops and cafés, until they slunk away. The best way to encourage doppelgangers not to linger was not to make a fuss but simply not provide what they needed.

I could have called Ethan—even if I didn't want to make up with Ethan at that moment, I could have called Ethan's dad or his uncle—and demanded that they sort out the situation with the hotel. It was in their best interests to keep Carwyn quiet and content.

I intended to do just that, but I remembered something, suddenly, about my mom, and it made me smile. Whenever anything like that happened in front of her, my mom would always order whatever it was the doppelganger had asked for herself, then hand it over.

I thought that it would cost me nothing to be kind and mean it, just this once. To be like my mother, just for one night.

"You said you wanted to see the Light city," I said slowly. "Let's go out and see some of it. I can show you around, and we can grab something to eat as we go. My treat."

Carwyn put his head to one side. I wasn't sure if he was assessing the sincerity of my offer or simply weighing the amount of fun he could have getting pot stickers in the Village with me versus checking out what the hotel cable television had to offer.

"All right, golden girl," he said slowly, "lead me to the light."

CHAPTER FIVE

I T WAS CLEAR EVEN BEFORE WE REACHED THE STREET that I had made another terrible mistake.

Carwyn had put up his hood before we left the hotel room, and we got a judgmental stare from the receptionist as we walked out. Matters only got worse from there.

We took the subway to the restaurant I'd decided on. It was only a few stops, but that was long enough. One woman who had seemed sleepy a moment before we stepped onto the train, her kid resting his sticky face against her shimmering Light-reinforced raincoat, went rigid as soon as she saw Carwyn. She stood vibrating with distress by the doors and exited, making for the next car, at the next stop. Other people were less obtrusive, melting away off the seats and through the doors or into the corner.

One guy in pink suspenders, who I thought might be trying to impress a beringed woman whose shoes were twined with Light magic so the spike heels became small bright towers that would not hurt her feet, stayed where he was. He sat only one seat away from Carwyn. The bright-shod woman watched Carwyn with obvious apprehension. The man in suspenders, I saw, was pretending to be nonchalant, and playing a hand-held game. He was a lousy actor. We could all see his shaking hands.

Carwyn shifted, and the guy dropped the game with a clatter and a flash of light that blinked out like a tiny supernova. He stared, and from under Carwyn's hood came a soft, sinister sound, something like a hiss, and Carwyn's pale fingers went creeping over the empty seat.

The guy made a low sound in the back of his throat and slid hastily along the row of slick orange plastic seats until he was at the other end of the car. I leaned over and rapped Carwyn's hand with my knuckles, making sure my rings were involved so it would smart.

"You're not helping yourself."

"No," Carwyn murmured, "I'm amusing myself."

"You're the only doppelganger that they have ever seen in person," I said as we left the train, to the visible relief of its remaining passengers. "Spreading fear and distrust is only going to contribute to the false idea of doppelgangers that they've built up in their heads."

"Please inform me on the subject of doppelgangers," Carwyn said humbly. "They sound like such interesting yet widely misunderstood creatures. Is it true that they only drink human blood?"

"I hope not," I said. "This place doesn't serve it."

The Star Bright was already in view, with its white façade and gleaming, tilted windows, the star on the black sign a burst of Light magic that looked almost like a real star. I'd had brunch there with Ethan a couple of weeks ago, and it was a warm, comfortable place to eat and talk. I smiled at the woman with the short black tie and moved toward an empty table.

"I'm terribly sorry," said the woman, stepping in front of me. "But these tables are reserved."

"What, all of them?"

The woman nodded, a jerky motion that made her earrings dance, jeweled little fish leaping into shimmering blue circles.

"All right," I said slowly. "Can we wait? How long will it take?"

"Could be hours," she said, twisting her hands together.

I glanced over my shoulder at Carwyn, a silent shadow at my back. He made no sound or movement, as if he really was a shadow.

"It's not my decision," the woman said, her voice very fast and very low. "It's just the policy of the management. They have to think of the other customers."

"Being thoughtful is so important," I snapped. "Come on, we'll go someplace else."

I stormed out into the dark street, banging the door shut behind me, and walked on with Carwyn following in my wake. We walked eight blocks, until we reached a Thai place I knew, where the bathrooms had shimmering curtains of magic light instead of walls. Tourists flocked there to use those bathrooms. I thought the whole thing was a little creepy, but the food was good, and outside the bathrooms the lights were low.

They must have seen us coming, because the man waiting at the door had the air of a manager and shining rings on every finger. Rings took money as well as magical talent.

"Miss, please, you can't come in here," he said. "This isn't that kind of establishment."

"The kind of establishment where people eat food and then pay for it?" I asked. "Because I've done that here before, and that's all we want to do now."

A woman eating nearby said, "Light's sake, *I* don't mind if the doppelganger wants to stay and give us a show!"

Her voice had a Midwest twang and she was looking at Carwyn with undisguised fascination, as if he were a combination of a dirty picture and something she might see at the zoo.

"You're welcome here, honey," she said, peering up at his shrouded face.

"Thanks, honey," said Carwyn, mimicking her accent. She jumped.

"Miss." The man touched his forehead with one hand and gestured to the door with the other, sparks cast by the stones trailing the motion.

I clenched my own hands, rings pressing hard against my palms, and fought back the urge to do what I had done at the train station for Ethan: shout who I was and demand better treatment. But I couldn't, of course. I couldn't link my name with a doppelganger's any more than it already was. Word would spread. That would be bad for Ethan.

Even going out onto the streets with Carwyn was a risk I should not have taken. I could have been recognized, and that would have reflected on the whole Stryker family. Ethan had already been accused of a crime. I was afraid for Ethan, fear cold as the knowledge that I was letting down the boy who had saved Ethan in the first place.

"Fine," I said, and whirled out the door.

I had taken a few steps down the street when Carwyn's voice sounded behind me.

"You were right," he said. "Once I stop upsetting people with my bad behavior, the world is all strawberries and sunshine. Or do I mean puppies and cream?"

"I'm sorry, all right," I told him angrily, as if the world's and my own cowardice were his fault.

"Sorry about what?" Carwyn asked. He drew level with me rather than being the shadow at my back. "Lucie, come on. It's not like anything's different in the Dark. The revolution you ignited hasn't changed things that much, not yet."

"The revolution *I* ignited?"

"The child who spoke out against the cages?" Carwyn

asked. "They chant your name down in the Dark. The *sans-merci* paint it in blood on the streets. There are whispers that say the Light city kidnapped you and the Light Council is holding you prisoner, that it is the *sans-merci*'s mission to free you. You're their princess in a tower. You're their excuse for the tower to be torn down."

I knew a little about the unrest in the Dark city. I knew about the riots, the fires, and the rumored assassinations, but there was always unrest in the Dark city. I knew all I wanted to. The chaos on the dark streets was not my fault just because they were calling my name these days.

The Light saw me as someone the laws existed to protect. The Dark saw me as someone who proved that the laws could be broken. But I didn't want to be either.

Except that wasn't true. I had stirred people up deliberately. I was responsible for some of the blood spilled on those dark streets. But I hadn't caused a revolution, for Light's sake. That was ridiculous. The buried were always restless, but they always settled in the end.

I shook my head to silence the voice of Ethan's uncle, which didn't belong in there. "It's nothing to do with me."

Carwyn just laughed. "Oh, right. You're the Golden Thread in the Dark, but it's nothing to do with you. The buried ones use you as a rallying cry, but that doesn't matter to you."

It wasn't that it didn't matter, I wanted to say. It was just that he was attributing power to me that I didn't have. All I'd done was follow the plan Aunt Leila had come up with: all I'd done was play a role to get what I wanted. Nothing they thought about me was true.

An icon didn't do anything of its own volition. A symbol didn't act of its own accord. Both cities projected what they wanted onto me, and wanted me to stay still as they did it.

We walked on through SoHo in silence, past a closed-up antique shop, a club with a sign that said SIZZLING, and into an alleyway that had a wall covered in intricate graffiti— the shadowy face and scared eyes of a girl lost in a psychedelic forest. Her eyes shone with Light magic, like a surprised animal's in the night.

"I didn't start it, and I can't stop it," I said at last. "I can't even get us a lousy meal. You think that I'm responsible for a revolution? I managed to fool everyone long enough to get my dad out. That's all. I'm not a hero. I saved one person. You saved one person last night. We're even. We're the same."

"Are you starving?" Carwyn asked. "Because I'm starving."

I walked into the alleyway with the lost-girl graffiti, then turned and stood opposite him. The hood obscured his face, so all I was looking at was featureless darkness.

"Put your hood down."

He pulled it away from his face without a word.

All day, ever since I had woken to find the one person

who meant love and safety to me in sudden danger, I had felt like I was back in the Dark. Like a rawly orphaned child, lying cold and exhausted and scared in Aunt Leila's house, sure that I did not have enough Light in me to go on.

Carwyn looked like Ethan, but an Ethan shadowed and starved, bones standing out in high relief in his face and with the sweetness gone out of his eyes. He looked like an Ethan who had been through some of what I had. He looked as if he might, just possibly, be able to understand.

I said very quietly, "Do you think you might need to go to the bathroom at any point in the near future?"

"Uh," said Carwyn, "what? No. What?" He paused. "I want you to know that was my first time," he added. "Not knowing what to say to someone. I always have something to say."

"Well, your first time didn't last long, but I guess that's always how it goes," I said.

I concentrated on my left hand, the sinister hand, so the rings on it glowed: lapis lazuli, opal, vermarine, emerald, and diamond, the colors of green and blue and moonshine mingling pale and bright as light underwater. When my hand was glowing, I inscribed a circle onto the night sky and made a loop of brightness that turned solid, like water transforming into ice, and landed in my palm.

I pushed the link I had made over my hand, so it hung around my wrist like a bracelet.

Then I looked back at Carwyn.

"I have conditions," I said. "This is only for one night. You're not going to argue with me. You're not allowed to beg or plead or try to make a bargain. You won't leave my side all night. You have to do what I say."

"You might be surprised at how often I've had conversations similar to this one," Carwyn commented, but he spoke in as low and as quiet a voice as I did, as if speaking too loudly in this lonely alley might tip off the universe.

Outside the alley, the city went rushing heedlessly along, like a river made of light.

A doppelganger's collar did not resemble any other collar in the world. It was a heavy strip of black leather, meant to last someone's whole life, and it was inlaid with metallic fittings like studs turned inside out. Glittering spaces like the setting of a ring when the jewel had fallen out. The spaces waited for the jewels to return.

"This is serious," I said.

I stepped toward him. Carwyn's gaze was fixed on me with steady attention. He did not move, but I saw him take in all of my movements. He was so absorbed in looking at me that he did not even seem to breathe.

I turned my rings so each large jewel was palm-side. I lifted my hands and laid them gently against his throat.

He tipped his head back. Moonlight poured down his neck until it was halted by the dull weight of his collar, a band of black pressed against the pale skin. The gems on my rings fitted into the metal spaces in his collar as if they had been made to do it.

Carwyn swallowed, and I felt the movement beneath my fingers, reminding me of the vulnerable skin beneath the metal and leather. He felt human, felt as if he could be hurt.

"I know," he responded. I felt the leather flex under my hand.

My rings locked into place. Light magic was tucked in these metal fastenings, calling to the magic in my rings, anchoring them. I pushed my will into the precious stones and saw them glow, even locked into the collar, like lamps behind a closed door. The dim, trapped light illuminated his face, slashes of shadow and eerie escaped radiance: the familiar and beloved turned strange and terrifying.

I wondered what I thought I was doing, even as I did it.

The heavy clasp of the collar clicked, the mechanical sound like the inner workings of a clock. The collar opened, the line of the doppelganger's throat abruptly naked, and the leather and metal fell into my hands.

I stuffed leather, metal, and hood into my pocket with one hand, and with my free hand I grabbed Carwyn's, looping the strip of light around his wrist as well as mine and pulling it tight. The Light magic bound him closely to me. He was my prisoner now, and my responsibility.

"We can go anywhere we want," I said, feeling both

the wild, desperate urge to laugh and as breathless as if I'd punched myself in the stomach.

I glanced at Carwyn, who nodded, looking lost. He followed me as I stepped forward: he could do nothing else, linked the way we were.

I said one more thing before we left the alley, a mumbled prayer. "Please don't make me sorry I did this."

"I can't promise anything," Carwyn answered. "You're already sorry. Aren't you?"

CHAPTER SIX

AFTER ALL THAT, WE BOUGHT STREET FOOD AND ATE it leaning against a fire extinguisher on the corner of Prince Street. I wanted to be outside, wind pressing cool on my heated face, as I tried to absorb what I had done and to convince myself that disaster would not come of it. Once I was finished eating, I crumpled up the tinfoil wrapper and the mainly lettucey remains of a taco and threw them in the trash.

Carwyn raised his eyebrows. "Uh, if you weren't going to eat that, you should have said."

"Doppelgangers: coming for your soul and your leftovers," I said, running on sheer bravado and fumes. "Follow me if you're still hungry."

We walked down streets full of restaurants and clothes shops until we got to the Moonflower Bakery, and then bought cupcakes. Doppelgangers turned out to be surprisingly fussy about baked goods. Carwyn turned up his nose at the strong suggestion I made that he should have a red velvet cupcake, instead selecting a vanilla cupcake with pink icing and sprinkles.

We went across the street and sat in the playground there, on the set of fragile swings with the paint peeling off the metal, our wrists hanging linked in the space between us.

"I just don't think cheese belongs on a dessert," Carwyn said. "I think it's weird and gross. Those are my principles. Okay, that's my one principle. I like mayhem and bloodshed and deviant sex acts. I disapprove of cheese."

"You'll see," I predicted darkly. "The cream cheese icing cuts the sweetness. This means that you can eat more of the sweet, sweet treat without feeling all sick and sugared out."

"You can say whatever you want to make yourself feel better about the fact that you don't have any sprinkles on your cupcake."

Carwyn put about half his cupcake directly into his face. I breathed in the night air deeply. It was getting easier to relax. It was difficult to be scared of someone who might soon have pink frosting in his eyelashes.

"Do the buried really think that they're going to start a revolution in my name?" I asked. "They think I want one?"

Carwyn nodded, licking frosting off his hands. "Some of them think you're part of the revolution. Some of them think you still need saving. There are people who believe you seduced one of the Strykers to take them down, and there are people who think one of the Strykers seduced you as part of a plan to silence your campaign for justice. The *sans-merci,* those psychos who wear red and black and talk about taking over, say that the Strykers captured you and your father to keep you from telling their secrets." He arched an eyebrow. "Imagine the Strykers having a terrible secret. Isn't that silly?"

I'd thought that I had seen weird stories about my personal relationships already. I'd been used to having no privacy before I even met my famous Stryker boyfriend. There had been brief columns about Ethan and me, photographs of us attending parties, sometimes reports that we had broken up or one of us was cheating with somebody we'd never met. I'd winced at a truly embarrassing picture of me in a blue string bikini on a yacht with Ethan.

That was bad enough. I hadn't dreamed people thought I was acting a part with Ethan. He was the last true thing I had, the only thing unsullied by all that had happened to me in the Dark.

"You seem to know a lot about what the people involved in the revolution think," I snapped.

"I'm a very knowledgeable guy," Carwyn agreed. "They say that doppelgangers can read human hearts and see all the fear and darkness in them. Pale companions of humanity, with their faces pressed up against the windows of the world. Seeing humans' pain and laughing at it."

The swing gave a tiny metallic shriek as he swung.

"Okay," I said. "You could probably also hang around in dive bars and talk to people. Doppelgangers have a lot to gain from a revolution."

"It's true a revolution might make the world a better place," said Carwyn. "But I'm not really the world-saving type. Lots of risk, very uncertain reward—you know what I'm saying? And even if the reward came . . ." He swung and shrugged. "A reward wouldn't stay a reward, not with me. You don't know me very well yet, but you'll see. Everything I touch turns to ash."

"What?"

I'd been worried that he would look too much like Ethan without the collar, but his hair was still shorter and his mouth crueler. He bowed his head, and his nape looked bizarrely uncovered, with an indentation below his hairline where the collar had been.

"This is how *I* think doppelgangers work," said Carwyn. "The doppelganger is created so the other, the first image, can live and prosper. But there has to be a payment. I think that one of us has to suffer. Dark magicians make doppelgangers to be living versions of those dolls people used to stick pins into. We usually die young, instead of them, but we don't simply die. We come to nothing, with none of our actions meaning anything, and none of our goals ever reached. We are those who might as well have died young: all our lives might have been. All our lives are lived elsewhere, by someone else."

Carwyn glanced over at me, and a smirk was born on his mouth, dark as ink spilled and spreading.

"Of course, sometimes the doppelganger can get its own back. Sometimes the doppelganger can make his mirror image be the one who suffers."

Legends say that a doppelganger will cause their original's death in the end, and try to take their place. There are records of doppelgangers who killed their doubles, their doubles' families, the magicians who made them, and innocent people. Doppelgangers are lethal. Making a doppelganger is illegal because it is making a weapon that will kill of its own volition.

I had listened to the stories but I had never considered, before this moment, how much a doppelganger might resent their original.

Except Carwyn had not killed Ethan. He had saved him.

"You know," I said, "you're right. You do talk an awful lot."

"Hmm." Carwyn flicked an eyebrow sardonically. "You were right as well," he said, and seemed to be chiefly addressing the remnants of his cupcake. "This is much too sweet for me."

"Someone should have warned you about that," I said, and ate the last of my own delicious cupcake with deep satisfaction. "Oh, wait. I did."

Carwyn tossed his cupcake wrapper and fragment toward the nearest trash can. It fell short by several feet, but Carwyn looked indifferent. Apparently doppelgangers were litterbugs, too.

"I talk, but I don't really listen. Where to next?"

I'd already given that some thought. I didn't want to go to any of my usual hangouts, because I worried we might be seen and questions might be asked. Carwyn kept talking about having fun in the Light city, and he would not be content with going home and being collared while the night was still young.

There was a place I had gone quite a lot when I was fresh out of the Dark city, and a few times since.

"I might have somewhere in mind."

The problem was, the place wasn't exactly legal.

I guided Carwyn through the streets and into Greenwich Village. He wandered along in my wake, looking amiably around as people passed by. At this time of night, it was mostly couples headed to dinner, single people looking for money or fun, and giggling groups headed to clubs. I saw one girl wearing an obviously fake doppelganger's collar, the material of her hood fraying and the collar plastic. Carwyn didn't look offended: he smiled the dark, smug smile from the playground and she smiled back, face shadowed but not hidden. Her smile reminded me of the way the midwestern woman from the restaurant had spoken to Carwyn. She stopped smiling when she noticed our linked wrists.

A lot of couples went around linked like this, which was why I'd done it. I couldn't risk us looking suspicious, or him getting away from me.

"This way," I said, going down another alley, this one between a bar and a closed shop that sold pottery and had shutters painted green. Behind the shutters, a tiny thread of Light shone, showing a security system was in place.

"Are we breaking in to steal urns?" Carwyn asked. "I could use a flowerpot."

I ignored him and walked around a Dumpster. There was a hatch, wood with wire mesh over it, heavy enough so it was extremely difficult to pull up with one hand, but Carwyn didn't offer to help and I didn't ask. I heard a siren and froze for a moment, but it went wailing past like a banshee late for an appointment, and I heaved the trapdoor open so Carwyn could go in before me.

Once I closed the hatch, it was dark there, standing on rough concrete steps, but I felt more than heard the beat of the music already. We negotiated the stairs tied together in semi-darkness, damp heat and smoke like mist rising to meet us as we went down.

It was a huge basement, a series of rooms like a network

of caves. The walls were the same rough gray concrete as the steps.

It was filled with Dark and Light magic. Shadows that nobody had cast moved on the wall, shadows of things that did not exist: beautiful naked silhouettes and flying dragons and clouds with lightning bolts and rain. The lightning bolts were jagged shimmering lines of magic that dissipated into glitter in the dancers' hair. One boy wore a neon-green bowler hat that spun continuously on his head, and always at a jaunty angle. A girl with bright wings tied to her back was blowing bubbles, fat globes of pure light that winked purple and blue and gold as they drifted through the room.

Everywhere you looked, there was Light and Dark magic dancing together, shadows and light lacing around people's limbs.

I'd been taken to this place by other formerly buried ones, some fresh from the Dark city and some hardly remembering it, people who helped me when I was just getting used to my new home. None of them went to Nightingale-Evremonde, and too many of them wanted to talk about what had happened to me in the dark. I hadn't been back to the club in more than a year.

Tonight, though, when I had already done something monumentally stupid, when I had tied a doppelganger to my side and was already drowning in memories, it looked just right.

"Welcome to Club Chiaroscuro," I said. "Come on, let's get a drink."

"I admit it's better than flowerpots."

Carwyn did look mildly impressed as we went to the bar in the next room. One of the girl's bubbles floated in between us, and I captured it in my free hand. It didn't burst, but glowed at the proximity to my rings, and I found myself laughing. Blue and green patterns flashed on the glowing sphere, and it went spinning and trailing sparks.

"Hey, Lucie! I haven't seen you in forever."

I tossed the bubble up into the air and threw an arm around Nadiya, who had been one of my first friends in the city and was still one of my best friends. Nadiya was almost always laughing but knew when to be serious, and she was always talking, but never about anything that might hurt me.

"You look amazing," I said, and she did: long, tight black dress, her hijab purple, and her eyes outlined with liquid eyeliner that I could never get the hang of. Whenever I tried, it looked like I'd taken to face painting. I was still wearing the dull, high-necked blue dress from the train station. "Don't say a word about how I look good or I'll never trust you again. Coming here was a spur-of-the-moment thing."

"I wasn't going to tell you that you look good," Nadiya said. "I was going to ask you to tell me more about how good *I* look. Oh," she added a little too casually, her eyes moving past me, and my heart sank. "And I see you brought Ethan."

I glanced at Carwyn.

"Well," I said slowly. "Yeah."

Carwyn's smile was unlike any smile I had ever seen on Ethan's face. "Hey. My Lucie is right as usual: you do look amazing."

Nadiya didn't know Ethan well. They were always perfectly friendly with each other, but he was a Stryker, and that made every interaction strained. Of course, she didn't notice anything wrong with this Ethan.

"Thanks. You look good too," she said. "Did you get a haircut?"

"I did!" said Carwyn, to all appearances delighted. "I did get a haircut. It was time, you know? Because, let's face it, my old haircut made me look stupid."

"No it didn't," I said.

"Lucie, lamb chop, it really did," Carwyn assured me. "It was a terrible combination of mama's little angel crossed with a poodle." He glanced at Nadiya. "You agree with me, right?"

Nadiya looked puzzled. "Uh," she said, "you look a bit thinner as well."

"I haven't been eating," Carwyn claimed. "I was . . . depressed by how stupid my hair looked."

"Ha ha," I said. "Okay, shut up, you big weirdo."

"Anything for you, pumpkin," Carwyn drawled.

Nadiya was looking at us very oddly. I cleared my throat. "Time to dance!"

On a dance floor crammed with laughing people, sliding shadows, and beautiful false lightning, Nadiya leaned into me and whispered in my ear, "Are you guys having a fight?"

"No," I said back, more loudly, watching Carwyn from the corner of my eye. "You know Ethan. Always talking. And then talking some more."

Nadiya considered this and then shrugged it all off. She leaned up and said something in Carwyn's ear, too low for me to make out. I glanced at her, worried she was suspicious.

I tried to sound casual. "What did you say?"

Nadiya bit her lip. "I know a guy who's got dust. You want some?"

"No," I said.

"Absolutely!" said Carwyn.

"Uh, wow." Nadiya blinked. "Well, if you want to unlink, Ethan and I could go get the dust and be right back . . . ?"

She sounded hesitant about the entire plan. Carwyn looked very pleased with himself.

"What a great idea," he said. "Why don't we do that? Come on, Lucie." He tugged at the link, our wrists bumping, and looked down at me with glee in his hooded eyes. "I'll be right back. I *promise*."

"Nope!" I said.

Carwyn's smirk faded slightly. "Ah well. Worth a try, gorgeous."

Carwyn tugged at the link between us again and, rather than get involved in a wrestling match, we followed Nadiya across the dance floor. She went to one of the farthest corners in the next room, where she had a brief but intense conference with a guy in a leather jacket. He squinted over at us.

"Aren't you . . . ?" he began.

"Lucie," I said, confirmation and a clear sign I didn't want to talk about it.

"Ethan," said Carwyn. "Kind of a dumb name, isn't it? I've never liked it."

"Is he drunk?" Nadiya whispered.

I laughed and shrugged at the same time. The laugh came out more like a panicked hiccup.

"Oh, well, Lucie," said the guy, who I had never seen before in my life. "We're going to have something to celebrate soon, aren't we? If everything goes right?"

I wasn't going to betray weakness or ignorance, especially not in front of strangers and doppelgangers. "I don't feel like celebrating, and I don't want any dust."

"We've got so much to celebrate," Carwyn put in blandly. "Such as our love. Our beautiful, beautiful love."

The guy reached into his jacket and pulled out a little pouch, which was also leather. He was clearly working a theme.

He put the pouch down on the top of the little table he

was sitting at, the tabletop a small circle of metal that shone with a few different metallic shades of color in the dim light. He drew open the zipper of the purse, and the chaotic roar of the club seemed to fade and fall away as the dust came creeping out through the zip and into the air.

Like grains of black sand that could float, the dust rose and spiraled over us. It spread out so far that it appeared pale gray, so anyone watching us would hardly have seen it. It would have seemed to them like an optical illusion, the palest of shadows, like that which comes from a cloud passing over a landscape.

Dust was created by Dark magic. I did not know how. But the word was that dust was particles of darkness made tangible. Shards of the dark ground down to dust.

Dust brought peace with it, like the feeling of dreamless sleep. I was almost tempted.

"Come on, guys, let's not," I said instead. "This isn't like you, Ethan," I added pointedly.

It wasn't much like Nadiya, either. I wondered what was going on with her, but I couldn't ask with a doppelganger attached to my wrist. She let herself be pulled away with little protest, and Carwyn had no choice about the matter. I looked around at the people dancing, the swaying and shimmying in the moving lights, and then at Nadiya and Carwyn, and found myself laughing again.

"Let's just dance," I said, and grabbed Nadiya's hand with

my free one so I could tow them both back into the midst of the dancers.

The music hummed and thrummed as we danced. Light sparkled all around us, in my eyes, glancing off my rings and sending beams out on all sides. Shadows wrapped me, sliding around my body and through my hair like black ribbons. Time seemed a little broken up, like the light, coming in flashes between the shadows. Nadiya shimmied down and then up again, purple sparks lighting her dark eyes. An older man with rings like mine on his fingers was tracing bright paths down a woman's back that flared briefly and then were absorbed into her skin. A boy in a neon brocade vest with nothing under-neath was dancing in a shimmering line of Light.

The strong line of Carwyn's arm was pressed up against the inside of mine, and I could feel his pulse, beating like another kind of music. I had him where I wanted him: I didn't have to watch him.

But I did look at him, curious to see if the doppelganger was enjoying himself, to see if I'd guessed right and this was something he would like. Doppelgangers do not work the same way real human beings do, everybody says. They do not have souls of their own, because there is nothing of light about them. Could doppelgangers even like things the way we did?

I could not tell. Carwyn's mouth was in a shape that was not quite a flat line or a smirk. When I glanced toward him, he responded by using the bracelet of light to turn me toward him as well, into the pull of his gravity, so we turned around each other in a slow circle.

He leaned down and whispered in my ear, "How well does this girl know Ethan?"

"Not well," I whispered back.

He murmured, "Are you sure about that?"

"Of course I'm sure," I said more loudly.

He didn't argue with me. He leaned away, shrugged, and kept dancing. The light did not illuminate him as it did Nadiya; his eyes remained dark and watchful, but the arm against mine was less tense than it had been all night. I could not exactly read his expression, but I did think he was having a good time. I smiled up at him as the shadows bled away into light and the light ebbed back again.

He put his free hand, fingers curled, on my waist. Still circling, I looked up at him for a cue to the next dance move. Light painted a shining pattern, bright and brief as a firework, silently against the line of his cheek and jaw. The music went throbbing on, and the light died another little death.

In that moment of darkness, Carwyn leaned forward and captured my mouth with his. It was a sudden, warm attempt at possession: his fingers light but sure, tilting up my chin. I had nowhere else to go but into the deep, intent kiss. I shut my eyes, and there were brush strokes of light, even on the inside of my eyelids. The world grew brighter and brighter, until I opened my eyes to find light shining crystal clear all around us, and his warm mouth still on mine.

It lasted only an instant longer, then Carwyn leaned away and said, his voice low, "When I first—"

"Hey," I said to Nadiya, dropping her a slightly embarrassed smile, "could you excuse us? Just . . . just for a minute."

She gave me an understanding thumbs-up and let the crowd sway her away. I used the link to drag Carwyn where I wanted him, into the next room, and then I got a better hold on him, grabbed his shirt, and used the purchase I had to throw him up against the wall.

"Very funny," I said. "You knew I couldn't protest in front of my friend, because she thinks you're Ethan, she thinks that's something I'd want instead of"—a betrayal—"nothing I'd ever want. Not with you. Why did you do it?"

My heart was pounding louder than the music, violently in my ears.

"Oh well," Carwyn answered, breathless with spite. "Because it *was* funny. And because I could."

"You can't," I hissed. "Not ever again. I'll collar you. I'll do it right now. And then I'll hurt you."

My rings spat sparks of burning light as my fists clenched in the material of his shirt. Carwyn was smirking again, that terrible darkness-spreading smile, and he did not seem cowed in the least by the threat. His whole body was vibrating with eagerness to lash back.

That was when the real lights came on, fluorescent and scalding white, making me blink hard. I heard the sounds of footsteps—serious steps, not the tottering of party heels or rush of sneakers—on those concrete stairs.

I did not let go or even relax my grip on Carwyn, but my hold on him changed all the same. Suddenly I was clinging. We both knew that out of everybody in the club, we were the ones in the most danger in a raid. Someone found with dust would only be put in jail.

If Carwyn was found, the Strykers' secret was out. If he was found uncollared, with the evidence that I had done it a suddenly heavy weight in my back pocket, we were both dead. I could see from one look at Carwyn that he knew all that as well as I did.

"Come on," I said to his sharp, intent face, like that of a hunted fox ready to bite. "This way!"

We went running through the crowd, elbowing the panicked mob aside. I thought we knocked a few people over as we went, but it didn't matter. I could hear loud voices in the first room and bodies hitting the floor, and I barreled toward my target destination.

"The men's bathroom?" Carwyn demanded. "You're a very surprising person, Lucie."

"You're a very irritating person, Carwyn. Nadiya's brother's friend, he used to have dust on him sometimes when the place was raided. I heard him say there was a window you could get out of."

It was a slim chance. But it was our only chance, and I was grabbing it.

We hurtled through the grubby bathroom door, paint splitting as if the wood beneath was trying to get out. A boy was at a urinal, doing up his fly. He looked at us, eyes wide and startled. His mouth hung wide too; he closed it and then opened it again, as if making the decision about whether to call out.

I knew that a guard could come through the door at any moment.

I threw a flash of Light magic at him, knocking him back for a precious instant.

"Tell him that he can't see us," I told Carwyn.

"I thought you grew up in the Dark city," Carwyn snapped. "How do you not have the faintest idea how Dark magic works? I could maybe persuade him he didn't see us if we were running past him in the dark, but he's looking right at us!"

"I know how Dark magic works," I said, and took a deep breath. I turned my hand in the link I had made for us, to hold Carwyn's hand. "I know secrets in the dark nobody ever told you, doppelganger. Tell him that he can't see us."

Carwyn looked ready to argue, but first he glanced at the boy.

"You," the boy began, "aren't you . . . ?"

Carwyn sighed, closed his eyes, and rolled his neck, as if working out a kink. When his eyes opened, they were covered with darkness, as if under a film of oil.

"You can't see us," he murmured, and there was a thicker sound to his voice. It made me think of blood.

"Keep saying it," I whispered.

"You can't see us," Carwyn murmured. I lifted my free hand and my rings blazed, bright enough to blind.

Something about the air changed. The boy's expression changed too, blanking out.

"You can't see us. You can't see us," Carwyn chanted. "Lucie, he really can't see us!"

Dark magic affected thoughts and emotions, and Light magic affected the physical world, created energy, and made everything work. I could blind someone only for an instant; Carwyn could make someone believe him, against the evidence of their own eyes, only for a moment.

But working together, it was different. If you could trick the eyes and the mind both, everything was different.

My aunt and I had done it for years in secret. I did not like to think about what Aunt Leila would have done if she knew I had shared this knowledge with a doppelganger. I did not want to think about what he might do with it. We had to escape.

We shoved the boy, blind and stumbling, out through

the bathroom door. He thought he was moving of his own volition. He would slow down the guards, and he would not remember us.

The bathroom window turned out to be real, but small and so high up that we'd have to stand on the top of a toilet to get out. And only one of us could possibly get out at a time.

We stood there for a minute, on the cracked white floor tiles. When I looked at Carwyn, he was looking away, neck bent and eyes fixed on the wall. He didn't plead.

"Screw it," I said, and tore the band of light off his wrist.

He grinned at me, danced one step back, and then made a running jump at the toilet, launching himself up off it with one foot and out the window with the force of a rocket. I hesitated for a second, cursing my own stupidity, as the strip of light in my hand grew thinner and thinner and then died out, leaving a trail of sparks across my palm.

From outside the window came Carwyn's voice, sounding both reluctant and annoyed. "Lucie," he grated, as if he had a particular grievance against my name, "come on."

I clambered onto the toilet and out the window, banging my elbow on the window frame, clumsy with sheer surprise. It was a much bigger drop from the window than I had hoped, but there were no other choices, so I leaped feet first. Landing hard and off balance, I would have fallen onto elbows and knees if not for Carwyn grabbing my arm and holding me steady. Almost as soon as he grabbed me he was pulling at me, his voice fraying with impatience as he repeated, "Come on —come *on!*" and we both ran.

We ran past the guards' cars in the street, so fast that my eyes were stinging and the car lights looked like blurred streaks of red and blue painted on the black night. We ran down dark alleyways and fiercely bright city streets and through a park where there were cool shadows and fireflies and where I had to stop, head hanging between my legs, and suck air in desperately. We ran so fast that my legs were aching to the bones and my rings were actual weights on my hands, dragging them down to the earth.

And then we were standing on the Brooklyn Bridge, wind dealing my face a series of night-cold slaps, the granite and limestone towers starkly white. For a moment I felt as if we could run back into the Dark: for a moment the bridge looked like a way home.

Beyond the towers and the glittering cable lines that hung from them, web-like, as though the whole bridge were a giant spider's castle, were the walls of the Dark city. Every Dark city had a wall built around it, even ours, which was separated from the Light city by a river. The walls were built with Light magic, and they would boil the blood of whoever tried to get over them. I remembered hearing the faint crackle of the bright walls near my home in the Dark, like the leaves of deadly trees in the wind.

I scarcely ever ventured this close to the edge of the Light.

It was a night of firsts.

"We made it," I said, forcing the words out in a series of gasps.

"Yeah," said Carwyn, still standing. He wasn't winded: his voice sounded normal. It sounded pleasant and distant, like he was thinking of something else.

I straightened up, wobbly but unbelievably relieved to be safe, to have both of us safe. The water whispered soothing promises, and even though it looked deep and black, the ripples caught edges of silver. Carwyn's face was serious until he saw me looking, when he showed me that ugly smile again.

"Thanks," I said unsteadily, ignoring the smile.

"Oh, Lucie, you shouldn't thank me yet," said Carwyn. "You had no idea what you were getting into, did you?"

It was dark and cold, and I was tired, and I didn't want to have to fight him to get the collar back on. But I would have to—that much was clear. I turned my face to look at the water one more time, to take a breath and grit my teeth. I felt the warmth of Carwyn's body as he stepped in, but he didn't grab me. He whispered to me instead, each word a puff of heat against my jaw.

"Someone should have warned you about me. Oh, wait," said Carwyn. "I did."

He didn't grab me at all. He didn't use Dark magic, which could cause pain even though it was not as strong as the Light. He just shoved me clear off Brooklyn Bridge.

I used the silver moonlight on the water, absorbing it into my rings, even during the long, shocked, shrieking tumble. I had barely hit the icy, disgusting water, which felt like chilled oil, when the river itself began forming steps up the wall for me to follow. I felt only an instant of black panic as the waters closed over me.

I wouldn't let myself panic. I climbed doggedly up the steps, concentrating on them, refusing to let the river become liquid and flow away until I was back on the bridge. Once I was there, my clothes hung impossibly wet and heavy on me, trying to drag me down as if I could drown on dry land.

The night streets were, depending on where I looked, blazing with lights, or shadowy and still. I saw strangers' faces passing me, a brief sympathetic glance, a wolf whistle from a car at the soaking-wet girl. No help was to be found anywhere: the city at night moved pitilessly on.

Carwyn, of course, was long gone.

CHAPTER SEVEN

I SPENT THE NEXT DAY VICIOUSLY ANGRY WITH MYSELF for being so stupid.

I stayed home from school because Dad woke up a little at sea, not frantic anymore, but with the look of a child lost in a confusing world, and I knew it made him feel better to have me there. The pressing need for me to always be there —always with the right thing to say to Dad, ready to touch his hand reassuringly or stay a safe distance away so he did not feel crowded—let me not think about the disaster I had single-handedly created. I was tired from a long night, body worn from spent adrenaline and using too much magic, but his needs came first.

"I'm not a child!" he said once, and I swallowed and said, "Yes, of course," and went to make him something he would like to eat.

I stroked his hair as he cried, for a long, wrenching half hour, and then he was quieter, listening to the stories I told. I tried to make them sound cheerful—all about Ethan and the holiday we'd had, and not how we had come home. I used the stories as comfort for myself as much as for my father, as if the gold curve of pears and leaves in the sunlight, the curve of Ethan's mouth under mine as we lay together in the long grass, could be made bright enough to blot away all that had followed.

"I'm sorry to be so much trouble," Dad said at last, his voice quiet and more even than it had been. He was so calm and reasonable sometimes, and then everything would go wrong. "It should be you causing trouble for me."

I shuddered, thinking of what would happen to him if the trouble I had caused last night came back to us both. I kept stroking his hair, and the reflected light from my rings trembled against the wall.

"You're no trouble at all," I lied.

Eventually Dad went to sleep, exhausted from the outbursts, just before Marie came back from school. She dropped her school bag, with its weird pattern of monstrous half-pony, half-kitten creatures with Light-jeweled eyes, on the floor and danced in.

"You're so lucky you got to stay home," she said, grumbling. "I'm so tired. And I'm so *hungry*."

"From working so hard, no doubt."

Marie grinned at me, sly and carefree at once, so I was able to grin back. I got up and went into the kitchen to make us grilled-cheese sandwiches, and when Marie asked how my day had been I said "boring," so she launched into a long story about her day. She was apparently having a feud with some guy in her class, and it had culminated in a game of kiss-chase, during which he'd grabbed her and she'd bitten him.

"But, like, it wasn't assault," Marie explained. "Because it was a protest for feminism, my teacher said, and establishing my autonomy over my body."

She pronounced the word "autonomy" with extreme care.

"I like your teacher, kid," I said. I vaguely thought that I should tell her not to bite people, no matter what the provocation, but that would be massively hypocritical coming from the girl who'd established her own right to bodily autonomy by threatening to send shocks through a boy's collar to every nerve ending he possessed.

Carwyn still shouldn't have touched me. And this boy shouldn't have touched Marie. I put a hand on her back, as if I could protect her, when it was already too late.

"I'm never to do it again, because if he'd needed stitches I would be in a world of trouble," Marie informed me.

"What's this about trouble?" Penelope asked, coming in early from the hospital for a change and unwinding her scarf, subtly shining with Light embroidery, from around her neck.

Marie and I exchanged a look and chorused "Nothing" in unison as Penelope laughed.

We ate our grilled-cheese sandwiches and watched TV, Marie curled up in the space between my body and Penelope's, fitting like a coin in a slot. I rested my chin on the top of Marie's cornrowed hair and envied her this thoughtless security. Having a kid act like a kid was fine; having one of your parents suddenly turn into a child was terrifying.

"Hey," said Penelope, looking at me, "you all right, Ladybird? Did your dad upset you? Or Ethan? Did Marie upset you? Because you should know that as her mother I have the right to beat her like a gong."

She reached over and took my hand, her fingers strong and a little callused, skin clear dark brown, rings bright and the metal thin and worn from long and continual use. I wished I had hands as steady and kind as hers. I wished I could tell her everything I had done, but that would just have been laying the burden on her instead of me.

She'd done enough for me already, and she wasn't my mother. My mother was dead, and I had betrayed her memory.

"Nobody upset me," I told her. "Nothing's wrong at all."

She opened her mouth to argue with me, but just then Jarvis came home. He came home late so often, ever since Ethan had got him the job in Stryker Tower. He walked in the door with his face crumpled like a piece of office paper that had been tossed at the trash can but fallen short.

Penelope's and Marie's faces turned to his, and Jarvis's expression smoothed. Marie scrambled off the sofa and ran to him, and he lifted her up to the ceiling, his Light-enhanced-for-perfect-vision eyes reflecting a golden rim. Marie laughed down at him, knowing for certain that her father would always protect her and always be there, his hold on her steady and strong.

The next day, I had to go to school. Nightingale-Evremonde did random checks on rings, sometimes, to see what the last spell you performed was. I used my rings to turn a traffic light red as I was walking to school, then ran across the street before anyone could leap from their car and yell at me.

Ethan and I had different classes on Tuesdays, and even different lunchtimes. It felt awful to be even a tiny bit glad about that.

I was punished for it. I was standing at my locker, staring and trying to figure out which books to take out and trying not to think about what I had done, when a hand ran possessively down the small of my back.

I started and spun around, knocking my elbow—skinned from climbing out the bathroom window at the club—hard into my locker door. Ethan held his hands up in mock surrender.

"Hey, Lucie, it's just me. I'm not one of those locker muggers who have been plaguing the school."

I'd been dreading seeing him, and yet unexpectedly it made me feel better. It was a relief to see this particular personality behind this face, to absorb all the bits and pieces that made up the person I loved: Ethan's gold-touched eyes, the hair curling over the crisp white collar of his school shirt, the way he'd removed his hand fast when I jumped.

I reached out for one of his hands and pulled him back toward me. I was wearing heels, so we were standing at the same level, cheek to cheek. I smelled his clean, sharp aftershave and felt the faint scratch of a spot at his jaw that he'd missed.

"I heard they were locker highwaymen," I said. "Stand and deliver your lunch money."

Ethan's free hand went to my waist, holding on. "Lucie," he murmured. "I have something to tell you. You're probably going to be angry, and you have every right to be." He took a steadying breath. "The doppelganger's disappeared."

"I saw him," I said. "The night before last. I went to see him."

It wasn't brave of me to confess that much. There'd been a guard at Carwyn's door, a receptionist who knew my face, and probably cameras in the hotel.

"I know," Ethan said. "The guard said you were going to get something to eat. He knew the place was paid for, and that Carwyn had money in his pocket. He expected him to come right back. But he didn't come back."

"They weren't delivering room service," I said. "I took him out because I thought he should have something to eat, but then I tried a few different restaurants and they wouldn't let us in."

Ethan's voice grew even more serious. "Did he get angry?"

No, I thought about saying. *No, he didn't get angry. I was the one who got angry. I broke the law and took off his collar because I felt bad about people being mean to the doppelganger. I fed him cupcakes and took him dancing with my friends. I basically took darkness made in your image out on a date. Why? I don't know why, Ethan. I guess because I am a crazy person!*

I couldn't say that.

"Yeah," I said instead. "He got angry. He ran off."

He had run off. That much was true.

"I thought he would just go back to the hotel," I said. I wished he had; that was like thinking he would. "Tell your uncle and your father I didn't—"

"Don't, Lucie," Ethan said, sounding tired, and my heart beat a frantic pattern against my ribs. "I thought you should know he was gone," Ethan continued. "I already told Dad and Uncle Mark that you had nothing to do with it."

"I just meant . . . I didn't mean to cause them any trouble," I muttered. "I'm sorry I did."

"Carwyn can make his own decisions. They're nothing to do with you." Ethan sighed, fingers curling around the stiff blue material of my uniform skirt, over my hip. "Maybe it's for the best that he went," he said. "When I first heard he was gone, I thought . . . I thought Uncle Mark or Dad might have had something to do with it."

Ethan meant that his uncle or his father might have ordered Carwyn to be killed.

I repressed a shiver. I knew they were capable of it. But I hadn't known Ethan believed that too. How could he live with them, if he knew? Ethan must have felt the shiver despite my efforts, because he put his arms around me, smoothing the hair that tumbled down my back, the big, solid muscles he got from the gym wrapped around me. I felt like he could shield me from anything, even though I knew it wasn't true. I rubbed my cheek lightly against his, catching the corner of his mouth with mine. It was wonderful to feel that way, just the same.

"I was always afraid he'd come back," Ethan continued, low and confessional. "I was afraid that Dad would suffer for what he'd done, and I was afraid to . . . to look into a doppelganger's eyes and see who he was, see if it meant I was doomed, like the stories say. Or if I was doomed for a different reason: that he was made because of me but we sent him away and we deserved whatever he did to us."

"Ethan," I said. "Ethan, you were a baby. I do wish you'd told me, but what happened to him was not your fault."

"When he did come back, I didn't like him," said Ethan. "I don't like that he had my mother for the first few years of my life. I don't like that he doesn't even remember her, that he doesn't care about her or about much of anything. But that doesn't mean he deserved to be treated like he was. He certainly didn't deserve to die. If he got away, I'm glad. I wish they could all escape."

I didn't know if he meant doppelgangers or all the buried ones in the Dark city. It didn't matter, since we couldn't change the world. We were just two kids in our school uniforms, clinging to each other in a corridor full of the noise and bustle of school, trying to pretend the world away.

"I'm glad too," I whispered. It felt like the first thing I had said to Ethan today that was not a lie.

I turned my face in closer to his, nuzzling, until we were kissing. My arm around his shoulders held him in, close against me. I did not want to let him go.

"And I'm late for class," Ethan said regretfully. He kissed me again, lightly this time, mouth and then my cheek, and stepped away. "Can you come back to my place after school? I have a special reason for asking."

"Sure," I murmured. "And you don't need a special reason."

I was late for class too, but I didn't go immediately. I sat on the sill of the window opposite my locker and fought back the thought of how much I had just lied to Ethan and how massively I had misjudged Carwyn.

I'd believed the fact that he'd waited outside the nightclub's window meant I could trust him, but that hadn't been true. He hadn't wanted me to get caught because if I'd been taken by the guards, I would have been found with the doppelganger's collar on me. He'd waited for me because he wanted a clean getaway, and once he'd accomplished that, he'd thrown me off a bridge.

He looked like Ethan. I hadn't confused the two of them, but seeing the familiar, beloved lines of his face, even on someone else, had confused me. I'd been able to be familiar with him, to take chances on him without feeling as if they were the deadly, life-altering risks they were.

Because of that, I'd trusted him, much more than I should have, when I shouldn't have trusted him at all. He was my best beloved's shadow self, an image made out of darkness, but worse than that he was a stranger, and I did not know what he was capable of.

I didn't think that Carwyn was going to run off somewhere, live a blameless life, and stay safe. I thought he was coming back. I knew he held our lives in the palm of his hand.

I knew I should tell somebody. But, like always, I was afraid to tell the truth. I knew it would condemn me.

I didn't tell Penelope, and I didn't tell Ethan. I didn't tell anybody at all.

Above the Strykers' apartment was a private gym, where all four of the Strykers had sessions with a personal trainer several times a week. I had only been there before to sit on the weight bench and read while Ethan finished up.

I had not expected this to be Ethan's special reason for asking me over. I had not expected my boyfriend to stand before me, in socked feet on the polished wood floor, with a sword glowing with Light magic in either hand.

"You scared me to death when you jumped onto the platform and leaped at those guys with swords," Ethan said simply. "I don't know what might happen in the future. I want to protect you — and I figure the best way to protect you is to teach you to protect yourself."

It was a sweet idea, but I hated to think of Ethan being scared and doubtful about the future.

"You're going to teach me?" I asked, keeping my voice light. I reached over and took one of the swords from him. I felt its magic crackling satisfactorily up my arm. "Since when do you know about sword fighting?"

"I don't have any Light magic, so Uncle Mark wanted to be sure I could always protect myself," Ethan went on. "He also thought it might be good PR if I joined the Light Guard for a year or so after college. I don't know. I'm pretty good."

He sounded shy, and a little proud.

"Are you?" I said, and I forced myself to smile at him.

"Yeah, and I'm willing to teach you everything I know."

"Lucky me."

We crossed swords, the blades flickering as they rang together, my blade glowing with a faint flare of Light each time I parried Ethan's thrust. It was like lightning and thunder, the gleam and then the peal, and it felt good. It felt familiar.

I had made so many mistakes. I had been so stupid. I lay awake nights thinking of all I feared and how I had failed. I could do nothing to fix any of it, but I could do this.

I parried again and sent power from my free hand to make Light burn too strongly in Ethan's sword. He almost dropped it. I pressed home my advantage and came at him with a flurry of ringing strokes, making him stumble back. He stared at me, awe and Light magic shining on his face, as if I had lit a huge match between us.

"You can fight!" Ethan exclaimed.

"I can win," I said, and forced Ethan's sword down.

Ethan did not even look at the sword points touching the floor, did not care that he had been beaten. He looked at me, frowning, and as my frantic heartbeat slowed, I began to realize I had made another mistake. "Why did you never tell me you knew the sword?" he asked.

What could I say? That my aunt the Dark magician had taught me in the little garden outside her house? That I had learned how to stand and move and fight for years, learned how to practice magic against a Dark magician as few Light magicians had the chance to—how to fight anyone, how to cheat, how to win? Was I supposed to tell him that my aunt used to say I could use these skills against a Light guard, and I had never dreamed I would, but years later, on a train platform, Aunt Leila had been proved right? That when I used too much Light magic and it poisoned my blood, my aunt would drain the poison away and drink my blood at her kitchen table, and then we would make cookies?

I'd told Ethan about my mother: that she had existed, that I'd known her, that she'd died. It wasn't much, but he was the only person in the Light city I had told about her at all.

I had not told Ethan anything about my Aunt Leila. I did not think he would like the sound of her, somehow, any more than she would have liked him. They were impossibly different people, from impossibly different worlds, and it would have made Ethan think differently of me.

Besides, Aunt Leila was safe, as safe as a Dark magician in the Dark city could be. I did not want to bring her to the attention of any Strykers, even the one I loved.

"It never came up," I said unsteadily.

Until the train platform, with Ethan kneeling and a guard drawing his sword. I had known the risk when I flung myself at the guard. I had known what to do. Ethan had just assumed I did not . . . because I had never told him anything else. I didn't want him to think of me as someone who could deal with these kind of situations, who belonged in that kind of world: Aunt Leila's world, in the Dark.

"I want you to tell me things, even if they don't come up," Ethan said. "Just as long as they're about you. I only want to know more about you."

It should have been a strange thing for a boy to say to his girlfriend of two years. I found myself looking away, as if I, not he, had been beaten.

"If you knew me more, you'd like me less."

"I don't think so," Ethan murmured.

I made myself smile, even though I was scared. "Come on —let a girl keep her mystique."

It was a weak ploy.

Ethan opened his mouth, and I knew it was to argue with me. I stared at him, mutely imploring him not to.

I thought it wouldn't work, but after a moment he lowered his eyes and put down his sword. "Asking you to spar was a mistake, huh?" he said, stepping forward and wrapping his arms around me. "I'm sorry."

"I don't want this," I said into his shirt. "I don't want us to be frightened. I want things to be the way they always are between us. I want everything to be normal."

Normal for me was keeping secrets. What was one more?

"All right," Ethan murmured. "Whatever you want."

There was an amazing sofa in Ethan's apartment, deep and soft as a cloud, and the color of excellent cream, the kind of sofa that meant price was not an issue and neither was the sofa owners cleaning it themselves. Six people could lie on that sofa like a bed.

That evening it was just me and Ethan, curled together and snuggled into the sofa cushions.

"I would love you without the fabulous luxuries," I informed him. "But they help."

"So what you're saying is that if I get fat, you'll keep me around for the sofa."

"You have a personal trainer because you're so afraid of losing your svelte figure," I pointed out. "But if you start balding prematurely, I'll consider keeping you around for the sofa."

"Well, that's a relief."

I levered myself up on one elbow, looking down into Ethan's face, soft with laughter and tenderness. The commercials buzzed along on television, little jingles and bursts of color, drawing into the news of the day, and everything seemed normal and safe.

"Besides," I said, laying kisses from his jaw to his mouth, feeling him smile under my lips. "I bet all your money could buy a truly awesome toupee."

I remembered an old poem that went, *What lips my lips have kissed, and where, and why, I have forgotten* . . . but I had not forgotten. There had only ever been Ethan.

The other one didn't count.

I had almost lost Ethan, a handful of days ago. It reminded me that it was a privilege to be close like this, the skin of his stomach under the flat of my palm, the curl of his smile against my mouth.

"You're such a romantic," Ethan mumbled.

"You have no idea." I kissed him again, my hair a curtain all around us, his mouth opening in a warm, easy slide under mine, and then a cough sounded like a door slamming, and I bit down on Ethan's lip.

"Ow!" said Ethan, and I reared back and stared around wildly.

Jim Stryker, Ethan's cousin, was standing in the doorway.

"Didn't mean to startle you," he said, with one of his stupid grins. "You were just getting your PDA all over the good sofa."

"Oh, as opposed to the extremely private stuff you were doing on it with Suzy at your birthday party."

"Come on, Lucie, be reasonable. I was drunk." Jim grinned again. He had thick lips, a thick bridge to his nose, gel turning his hair into a solid mass. Other people thought he was handsome, but he'd always looked like an overblown version of Ethan to me. "I wouldn't do anything like that sober. Unless you're finally willing to drop Ethan and try a real man."

"I'll do it!" I declared. "Now, tell me more about this real man. Will you take me to him? Because I haven't seen anyone like that lately."

In some ways, Jim was restful to be around, since he took

everything any girl said to him as flirting. Occasionally he looked confused by something I said, but the whale of his self-esteem always ended up making short work of the plankton of doubt.

It occurred to me that if Ethan's doppelganger had acted like Jim, I wouldn't have felt any urges to sympathy, and I certainly wouldn't have taken off his collar. Carwyn might have been soulless, but at least he wasn't an idiot.

I couldn't think about that right at that moment, and I certainly couldn't be such a nervous wreck that I was jumping at the least little noise. I rolled my eyes at Jim and reached for Ethan's hand.

Ethan jerked away from me, and I stared at him. He was sitting bolt upright, suddenly tense, his jaw held tight. I felt my heart trip in my chest, felt the lurch and the chill, like a little kid stumbling over her own feet into a freezing-cold puddle.

"What," I said, my voice trembling. "What—what is it?"

"Guys, look at this," Ethan said, voice and body strained as if the television were going to attack him.

We both turned our attention to the television. I had been tuning out the drone of the reporter's voice, but now I looked at the shimmering Light magic projected against the wall, resolving in my sight until the voice and the picture came clear.

". . . violent disturbance within the walls of the Dark city, during which six Light guards lost their lives," said the news-caster's voice, flat and noncommittal, turning the words into boring nonsense. I wondered if that was why these people were hired, because they could make disaster sound dull and give people the distance they needed from it.

The feed from the camera was grainy, showing footage taken at night on someone's phone. But I could see enough of the entrance gate: it was just outside Green-Wood Cemetery.

I could recognize it even though it looked different. The whole scene was painted gray by night, and in the street itself were streaks and dark stains, still shining fresh. The rough, irregular stones of the street had dammed flowing blood into small dark pools.

The camera followed the path through the gate and into a scene of chaos.

It looked as if lightning had struck every tree. They were ripped to splinters and shards of wood, cast over the grass like the remnants of a shipwreck, and amid the wood were the iron cages.

Some of the cages had bodies still huddled in them. Some of the bodies were skeletons, left in place as a warning to oth-ers not to cross the Light. Some of them might have died last night, died of terror at the idea of freedom.

Some of the cages lay twisted and empty, the black iron melted, the cage doors gaping open.

The cages were down. Nobody would ever be strung up

like my father had been, ever again. They were the symbols of the Light's power, the awful threat of the Light's worst punishment.

Nobody had ever dared attack the cages before.

I remembered that guy at the club who had told me we might have something to celebrate soon. Was this what he had meant? Had somebody planned this?

Why had he thought I would know?

A shrill sound of laughter rang out, and the camera zoomed back up the hill, through the gates, to the blood-stained street.

There were people there, and one side of my brain just said, *Yes, normal people. That's what people look like,* and the other side of my mind, the side accustomed to the Light, said that they were gaunt scarecrows. Food had to be brought in past the walls, and the Dark city was never given quite enough. I'd been overwhelmed by the lunatic abundance of food in the Light city when I'd first arrived, but I hadn't realized how used I had become to the Light citizens, smug and sleek as housecats.

There were people laughing, dancing, people openly wearing the black and scarlet of the *sans-merci*. Dark magicians were on their knees, doing spells with the spilled blood. Ethan and Jim would not be able to differentiate between Dark magicians—one would look the same as another to them—but I could see from the edges of their clothes under their dark robes that they were not among the Dark magicians who served the Light Council. They would not have been permitted to drain people often. They were holding more magic in their hands now than they had ever before touched in their lives.

My own hands were twisted together in my lap. They felt colder than my rings, shivering flesh under a weight of metal. My Aunt Leila, whom I loved and who was the one person I knew I could count on, was a Dark magician. I had only ever felt sorry for them, known that they suffered for something that was not their fault, and that they were starved of their power because people feared it.

I was afraid, I realized, of what they would do with power now that they had it.

Over the shoulder of a child, his cheeks fat with a grin and daubed with blood, I saw a message glistening on bricks.

Scrawled upon a wall with a finger dipped in blood were the words FREE THE GOLDEN ONE.

It was as if I was seeing the words of Carwyn and the man from the club written on a wall, a message spelled out all too clearly now that it was too late.

"Oh God, they mean me," I whispered. Ethan took my hand and held on: Ethan was all I had to hold on to. "They did this for me."

CHAPTER EIGHT

WHEN I GOT HOME FROM ETHAN'S HOUSE, I
waited until Dad was asleep. Then I crept into
the long skinny hall that we didn't call a corridor, the wood floor forgivingly quiet under my bare feet, and
listened outside the door of the other bedroom. I could hear
Jarvis's deep breathing and Penelope's faint snore, and I was
almost sure I could make out the soft sound of Marie sighing in her sleep. I was the only thing moving in that dark
narrow apartment, shadows on exposed-brick walls, with a
beam of moonlight and the orange slant of a streetlight filtering through a tall, black-trimmed window.

I stole back into my room and opened my wardrobe,
snaking my hand under the mountain of clothes and shoes at
the bottom to the very back, where I had hidden the doppelganger's hood. For a moment, I could not find it, my fingers
making a blind, futile journey over the fuzz of a sweater and
the rubber sole of a shoe. Then my skin caught on one of the
metal slots, fingertips brushing the cracked leather. My rings
almost hummed in recognition.

I pulled the collar out and heard the tumble and slam of a dislodged shoe against one of the wardrobe walls. I stayed frozen in a crouch as my father murmured, disturbed and discontent, and then settled back into sleep. My pajama top stuck to my collarbones with sweat.

At the train station, the guards had said somebody who looked like Ethan had been distributing security information to a member of the *sans-merci*. And a few days later, the cages were shattered and the prisoners had gone free.

Anyone under suspicion of consorting with the *sans-merci* would be suspected of involvement with the attack on the cages. Ethan was going to be under investigation, and his connection to me would make it worse. The *sans-merci* were acting in my name: the Light Council might decide we were both in league with rebels.

I knew that I had done nothing, and I was certain Ethan had done nothing. I had another suspect. Carwyn had been talking about revolution and blood in the streets. Carwyn must be involved.

And I had made it easy for him to move about the city, unmarked by his hood, people all around him never dreaming what he was or what he was planning.

I should take this hood and collar to the Light guards, should explain the threat I had unleashed on the city. But what would they do to me then? What would happen to my father without me?

I knew better than to expect mercy.

I wrapped the collar in the hood to muffle any betraying clink of metal, then crawled across the floor with it clutched in my fist, to my school bag. Inside my bag was a small brown leather pouch containing a handful of ashes I had taken from the fireplace in Ethan's living room. I tucked the doppel-ganger's collar into the little bag, blindly fumbling, and then crawled around the side of the wardrobe, to the brick wall.

If I crawled, nobody could see me through the windows. Just in case someone was watching the apartment.

When we had come to Penelope and Jarvis's, I had been constantly on edge, relentlessly terrified that someone would show up to take back the pardon and take Dad in to be tor-tured, so terrified that I had burned Dad's books on Dark magic and the very few letters Aunt Leila had sent. I had never written back to her, and she had soon stopped writing. I spent my time back then, whenever Dad was drugged into calm, scraping away at mortar until I could pull out a couple of the bricks.

If someone looked at this wall, they would have noticed two bricks that were obviously displaced. I had taken a fork to the crevices between those two bricks, and the mortar around them had a slightly gnawed appearance.

The real loose brick was seventeen across and five up from the bottom, in the shadow of the wardrobe. I slid the brick out, feeling its rough edges nip into my palm, to reveal a tiny hollow space. I shoved the pouch almost to the very back, then crammed in ashes, hoping the dull brown of the bag would be entirely obscured even if someone took the brick out.

Although I had burned Aunt Leila's letters and Dad's books, I had kept one thing: the pendant necklace with the single jewel my mother had worn and worked magic with in the confines of our home. I didn't deserve to have a keepsake of her, but I had not been able to leave it or get rid of it.

I had never hidden anything else in there, until then.

I slid the brick back into place, stood up, stepped away, and surveyed the innocent expanse of the wall. Then I came out of the bedroom, pulling the door open and closed as softly as I could, and went to sit on the sofa. I put my guilty head in my ash-stained hands and sat there for what seemed like a long time.

I do not know why I looked up to the silver square of the window, its pale reflection cast on the floor at my feet. Perhaps it was a strange noise, or perhaps it was something the Light Council says all Light magicians have: an innate sense of when the darkness approaches and encroaches on the illumination we give out.

A dead streetlight stood in my line of vision, its magic failed, staring like a socket in which the eye had been put out. As I drew closer to the window, I saw the windows of the buildings across the street, all glossy black save for the sharp lights of cars reflected as they went by. The city was indifferent and distant, as close to sleeping as it ever was.

Underneath my window, my devil was waiting, wearing my true love's face. The moon bleached that face and the street beneath, so Carwyn looked as if he were standing on a ray of moonlight, a shining silver expanse that stretched from the sky to his feet.

His face was so pale, the color of alabaster or pearl, the poetic peaceful color that people turned in stories when they died. But I had seen the dead in their cages, had seen them livid and ashen, and I had learned long ago not to believe in stories.

The dead are defeated, the dead are lost. But this, I thought, with all the whispers about doppelgangers I had ever heard suddenly crowding my mind, was something that had been sent back from the land of the dead. This was a shadow of a person. This was death triumphant, walking among the living.

And I had set him free.

He had not changed position or expression as he looked at the window. All he did was stand beneath the window and stare, but I knew he saw me. His eyes looked dark and empty, in contrast with his salt-white face, like holes burned in a sheet.

I do not know how long I stood at the window.

I do not know how long my pallid companion stood

looking up at me before he seemed to dissolve away, slipping from the moonshine to mingle with his fellow shadows.

I did not know if it was a warning or not. I didn't know if he was telling me that he'd had something to do with the spectacle at the Green-Wood Cemetery, or that I was guilty by association, if he wanted only to frighten me or to ensure my silence with fear.

It was a wasted trip for him. I had seen the blood in the streets and on the wall, and I had told nobody what I had done. I had made my decision. I had hidden the collar. I could not betray him without betraying myself.

All the streets could run with blood, and I would not go to the authorities. They had taken my mother forever, taken my father, and I had only gotten him back through being able to lie and pretend we were somehow different from the other victims. Only a few days ago, they had tried to take my Ethan.

I needed no apparitions in the night to urge me to evil.

I had made the decision long ago: better to be safe than good.

The next morning, I got up early and made everyone breakfast. I tried to cook and clean as regularly as I could. Jarvis, Penelope, and Marie might care about us, might feel sorry for us, but it was smart to make them like me. The last time I ever saw her, my aunt had advised me to make myself useful.

Be clever. Be careful. Remember they are not like family, she'd said. *Wait for me to come and get you,* she had added, but I'd known she was dreaming, and I was on my own.

I forgot sometimes, with Penelope especially, but I tried to remember. I didn't want to be stupid or careless.

Now I had been stupid and careless, and I had to make up for it by trying even harder.

"You're a treasure, Ladybird," Penelope declared, coming into the kitchen to snatch a piece of bacon and patting Marie's cornrowed hair. "What we'll do when you go to college I can't imagine."

Nothing would change when I went to college. I was going to college in New York, of course. My father couldn't manage without me.

My father emerged into the kitchen last of all, glasses askew and hair ruffled, looking like a baby owl confused by the world. He sat down at the kitchen island, and I set his plate in front of him and poured his juice.

"You effortlessly make the morning shine, my dear," he said, sounding like a gentleman from days long gone by, and I could see he felt better. He started talking with Penelope and Jarvis about the deleterious effect of dust on the minds of the young. He was doing research on the subject, writing a paper: there were days he went to the library and talked to strangers, and they thought he was such a charming, intelligent man. He was going today, and I was sure every stranger he spoke to would be fooled again. They would never have imagined there was a thing wrong with him.

I'd burned the side of my thumb cooking the bacon and eggs, and I took this opportunity to press the burned skin to the metal of the refrigerator sneakily, so nobody would see me do it. Nobody ever guessed how much effort looking effortless took.

"I'll walk to school," I said. I always got up in time to do that, because only four people fit in the car without being cramped, and dropping me off meant making an extra stop.

"You don't have to," said Jarvis. He always offered me a lift, as if it was his job to look after me, as if I was Marie. He was always so kind, and it made me nervous: I always wondered when his kindness might run out.

"I want to," I told him.

I wasn't lying. I usually walked, and Ethan usually met me on the way.

Ethan could not come by my place much, because my father got upset when he saw him. He got upset at the very name of Stryker. I couldn't blame him, not really: I knew as well as he did what anybody on the Light Council could do to us, let alone what Mark or Charles Stryker could do.

I gave everyone a round of kisses and goodbyes and walked

out into the sunshine. It was a bright morning, but sharp around the edges. The sun was a golden disc so high up in the sky that it made sense that its warmth had not reached the city yet. I pulled my coat tighter around myself and walked on, watching the glitter of sunlight on the tin roofs of warehouses and faraway spires alike.

I smiled when the long black car purred up to the curb and stood waiting, like a cat expecting to be petted. The richest cars were the narrowest, in a classic style built to show off that they had no need for engines now that they had Light magic, with no thought for packing a family or a car seat inside the vehicle. This was an impractical and gleaming black sliver of a car.

Usually Ethan walked to meet me, but now and then he took a car if it was cold or he'd overslept and was afraid that he would miss me. He was a child of luxury: he never needed to think twice about taking one of the cars, in the same way normal people never needed to think about grabbing a cup out of a kitchen cabinet. There were always plenty, and it was no big deal.

Talk about someone effortlessly brightening up a morning. I stood with my cold hands in my pockets and beamed at the darkened windows of the car.

Then the window rolled down, and Mark Stryker was looking at me. I looked past him and saw his face in a weaker mold. Charles Stryker. Both Ethan's father and his terrifying uncle had come for me. That meant they had something specific in mind—they only came hunting in pairs on matters of utmost importance.

"Lucie," Mark said mildly, "jump in the car, would you? We'd like a word about the *sans-merci*."

CHAPTER NINE

A DRIVER IN THE STRYKER LIVERY, ELECTRIC BLUE lines on a background of lambent gold like the sun's rays in reverse, unfolded himself from the front seat and opened the door for me. Neither Mark nor Charles Stryker could be expected to sully their hands with car doors.

I crushed my impulse to flee like a scared animal. There was nowhere I could run where they would not chase me down.

Instead I got reluctantly into the car. The leather was so expensive, it did not squeak as the skirt of my school uniform slid over it. I sank backward into the seat and felt enveloped by the whole dark car, carried off like a maiden in a story, never to be seen again.

I found myself twisting my hands in my lap, barely even able to look at the men I was facing, and realized I was sitting as if I was at a job interview or worse: as if I was suspected of a crime.

Even if they knew I was guilty, that was no reason to act guilty.

I looked up. Charles was leaning forward and looking tense, because he was the clumsy one. Mark was sitting back, his face relaxed.

The windows of this car, I remembered, were black and opaque as jet from the outside. It was very dark in the car, a little stuffy, smelling like the ghost of expensive cologne. The only light was that shimmering around all our rings. The Strykers had glowing, lucent jewels, the best money could buy. Next to them, mine looked like glass.

Charles coughed. "We wanted to talk to you about the recent trouble. With Ethan."

"I won't breathe a word about—" I stopped before I said Carwyn's name, but I should not have spoken at all. It betrayed nervousness. "About anything."

"No, Lucie, of course not," said Charles. "You're a good girl," he added anxiously, as if to appease me.

"We all know that," Mark slid in.

The statement hung in the air, like a sword over my head. I waited for it to fall.

"The charge laid against Ethan is a very serious one," said Charles Stryker, rubbing the loose skin over his knuckles. "The guards who apprehended him have been dealt with, and the guards in this city have been told it was a case of mistaken identity. But the fact remains that he was charged, and now there is the civil unrest of the cages being torn down, and your name is being thrown around by some very unsavory people. Of course we do not believe that you are in any way involved with the thugs who launched the attack on Green-Wood Cemetery. They are using your name and fame for their own purposes and may plan to do worse. Who knows what sinister intentions the *sans-merci* harbor toward you, but do not worry, Lucie. The Light Council will protect you."

"Thank you," I whispered, and waited to hear the conditions of my protection.

"If people begin to believe Ethan is mixed up with the *sans-merci,* the consequences could be very serious. For all of us."

I remembered the blade that had been laid against Ethan's throat, and my own fear stopped choking me. It was easier to devote myself to someone else: it was what I knew how to do.

"It's ridiculous to think that people might suspect Ethan of doing anything wrong," I said, and my tone was as assured as Mark's had been earlier.

Mark smiled. "Exactly."

"But still, we cannot defend Ethan's innocence as vigorously as we might wish, lest certain unfortunate matters come to light," Charles said.

They could not let people know it was Carwyn who had committed treason, not Ethan, because they could not let people know that Carwyn existed. I nodded to show I understood.

"As Charles said, the guards who made the rash accusation, and the commander who gave the orders to apprehend

Ethan, have been dealt with," Mark contributed. "But . . ."

That meant that they had been killed. I wasn't sure if I was supposed to understand that, so I just looked at them.

"Ethan is going to have to make a public statement about the unfortunate misunderstanding," Charles continued. "On a live morning show today. Just to clear everything up. So that he will be found innocent in the court of public opinion."

So that he would not mess up the Strykers' chances in the next council elections.

"You have a certain well-deserved cachet with the media," Mark commented.

"And of course, a lovely young couple, side by side . . ." said Charles helpfully.

For a moment, I wondered how much of his weakness was real and how much was for show. With Charles there, everything Mark meant got said, and Mark did not have to be the one who said it. The way they worked meant Mark's standing was untouched and Charles was underestimated.

I looked from Mark's face to Charles's, then back at their hands, with their nails buffed and their rings shining. Of course they would not ever have killed anyone themselves. Of course their hands were clean.

"Whatever I can do to help Ethan," I said. "I'm happy to do it."

· · · ·

At Home with Seth and Gina was the most-watched morning talk show in Light New York. Every time a politician committed an indiscretion or a celebrity had a scandal, they tried to smooth it over on *At Home.* People trusted it more than the prerecorded shows, because they knew it was live, but they never considered how carefully every appearance had been prepared for.

Except for this time.

Mark and Charles must have bargained that the more I was caught off guard, the more likely I would be to agree to do it. Even if it meant going on television totally unprepared the day after rebels rose up in my name.

A bevy of makeup people ushered me into the building and instantly away from Mark and Charles, carrying me in an inexorable tide from hall to elevator to dressing room. A woman blew my hair out very carefully, the shine in her rings lending my hair an extra luster even after her hands had left it. Two more women painted my face like it was a canvas, with tiny brush strokes and tints of magic. They had laid out a white bandage dress for me. When I stepped into it, I felt the cool heavy weight of silk on my skin and saw that it fit me well enough.

The women had turned off the bright lights that surrounded the mirror. I stood and looked at my reflection, my hair shadowing my face, my body a woman's body.

That was television: if you had a woman's body, you were expected to show it off. But they were making a mistake. The wardrobe people clearly knew I had always worn white for the media, but they did not seem to realize why: draped white on a child made her seem pure, as though her soul were snowy white and free of stain, as though every word out of her mouth must be truth. Audiences believed children's words. They did not believe the words of women. Just having this body made me suspect. Putting it on display was even worse.

I remembered the guards on the train platform, who had not believed me when I said who I was.

I didn't look like the innocent child, like the Golden Thread in the Dark anymore. I didn't know if this was going to work.

Ethan was standing outside the studio, waiting for his turn. I laid my hand on one of his shoulders, resting it gently against his perfectly pressed shirt.

When he turned around, he looked stunned. "Lucie. What are you doing here?"

I hesitated. It was strange for him to be anything but happy to see me. "Your father and your uncle asked me to come."

"And you *came?*" Ethan demanded.

I straightened my back and gazed up at him. "They said I could help you. Of course I came."

I expected him to be grateful. I certainly did not expect the look of agony on his face, as if I had hit him.

"I don't want you anywhere near me right now," Ethan whispered.

I was left speechless, my hands hanging empty, and it was at that moment the door opened and a woman with gelled silver hair that made her head look like a tiny moon said, "We're ready for you."

The two presenters were a man in a shirt his stomach was trying to break free of, and a woman in a shiny pink dress so stiffly constructed, she had to perch at the edge of her chair. Ethan and I were shown to a sofa.

"So you're just here to set the record straight, young Ethan," said Seth in an avuncular tone.

Maybe it was my presence throwing him off. Maybe it was the tone that was the mistake, since Ethan's actual uncle was as cuddly as an anaconda. Ethan stared for a second too long before he said, "That's right."

I saw both of the hosts' faces change, the first hint of hostility creeping in.

"And what are you doing here, Lucie?" asked the woman, Gina. She laughed at the end of the question, but it seemed a little too pointed.

"I'm here for moral support," I said, and tried to laugh too.

"Love's young dream still going strong, then?"

"Very much so," I said, and reached for Ethan's hand. He

pulled his hand away, as if by instinct, and then hastily corrected the gesture. I knew the camera would record it, and tried to pin on a smile. I feared that the smile was not terribly convincing.

"Let's get right down to it," said Seth. He was the one whose job it was to ask the important questions, I knew, because audiences would listen to a man's words and take them more seriously. "Mr. Stryker." There was a weight to the way he addressed him, as if Ethan was not to be thought of as a child anymore but was to be considered and condemned as an adult. "I hear that you were recently involved in an unfortunate incident outside the borders of our city."

"I was charged with treason and almost beheaded," said Ethan. "I guess you could call that unfortunate."

I pressed his hand warningly. The worst thing he could do was treat this as a joke.

Ethan shifted slightly away from me. I could not understand why he was acting this way.

"The charge was passing secrets to the rebels, was it not?" the interviewer asked. "Details about the lives of people on the Light Council, how to get into their homes and workplaces. It is obvious that the person who passed them meant to attack the very foundations of our city."

"Yes," said Ethan. "So it'd be a bit of a weird thing for me to do."

That was better, but his polite smile looked stretched at

the edges, like rationed butter scraped over bread, as if he had only so much diplomacy in him.

"The passed documents also contained details of the magic used to set up the cages—information that was deployed in the horrible attack on Green-Wood Cemetery that destroyed the instruments of the Light's justice," Seth went on relentlessly. "The man who passed along those secrets must be a member of the *sans-merci*. And he is a man who looks very much like you. But you and your family declare that this is just a strange coincidence."

"That's right," said Ethan.

"A sad misunderstanding brought about by an unlikely look-alike."

"That's right!" snapped Ethan.

The lady interviewer in pink leaned forward, her body language mirroring her colleague's, their shoulders hunched and their gazes intent. They resembled vultures dressed up in fancy clothes, their true natures obvious despite their costumes as soon as they spied a wounded creature.

"What is your opinion about the cages?" she asked. "Of the criminals who are put in them?"

Ethan hesitated. I did not dare look at him, add the weight of my gaze to the watchful eyes of the vultures and the glinting, unrelenting eye of the camera that meant the eyes of the world. I felt the tension of his body through his fingers, cold and unmoving in mine, and in the hush after the woman's question, I heard my dearest love's indrawn breath, heard the small wet sound of his tongue swallowing back both lies and truths. I was sitting beside him, my hand in his, and my father had been caged. The cages had been wrecked by rebels. Nothing was safe for Ethan to say.

"Did you think that the criminals deserved the cages?"

"I do not think anybody deserves that," said Ethan at last.

"You're glad they were torn down?" Gina asked, her voice like a predator slinking after the last wounded animal in a herd. Ethan said nothing. "You disagree with the punishment of the cages. Do you disagree with food rationing for the Dark city? What other complaints of the *sans-merci* do you agree with?"

"I think everyone should have enough to eat," Ethan snapped. "I think we need to talk about these issues, I think we need to listen to the *sans-merci*."

"Listen to killers?" Gina asked, the question very precise. Ethan flinched. "Does Lucie agree with you?"

I opened my mouth.

"Lucie and I don't talk about that kind of thing," Ethan said shortly. I wanted to scream at him. He knew the *sans-merci* were talking about me as if I was a princess in need of rescuing. He should not make them think they were right.

He was going to infuriate the Light Council and give the rebels further reason to fight.

"So this mystery man, the one who looks so much like

you," Seth continued, picking up smoothly where Gina had left off. "You have more in common than your faces. You agree with the message he was spreading? You two have the same face and the same beliefs, but you claim you are not the same person?"

"I understand why people find it hard to believe," I said. The attention of everyone was suddenly and sharply focused on me.

It was strange how difficult it was to speak while wearing a false smile. I wished I could control my body in precisely the way I wanted: what use was it if I could not use it? A puppet would obey me better than my own flesh. I wished I could be a puppet, could be some smiling, dancing thing that would make all the right moves and save him.

"Two boys that handsome in one city," I said. "I find it hard to believe myself."

The joke fell utterly flat. Nobody laughed except me, and my laugh shook.

Of course, the idea that there was someone who looked exactly like Ethan who was wandering Light New York committing crimes sounded like a very weak excuse indeed. To everyone else, it was a ridiculous, obvious lie that nobody would believe. Only I knew that it was the truth. Only I knew that if people found out the truth, we would all be in even worse trouble than we were now.

• • • •

That afternoon, we were in Stryker Tower, escorted into one of the rooms where the council met. We sat at a long oval table watching our interview play. Even at the very beginning of the interview, before disaster struck, we were both stiff and uncomfortable. I was visibly trying hard to be charming and thus was not charming at all. Ethan turned his chair away slightly from the screen, as someone who was not used to and could not bear to see unpleasantness.

I was used to seeing people hurt. I could watch and try to measure how hurt they might be.

I had known the interview was going wrong even as it happened, but I had not dreamed it could turn out as badly as this.

It was not Ethan's father, Charles, who had brought us here. It was Mark Stryker, and he was looking at Ethan as if Ethan was not his nephew but an unexpected liability.

"Have you two seen the papers today?" he inquired.

"I've seen the *Times*," I said.

"So you haven't seen a paper that counts," said Mark.

We were sitting but he remained standing, the better to tower over us. He made a gesture at one of the men behind him, one of the usual anonymous drones always wearing gray. Even the man's shining rings seemed like a uniform as he handed a sheaf of newspapers to Mark and Mark tossed them one by one onto the table. Their lurid colors, the twisted bright repetitions of mine and Ethan's faces, turned the table into a nightmare carnival.

"Paper after paper discussing your obvious guilt, and what that will mean for the future of the Light Council," Mark said. "Splendid. Just what we wanted. I thought having the girl with you might help, but I suppose it was too much to hope for. We can't expect her to have the same popularity as she did a couple of years ago."

"Why not?" Ethan demanded.

"Because I don't look the same," I said. "And because I'm with you, and the citizens of both cities either hate the Strykers and think I need to be rescued, or they support the Strykers and worry I am undermining you. No matter what they believe, I'm an easy scapegoat."

I remembered my changed shape in the white dress. A child, a daughter, could be innocent in a way a woman—a woman with her man—could not be. Especially not a woman whose name the *sans-merci* were using as a rallying call, a woman who might have seduced a Stryker to the rebels' cause or who might have been the Strykers' victim. I could imagine a dozen dark rumors about me floating around the Light city.

I had always known that the way others saw me had nothing to do with the truth. Now new lies were being told about me, and I knew how easy it was to make people believe lies.

Ethan looked at me, his face a picture of angry confusion.

I didn't want to explain to him. I had always been innocent in his eyes, and I wanted to remain innocent.

Mark looked toward me as well. "So only one of you is a fool," he said. "What a pity that means there is a fool in my family."

"This whole interview fiasco was your idea," Ethan said. "So maybe our family can boast of more than one fool."

He always spoke to Mark like this, as if it was safe.

Mark did not even look at him. He kept looking at me.

"You do have some sympathizers left," he said. "However, Ethan giving you the cold shoulder throughout the interview did not help his cause with them. There are theories that the Strykers are threatening the Golden Thread in the Dark into a false relationship with their guilty child. They are saying that because of your protests against the cages when your father was imprisoned, you and your father were taken into our custody and that you are little better than a hostage, being used to increase the Strykers' popularity because the people love you. The rebels are calling for the Dark city to rise up and free you. The crowd loves a good story. People are listening."

Carwyn had said much the same thing to me as we sat on swings and ate cupcakes.

I supposed I could see why somebody might believe the relationship was fake, I thought, looking down at the papers. I was all-right-looking, but nothing special: not beautiful, not arresting. Ethan could have any thin blonde in the city, if that was the way his tastes ran. He could have a different blonde every night. Only one thing made me special: my fame, and how it could be used.

I had been able to make people see that I loved and grieved for my father, but that was my father. People understood blood, but nobody could quantify romantic love, the alchemy that could transform a stranger into someone as close as family. Kissing and holding hands, all the outward trappings of love, could be faked. People performed the acts of love without meaning love. Love was the mystery nobody could solve, the fairy tale everyone loved to listen to and not quite believe in.

I did not know how to prove what I did not understand myself.

"I don't care what people believe," said Ethan. "As long as being associated with me does not hurt Lucie."

"You should care," said Mark. "Charles and I share everything. We always planned that our sons should do the same. If, however, you do not have the same loyalty to the family as your father does, if you continue to be softhearted and weakminded, then all the privileges you have enjoyed—vacations and your fine school and your shining future—could very quickly come to an end."

"Is that so?" asked Ethan. "Good thing I don't want any of it, then."

"You don't?" Mark inquired, his voice like silk wrapped

around a knife, the smoothness snagging just once on a sharp edge.

"The people hate us," said Ethan. "The Light guards terrify people. The cages terrify people. They shudder as they walk through the shadow Stryker Tower casts."

I tried not to react. That was all true, but I had not realized Ethan knew any of it.

"Hatred is the compliment the weak pay the strong," said Mark. "A couple of dogs bite, so you put them down. But most dogs obey their masters."

"I don't want people to fear and hate me," Ethan said. "I don't want any part of that kind of deference."

"That deference will keep the people slinking in our shadow as long as Stryker Tower stands. Think of this. If you were anyone but Ethan Stryker, you would be dead now. Your name saved you."

"I remember what saved me," said Ethan. "It wasn't my name."

"Wait for us outside," said Mark, nodding to the gray-suited shadows behind him. "Stand up," he told Ethan.

At the same moment the door swung closed behind the men, Mark hit Ethan: a swift, controlled blow in the stomach, where there would be no visible bruise.

Ethan doubled over from the impact of Mark's beringed fist, gasping and grasping at the table. I jumped up out of my chair and slipped into the space between them. Mark was a good deal bigger than I was.

He looked at me, eyes icy and intent, but I had looked into the doppelganger's face. Neither Mark's likeness to Ethan nor his coldness could even make me pause.

"You don't touch him again."

"Lucie," Ethan said, his voice hoarse, "don't."

"Are you where he's getting all this new philosophy?" Mark asked. "You do not want justice, Ethan. Justice would mean your death. Who do you think disposed of the guards who accused you and who saw your double? There are different laws for us, but the system will only benefit you so long as you uphold it. Your doppelganger did not save you. I saved you. And I will not have you refer to him ever again."

Ethan put one hand on either side of my waist and drew me back toward him. "I wasn't talking about the doppelganger."

"Oh, you were talking about Lucie? Yes, she's a sweet girl, isn't she? I know how fond you are of her. Consider how terrible it would be if something were to happen to her. I want you to be smarter than you are being. I want you to think, Ethan," Mark murmured. "Think of all you have to lose."

He stepped away from me and Ethan. He did not even cast a glance over his shoulder at our united front. He opened the door and joined all his bright-ringed shadows outside.

I could feel Ethan's heart beating too hard and too fast,

like a fist hammering on a door, a prisoner desperate for freedom.

"I'm sorry," Ethan breathed into my hair. "I never meant to mess up this badly, I never, never meant to draw you into all this. That's why I treated you like I did on the show. I don't want you associated with any of the trouble I've caused. I'm so sorry."

He didn't seem to realize the implications of all he had said on television: that people truly would think he was guilty of conspiring with rebels. He'd led a charmed life, easy and luxurious. He'd never had to face horror and death. He could not help being naïve, expecting there to be no consequences forever. I could not help wanting to shield him from those consequences.

"It's okay," I breathed back. "It's going to be okay."

But I had lost the power to convince other people of a lie, and I had never been able to convincingly lie to myself.

I covered the back of his hand with mine, and he laced our fingers together. We stood like that for a little time, skin to skin, our hearts finding the same rhythm.

"It's too late to go back to school," Ethan said. "Let's go home, you and me. We can talk about all this. I have some stuff to tell you that I don't want Uncle Mark to hear, and my dad will come home soon. He will help me."

"How often has Mark hit you?" I asked.

"Never," said Ethan. "He never has before. My dad would

never stand for it. My father loves me, Lucie. He's not a good man, but he loves me. He'll stop my uncle. You'll be safe."

"I'm not worried about myself."

"I'll be safe too," said Ethan. "Come on. We're going home, and it's going to be okay."

I made a mistake then. Yet another mistake.

I believed him.

CHAPTER TEN

WE WENT THE WAY WE HAD GONE A HUNDRED times before, past the doorman and through the double doors, into the gleaming elevator and up until we could cross the shining marble floor. I was shaken, holding Ethan's hand tightly, but it was a comfort to be somewhere familiar.

Ethan's key turned in the lock. A flare of light followed as it clicked open and the mahogany door followed, and I stepped over the threshold into the apartment. I was already thinking of the luxurious softness of the cloud-colored couch, of resting and being consoled by wealth that felt like security, and Ethan's arms.

Behind me, Ethan fumbled and dropped his keys. The tiny jangling sound of metal on marble made me spin around as if it had been the sound of a sword scraping from a sheath. It was only Ethan, though, stooping to pick up the keys with an apologetic smile on his face.

I turned away again. The walls were windows, clear glass, and it seemed as if the city was spread out at my feet. It looked bright but small, a child's toy town, not full of human unrest and danger. The other city, the Dark city, my old home, was nothing but a black ribbon on the edge of the Light.

"Sorry about that," said Ethan, swinging the door shut. "I just—I saw my father's coat hanging there, but I thought my father was wearing it when he left today." I turned back toward him and saw him pause, hope and fading sunlight warm on his face. "Maybe he's already back. Dad? Dad!"

Ethan's call echoed off the high ceilings. The large chandeliers, each crystal in them lit with magic to create a huge, coruscating proof of wealth, tinkled overhead.

That sound was the only answer he received.

Ethan glanced back at the coat on its hook. I saw his face change.

"Dad," he said, his voice sharp with alarm. He set off for the kitchen, calling for his father. I stood there and let him search.

Ethan was wrong about which coat his father had taken to work, I told myself. We had the apartment to ourselves, that was all. We were alone together and could make a plan. His father would be home soon, ready to shield Ethan from any threat.

That was what I told myself. Except Ethan came back from the kitchen shaking his head.

"Dad!"

"Wait," I said, but Ethan didn't wait.

He was already running down the corridor toward the bedrooms and I was running after him, fast enough that I seemed to outrun all the assurances I was giving myself. All possibilities of comfort seemed left behind, trailing me uselessly like ghosts.

We burst in through the door of Charles Stryker's bedroom. It had a vaulted white ceiling, skylights set like a cupola in the center. The wall on one side was all mirrors, and the wall on the other was all windows, and in the wall facing us was an entrance I had never seen before: a hole that led to a shadowy passage.

Aside from that no-longer-hidden doorway, the whole room was bright. The sheets around Charles Stryker were brilliant white, and the blood on the sheets and on his white shirt was a vivid spreading stain.

Ethan shrank from the sight of his murdered father, back against the mirrored wall. I glanced at him over my shoulder as I advanced toward the bed, and it was as if there were two of him watching me with haunted eyes.

Charles Stryker's face had always seemed to exist in relation to the stronger personalities about him, and that had not changed even now. He looked like a stone likeness, a death mask that could be lying under dust in a family tomb. I could see Mark Stryker's death in this face, I could see Carwyn's, and I could see my Ethan's.

A knife had been driven into his heart. It had pinioned

him as if he were a butterfly transfixed against a corkboard. The hilt was decorated with writhing shadows, Dark magic making the markings twist and turn. Around that shadowy hilt was a crumpled strip of pale paper, fluttering like the frill of a petticoat.

Ethan made a thin, terrible sound as I reached for the paper. "Lucie," he whispered. "Don't—" But I straightened it in my shaking hands and read the words written there in ink made of shadows that curled darkly and obscenely across the page:

Put him down into the dark. — The sans-merci.

Bury him, the buried said.

As soon as I had read the note, the shadows swallowed the paper at a gulp. Dark magic turned the paper into black ashes slipping between my fingers.

"We should . . ." Ethan said, and swallowed. "We should call the guards, but we can't, can we?"

I was not surprised Ethan wanted to call the guards. I was surprised that he realized we could not: I'd thought I would have to fight to make him understand that he was suspected of treason already and he could not be found at a murder scene.

Charles Stryker's death meant the Strykers' power was more than halved: one less member on the Light Council, a blow to the perception that the Strykers were invulnerable. I did not know if Ethan realized that we were all in danger.

I looked at his lost, hurt face — the face of an orphan child, which is what he suddenly was. I remembered that moment, when the whole world felt like it had turned on me like a wild animal and gone for my throat, when I understood that the world had always been a cruel, hungry thing.

"Call your uncle," I said as gently as I could.

Ethan took out his phone and called his uncle. His hands were shaking as he did so, as mine had shook unwrapping the message around the knife.

"Uncle Mark," Ethan said, and his voice trembled as he burst into tears. "They murdered Father."

I leaned in, my forehead touching his, so we could both hear the voice of our salvation. The voice of the man who had hit Ethan less than an hour ago, the voice of the man we were nevertheless going to obey.

"Where are you?"

Ethan swallowed. "I'm at home. Somebody used the plans of our home to get to him. They came through the secret entrance to his bedroom, the one we were meant to use if we ever needed to get away. They invaded our home and killed him, Uncle Mark, and I—"

"Get out of there. You are not the one who should make this discovery. I'll handle it. Get out now!"

Ethan had barely been able to look at his father, but now that it was time to leave the room, he hesitated. It must be hard to leave someone knowing it is for the last time: it must be so hard to say goodbye. I had never had the opportunity.

I could not let him linger. I took his hand and laced his fingers with mine. His hand was shaking.

"We have to go."

"Will you stay with me, Lucie?" Ethan asked quietly. He sounded humble, as if he was beseeching a queen for a favor he knew should not be granted. "I know it's asking a lot. I know this is bound to bring back bad memories for you and this is all my fault, but I don't know how to bear it without you."

"Stay with you?" I said. "Let someone try to part us, now or ever."

We went stumbling out of the building, almost blinded by tears and terror. I did not see the mirrored hall or the doorman. I could not see anything but the still, white face of Ethan's father until we burst out into the streets and found them alive with light.

It seemed an optical illusion at first, born of our dazed and dazzled brains. Then we realized what was happening—the setting sun was aligned with the pattern of our city's streets, turning each one into a comet's tail. The air above the sun was illuminated, golden crowns on the tops of every tower. Each street became a different glittering ray. Points of light hit window glass and turned into tiny sunbursts themselves, and the whole bustling human city transformed into something glorious.

It seemed as if we could walk up a shining path to the very heart of the sun and be wrapped in warmth so intense, we would forget what it was like to feel the cold of knives or dead hands, and have our eyes so filled with light that we would never see anything dark again.

Manhattanhenge happened twice a year, once before and once after the summer solstice, the streets aligning perfectly with the rays of the setting sun. It had come even in the old days of our city.

Now that light meant so much to us, an unclouded Manhattanhenge sunset was almost sacred. I saw people wandering out into the orange-painted streets under a honey-bright sky, their rings ablaze and their faces radiant. I wanted to run, to escape by any means necessary, but there was nowhere to run to. Death waited in both the light and the dark.

We stood in the street for a long time. The light drained slowly out of our city and the night came, and with it Mark Stryker and his guards, attracting attention to us at last. Then came the snapping lights and snapped questions of the press, the throng of people who were curious and surprised and whose murmurs seemed vaguely threatening. I thought I saw a group of people who were armed, but I did not know if the weapons were for attack or defense. The crowd hung back on the other side of the street in a purposeless way that seemed as if it might explode into purposeful violence at any moment, and yet never did. I saw a few people looking from me to Ethan, and their looks were not friendly.

"Maybe we should go to my place," I whispered to Ethan.

Ethan had seen the glances too. His face was white, but his lips were set in a determined line. "I can't go. This is all my fault. I have to see them—bring him out. I have to see. You should go, Lucie. I don't want you involved in this."

"When will you get it?" I whispered. "If you're in, I'm in."

He looked even more distressed by that. I felt as if nothing I could do would comfort him.

A commotion broke out in the back of the crowd: people pushing against guards in a way they would never have done before the cages fell. I saw the Light guards' flashing swords, and I saw ordinary knives as well. I did not hear the commotion long—the Light guards crushed it efficiently. I wondered how many more people in the crowd might rise up. I wondered how many people were going to die tonight.

I still could not leave Ethan.

We all waited, strangers and family, and at last we saw Ethan's father brought out. The black car that carried Charles Stryker's body away drove off with a furious rattle, as if it were charging at an enemy.

There was nobody left alive on earth who loved Ethan but me.

I knew who had reason to hate the Strykers. I knew who

could have walked past the doorman without a soul questioning him because he wore Ethan's face and no collar.

I knew Carwyn had done this, and I was the one who had
let him loose.

We were allowed back into the Strykers' apartment, though
Charles Stryker's room was sealed off. I did not leave Ethan
through all that long, dark night. I was with him when
the light returned and Mark Stryker with it. The morning
dawned pale and sickly. All the faces around me looked the
same, worn down by sleeplessness and the camera flashes that
felt like tiny strikes of lightning.

Jim had come in and gone to sleep on the sofa beside us,
while Ethan had sat pale and tense all night, his eyes wide but
blank, seeing nothing. The only sign of awareness of the outside world that he gave was the tight grip he kept on my hand.

Ethan grieved, Jim slept, and I waited.

When Mark came in, I was reminded that Charles's face
had looked like a mask, because I saw Mark's mask slip away.
Mark looked tired but noble, grieving but patient, and then
the door of his home shut behind him.

The mask dropped. His face fell into a different expression, closed off and betraying nothing but impatience. I did
not think there was much else to betray. There were small,
straight lines bracketing his mouth, nose, and eyes that told
the story of his character to me, that gave an air of cruelty

to his stern, handsome face already. But it would be years, I thought, before the lines became so pronounced that nobody would be able to look on his face and find it possible to trust him.

The first thing he said, to everyone's surprise, was my name.

"Lucie, you know quite a few of this family's secrets already. Naturally we trust you with them, and naturally we would be deeply wounded if you betrayed them. Now, however, your silence is not going to be enough. If you wish to leave, we will let you. If you stay, I will consider that a promise that you mean to support us in our plans."

Ethan turned his face toward me for the first time in hours and whispered in my ear so softly that his breath barely stirred my hair. "You should go. I don't want this for you. All I want to do is protect you from things like this."

I had told Ethan, *Let someone try to part us,* and I had meant it. I did not answer him with words. I simply tightened my grip on his hand.

"Excellent. Now, Ethan: the doorman has been dealt with. Nobody knows you were the one who found Charles's body, so nobody can suspect that you let in the rebels or wielded the knife yourself."

A shudder of horror passed through Ethan. I held his hand as if I could hold him together, as if no matter how he shook I would not let him shake apart.

"In the eyes of the public, you have become a tragic orphan. Here's how we're going to use that."

I wondered if the doorman had been killed or simply bribed.

"We are going to redeem our family's name and build something from this disaster," said Mark. "You, Ethan, are going to go to work for the council as a page. I want you in the public eye, serving the Light in small, useful ways, until all doubt of you is slowly removed as sympathy for you rises."

"I can't even do magic," Ethan said.

"Half the council can't do magic," Mark told him. "That does not matter. What matters is that you uphold the Light."

Once, everyone on the council had worn rings of Light, but they had passed power down to sons and daughters who did not. Now some of them wore rings and some did not. Magic was like beauty: you were pleased to be born with it and happy to marry those who had it, and you hoped your children would be blessed with it if you were not. But you could be powerful without it, as long as you were rich and committed to keeping the structure of society exactly as it was.

It made no difference to me. A man was not any better simply because he wore the rings and wielded magic. Mark Stryker was proof enough of that, and Charles Stryker had been too. Was life any fairer back when all the council had magic? Or before the magic came, when power depended on wealth and cruelty alone? Had anything ever been fair, in the history of the world? I didn't think so.

I knew what Mark intended for Ethan. People would look at him, the orphaned boy in the public eye, and pity him. It was not a glamorous job he was being given, and that was smart, but it was a job that made Ethan's allegiance clear. The shadow of suspicion that had fallen on him would vanish. Ethan was young and handsome, ten times as charming as Jim, and dating me, Lucie Manette, the Golden Thread in the Dark. He could make the whole Stryker corporation look good. Mark's plan was for him to be a figurehead, and at the same time to make accusations against Ethan look absurd.

"Uphold the Light," Ethan said. "What does that mean?"

"It means that you will follow my lead. The filth of the darkest streets are rising up, and they need to be put down and shown their place. Do you want the same thing that happened to Charles to happen to me, and your cousin? Do you think that the people who came for your father's blood will show any mercy to you? There's no mercy in them. We stamp them down or they stamp us out."

Mark took a deep breath and gave us the smile he usually saved for the cameras.

"Stop being a child, Ethan. Start being your father's son."

He stood at the glass window overlooking the city, framed against a new day and a brightening morning. He looked supremely confident. I knew Ethan would join the council: I knew none of us had any choice but to do what Mark wanted. What else could we do? Ethan's father had been murdered, Ethan was under a cloud of suspicion, his doppelganger was wandering the streets of the city, and ultimate power lay in Mark Stryker's hands.

I took a deep breath. "What can I do to help?"

"I'm glad you asked me that question," Mark Stryker said. "I do think you owe us, Lucie. All this nastiness is being done in your name, and it reflects very badly on us. You must want to make up for that. Don't you?"

"She doesn't have to make up for anything," Ethan said loudly.

"I'll do whatever I can," I said, even more loudly.

"I thought about you making a public statement," Mark said. "But considering how the interview went, that might not be the wisest course of action at this time. We do not want anything to seem coerced. What we want is to see you by Ethan's side, serving willingly as his partner. What do you think might accomplish that, Lucie?"

"She doesn't have to do anything!" Ethan shouted.

"I'll do it with Ethan," I said. "I'll serve as a page as well."

Mark Stryker smiled. I feared him and hated him so much, I would have done anything he wanted.

Even then, even when I had seen Charles Stryker lying in his own blood less than a day ago, I believed the Light Council was too strong for their power to ever be broken.

CHAPTER ELEVEN

MARK TOLD ME TO BE QUIET WHEN WE SERVED the council, and I did what he said. Ethan was just as quiet as I was.

The meetings were held in Stryker Tower. It made sense to gather there. The tower was one of the most notable buildings in the city, a column of steel and glass that people could look toward as they had once looked toward old idols, pyramids, the sun itself.

And any foes, no matter how powerful, would be less able to fight the Strykers on their own turf. The very people who served the coffee were Stryker employees. Now the people making copies and taking minutes were one of the Stryker heirs and his girlfriend. Mark had everybody at a psychological disadvantage.

At the head of the table sat Anton Lewis, the abbot of Light, with his brilliant rings casting light upward onto his soft, jowled jaw and his wet, trembling mouth. He was said to be the most powerful Light magician in the city and to act as a channel between the people and the Light. Years ago, he had tried to enact reforms of the treatment of those in the Dark city, laws that would abolish the cages and allow Dark and Light citizens to travel more freely between cities.

The rest of the council had made sure those laws did not pass, and Anton Lewis's failed attempt had only made the Dark city more discontent. They hated him for trying and failing more than they hated anyone else. My Aunt Leila had despised Anton Lewis more than all the other members of the council combined, unless you counted his wife. She was a former supermodel who had been known as Bright Mariah and whom the Dark city called Bitter Mariah.

She sat at the council table, her silver-fair hair and makeup always impeccable and her clothing as clearly expensive as if it had been made with gold thread. I had seen pictures of her when I lived in the Dark city, and had hated her shining face and all the useless finery she was draped with, as if she was more a mantelpiece full of baubles than a woman.

Aunt Leila thought that Anton was a coward and Bitter Mariah was worse than that. I'd agreed with her, once, because I'd agreed with her about everything.

I'd seen a lot of women dressed expensively since those days, and I did not think finery made Bitter Mariah guilty. Then again, I did not think she was innocent. She supported and upheld the Light Council and all their cruel laws: she was just as guilty of murder and callous indifference as the rest.

There were many other faces, among them David Brin,

who administered the city finances, and Gabrielle Mirren, the moderate of the council who was kept on for her popularity and whom Mark did not allow to speak often.

I had seen these people, mostly old men with expensive suits that were sleekly smooth at the shoulders and straining at the stomachs, on television many times while I was flicking through channels. It was strange to be in their immediate presence, to hear the small bad jokes they told and the way they grunted, or scratched at their heads. Brin peeled and ate oranges throughout the council sessions, leaving spirals of orange skin in a heap at his place every time.

It was like being in the teachers' lounge at school, staring around in startled amazement that those in authority were just people, flesh and blood and often boring, just as likely to be stupid or wrong as anybody else.

And yet these people held all our fates in their hands.

"Obviously, one of the first things we must do is restore order to our cities, both the Dark and the Light," said Mark Stryker.

The first meeting we attended was all about putting more Light guards on the streets of the Light city—to reassure citizens that they were being protected, of course. I saw Ethan open his mouth several times, but I sent him imploring looks and he stayed quiet.

Gabrielle Mirren said at one point, "We don't want people to feel as if we are tyrants—"

"But we cannot allow them to think we are weak," said Brin. He got a nod from Mark for his trouble.

I walked home that day and saw the new Light guards patrolling and people rushing for home with their eyes on the ground. It reminded me of being back in the Dark city, everyone being guarded and watched as the buried were.

It was like Manhattanhenge, but the streets were filled with fear instead of light.

The second meeting was full of plans for the Light city as well. It was not until the third meeting that the council talked of what to do with the Dark city. There had always been guards patrolling the streets, and a garrison of guards at the gates examining everyone who went out and came in, but now the cages were gone and there was rioting inside the walls.

The Dark city was under martial law, and the garrisons needed new officers. Mark Stryker said we needed to send in people we could trust, who would control the situation. I did not know most of the names discussed, and I sat there with a distant expression on my face. I looked at the rings on my fingers as if they were strange new constellations, their light coming from a very long way away, beautiful but basically useless.

"What the Dark city needs is a firm hand," said Mark Stryker. "It is regrettable, but some harsh measures will have to be taken."

"The people of the Dark city live harsh lives already," said Gabrielle Mirren, but she did not protest when Mark read out the names of a few men that even I recognized by reputation: men who sent people to the cages without trial and armed all their guards with both the whip and the sword. They were sending in troops to crush the rebellion.

People who passed out pamphlets or spoke out against certain laws would be arrested. *Aunt Leila will be taken in for questioning,* I thought. I could imagine what they might do to her. She could disappear like my mother had.

"These are men who can annihilate the *sans-merci*," said Mark.

I kept silent but looked at Ethan. He must have seen the horror on my face. I saw the angry look on his.

"And anyone else who gets in their way," Ethan said recklessly. I reached out and touched his arm because I wanted the support, and as a warning.

Mark looked up at Ethan, a sudden sharp glance that showed exactly how much he did not appreciate having his decisions called into question in front of the council and by a member of his own family.

"Do you have an objection, Ethan?" he inquired.

I tried to get Ethan to look back at me, tried to get Ethan to shut up, but my wish for him to be safe was just as useless as my wish for Aunt Leila to be protected.

Ethan was looking at his uncle, his dark eyes steady: angry, but with a flame in them that burned beyond anger. "There are better people to send," he said. "People who could bring peace instead of creating a wasteland."

"By the Light," said Mark, his voice amused. "And can you name some of these remarkable people who can turn violent and dangerous revolutionaries into courteous guests at a tea party? Feel free to speak, Ethan. Tell me who you would choose."

Ethan said, "I would choose Jarvis Lorry."

My hand clenched on his arm.

"My father hired him. He's been working for us for more than a year now as our head of security in Stryker Tower, and in his position he has settled conflicts with former employees and disaffected crowds alike in a way that did not end in violence and did end with both parties satisfied," said Ethan. "He's absolutely honest, and concerned with justice above all. He will make sure the laws are upheld and the people of the Dark city are treated fairly. These people need help, not punishment."

Gabrielle Mirren murmured agreement, and Mark's eyes narrowed. "These people," he pointed out softly, "killed your father."

"The whole Dark city killed my father?" Ethan asked. "How did they all fit in the apartment?"

There was an uneasy silence then: people did not know

whether to be horrified or to laugh. I was almost amazed at how Ethan refused to play the game of making people like him in order to achieve his ends. He could have done it. He was handsome and charming, and when he smiled at people, they wanted to smile back. He seemed to believe that it was beneath him in some way.

He was not like me. He would never have done what I did.

"What do you think of this?" Mark Stryker asked. It was the first time anyone had addressed me at the table.

Ethan squeezed my hand hard. I had sent silent messages to him for help, for quiet, so many times, and he had not listened. Yet I did not know how to refuse him.

Jarvis was a kind man. I was sure he was good at his job. I was sure that he would try to resolve matters in the Dark city without violence. And my Aunt Leila was still in there. What if sending him could save her?

But I was scared of the Dark city and scared of what might happen to Penelope's husband and Marie's father in it. I knew what happened to people with good intentions, down in the Dark.

I swallowed. "He and his wife were kind enough to take me and my father in when we arrived in the Light city—"

Mark's eyes narrowed further, like a trap slamming shut, when he smiled. "Excellent point," he said. "You are still very popular in the Dark city. Sending someone connected with you would be a good move for public relations. I suppose we can grant the man a promotion, considering the circumstances—and given Ethan's enthusiastic support."

I opened my mouth to say that was not what I meant, but I did not want to cross Mark in front of the council. I looked to Ethan for help, but Ethan's face was set in determined lines. Ethan was getting what he wanted.

Mark smiled and kept his gaze fixed on me until I had to smile back. "I think this is an excellent idea. Don't you agree with me and Ethan, Lucie?"

The word stuck like a piece of apple in my throat, but I forced it out. "Yes."

I was not like Ethan. I would never dare argue with Mark Stryker or the Light Council.

"Then consider it done. No need to thank me," Mark added, and kept smiling.

"Thank you," Ethan said to me when we had left the meeting room. "I promise you this is the right thing to do. We can't go on this way. The Dark city has to be treated more kindly, not less. We have to act."

"Don't thank me," I said. "Don't tell me that this is the right thing to do. Promise me that he will be okay."

Ethan was quiet for a little while. We got out of the elevator and walked through the glass and steel hall that led to the revolving doors. It was like walking through a greenhouse full of glittering metal and gleaming marble instead of flowers.

"I promise," said Ethan.

Over dinner, we all discussed Jarvis's promotion. I made the food carefully, made even the bread rolls from scratch, as if putting extra effort into a meal would make up for what I had done.

Penelope and Jarvis were both smiling and talking brightly. It was Marie whose small face showed distress. She kept looking warily back and forth from her father's face to her mother's, as if they were trying to trick her by smiling when their whole bodies were tense.

"Good bit more money in it. He'll be able to keep me in the style to which I wish to quickly become accustomed," Penelope said, and tapped her glass against Jarvis's.

"Guess I'm doing a good job. Or somebody put in a good word for me."

Jarvis twinkled at me, and I wanted to shout and disclaim responsibility, but I was responsible. If it wasn't for me, Jarvis would never have met Ethan; Jarvis would not be involved with the Strykers at all.

"Didn't need to. Anyone can tell good work when they see it," I said.

We were all pretending, but there was a value to pretending.

When you pretend hard enough, for long enough, you can convince yourself. It was not likely Jarvis could be anyone's target—he was not even a Light magician. He would be trying to establish order, and doing it kindly. This job brought in a lot more money, and it was not so dangerous. Maybe it was not dangerous at all. Maybe Jarvis would be safe and Aunt Leila would be safe and Uncle Douglas would be safe. Maybe Ethan was right to hope and I was wrong to doubt and everything would be well.

We ate the dinner I'd made, and from picking at the salads we progressed to fighting over the last brownie. By the time dinner was over, Marie was laughing on the sofa while I made coffee and Jarvis tickled her and explained that he would not be gone for long at all.

"There's a nice house in the Dark city for important officials such as myself, and I have a card which ensures that if there is any need, I have priority transport out. Do you know what priority is, Marie belle?"

"My name's not Maribel," said Marie, raising her eyebrows, and Jarvis laughed. The extra money would go to Marie's future, I told myself—she was so smart. This could be good.

"Mr. Stryker said that I would never be gone longer than two weeks at a time, and that usually it would only be a week. I will see you every weekend, and now that your father is rich we can go to a Broadway show every Saturday night if you want."

I was bent over the sideboard, pouring Penelope's coffee. The sound of a gasp and glass breaking made me spin around and spill the coffee over myself and the floor in a dark scorching trail. I barely noticed I had been burned. All I could think was that it was the window breaking, that Carwyn had come back.

My father had dropped his cup. I thought for a moment he was having one of his attacks, but when I looked at him, his eyes were clear.

That was almost more terrifying.

"I'm sorry," Dad said, and laid his hand on Jarvis's arm. "I've been trying to hold it in, but I can't. You have to listen to me. You have to believe me, Jarvis: you can't go. It's too dangerous, and you won't be able to help. Josephine thought she could help people, and they killed her for it."

I willed tears back. We had never, never talked about Mother.

"Everything's absolutely fine," I told him. "Jarvis just got a promotion at work."

"At work with the Strykers?" Dad asked, his voice suddenly sharp. "In the Dark city, where they are rioting? I tell you, he mustn't go! We all have to run away, get out of both cities while we still can, before they burn—"

Jarvis jerked his arm forcibly out of Dad's grasp.

"Leave off! You're scaring Marie."

"Dad," I said. "Dad, please. Please come lie down. For me, for Mom."

Dad fumbled for my hand as he came toward me. "This isn't madness, Lucie. It's the truth."

I would rather have listened to madness than truth. At least madness had some hope in it.

"Aren't you tired of the truth?" I said in a low voice, so the others could not hear. "When has it ever helped us?"

My father looked at me. I couldn't hold his gaze. I had to lower my own, and as I did I felt hot tears creep out from under my lashes.

"All right," Dad said finally. "I'll lie down. You're right, Lucie. I am tired."

I guided him through the door. I sent what magic I could through my rings—small, soothing pieces of magic, like sprinkling a few cool drops of water on a brow hot with fever, all I could do to comfort him. I smoothed his pillow with a hand heavy with rings, smoothed his thinning hair as gently as I could, as if he was a sick child.

"Jarvis has to go," I whispered. "If he can help the people in the Dark city, he has to."

"Josephine always said that. No matter what the danger is, no matter what you might find, she said, you have to go, you have to heal. She had to heal him, Lucie. She told me she had to."

I didn't know who "him" was: probably just another one of my mother's patients. I didn't know why my father was suddenly talking about her.

"Shhh," I said, my throat aching. "We are all perfectly safe. Nobody has any reason to hurt us. Everything is all right."

His eyes opened and he looked at me with disbelief, as if I was the mad one, as if I always had been.

"Nothing is all right. They killed your mother."

I felt pierced through with guilt. I wondered what my father really thought of me, about my lies, about my consorting with the Light Council, whose guards had killed Mother. I had nothing I could say in my defense. I just kept stroking his hair.

"Hush," I said. "I know. I know."

CHAPTER TWELVE

I DO NOT REMEMBER MUCH ABOUT THE NEXT FEW days except for the tension of how busy I was. It was as if time were a suitcase filled too full, about to burst and break. Jarvis had to be sent off. The council meetings had to be attended. My secret had to be kept.

The times of desperate rush whittled down my priorities, made them terribly simple and clear: food, drink, rest, and this, his hand in mine. Ethan held my hand loosely, gently, as if he was not afraid of losing me and he would let me pull away anytime I liked.

"You don't need to worry about Jarvis. He's already doing a great job. He's making sure the people in his district of the Dark city are being looked after. He's helping more than I can say."

"That's good," I said.

Ethan's hand closed around mine a little tighter. It had not been true, I realized, the thought I'd had: that he was not afraid of losing me. That was just something I told myself because I never wanted him to be afraid. It had seemed beautiful to me, the easy confidence he had not just in me but in his belief that the world he trusted would leave him intact. But the world had hurt him now, and there was no way for him to regain innocence. Even for him, in his warm golden life, there had entered the cold shade of fear.

"I understand. Your dad needs you. And I understand that you have been trying really hard to help me, with these meetings, with everything," Ethan said. "I need you too."

What I had been doing at the meetings was not so difficult —be silent, smile. It was sickening to do and sickening to be complimented for. There would be another meeting early tomorrow morning, and I would give them all the smiles and silence they wanted.

"I've made so many mistakes. I feel so guilty. I don't believe I could have survived these last weeks without you," Ethan continued. "That's what I'm trying to say."

"You could have survived alone," I said at last. "But I didn't want you to be alone."

Ethan let go of my hand so he could put an arm around me and draw me in close. The sun was sinking in the sky, but it was just low enough for light to catch the windows of the buildings it was sinking behind. It was as if the sun wanted to be close to the earth, as if the sun was in love too.

The whole city seemed so beautiful suddenly, like a glass

filled not with liquid but with light, a crystal glass on the very edge of a table, tipped just a hair too far. Sunbeams quivered over glass, tossed ribbons of light over and around buildings. It was like seeing the trembling instant before the glass fell.

All the more beautiful because it was fragile. Never more beautiful than at the instant before it was destroyed.

The next morning, Ethan found me outside the meeting room in Stryker Tower, in the long hall with its glinting tapestry that had light woven into the fabric to look like electric gold. He was pale, and he reached for my hands as if I was in danger of falling off a cliff and he had to save me, and I knew that Jarvis was dead.

"He's not dead" was the first thing out of Ethan's mouth, but I did not feel relieved.

My father had not been killed either. And my mother had vanished and we had never seen her body. Worse could happen to you than a clean death, down in the Dark.

"What's happened to him, then?"

My voice sounded tight and closed off. I stepped back, away from his offered hands and comfort. What I wanted was to be so strong that nobody would be able to touch me. All I would take from him in that moment was information.

"He was reported missing from his home in the Dark city," said Ethan. "There was no sign of a struggle or forced entry. He has been gone for less than twenty-four hours. He may have gone somewhere of his own accord. He might be back at any moment."

I laughed, and he jolted at the sound. "Come on, Ethan. You don't believe that."

He stopped trying to reach for me.

"No," he said. "I don't believe it. But I don't know what else I can say to comfort you."

"You could start by not lying to me, or yourself. I don't want comfort."

"You comforted me," said Ethan. "You supported me at every turn, and you made it look easy. Let me try and do the same for you. Let me just try."

My father thought I was able to care for him, carry both his and my weight in Penelope's home, be a daughter, a student, a famous victim, girlfriend to a celebrity, and as good as a mother. He thought because I smiled and pretended like it was no trouble—because smiling was one of the things I was expected to do—that the weight of expectations was not absolutely crushing.

So many expectations weighed down on me. I felt as if I was in a story I had heard once, of a man who had stone after stone pressed to a board over his chest. As long as he had had breath, he had asked for more, and I understood why he had asked. After a certain point the idea of a world where you were not under pressure seemed like a dream, and all you could imagine was more weight being added until you broke, and sometimes you wanted the relief of breaking sooner.

I broke then.

"You can't comfort me," I said. "Especially not when you say stupid things like this. You think it's easy? To be everything to him, to you, to the council, to be so much and never be anything objectionable? You think it's effortless because it's supposed to be effortless—"

"I never said that," Ethan protested. "I never said anything like that. I said you made it look . . . I know how hard you try."

That didn't make it any better. I wanted how hard I tried to be invisible but appreciated all at once: I wanted what I could not have and I wanted Jarvis to be safe and I did not know how to stop being angry.

"And it suits you for me to try, when you need me to be strong. But not when you want to feel better about yourself and what you did—who you sent to his death. When you want to feel like a big strong man consoling a weak, weeping woman, things are different. Then you act as if I am something to be protected, like I'm a piece of china to be kept in a glass case. Maybe you want me to be breakable, so you can shield me. But I'm not. How can I be fragile and do everything I have to do?"

Ethan's hands clenched into fists when I said "death." He did not interrupt me, but with every word his face grew paler and paler. We stood as far apart as that richly decorated corridor would allow us to stand, and I wished we could be even farther.

"You're the one who always tries to protect me," said Ethan, and he was shouting suddenly back at me, as he'd never shouted before. "As if I'm the fragile one, as if I can't understand anything. Do you have any idea how frustrating it is to love someone who will not let you help them?"

"I treat you as if you can't understand anything because you *can't understand anything.* You've lived your whole life in the Light. You've never been hungry or cold or left bleeding in the Dark. You think I'm wrong? You think you do understand? Tell me, Ethan Stryker," I said, and I wielded the name as if it was a blade, and saw him flinch as if it had been one. "How can you?"

"Just because we've had different lives doesn't mean we can't try to understand each other," Ethan said. "Just because I've lived a life of privilege doesn't mean that I can't sympathize, that I don't have a heart to feel or a mind to know that what you suffered and what other people are still suffering is terribly wrong. The laws against the Dark are disgusting and cruel, and the whole system needs to change."

I felt myself tense all over, and I looked toward the door

behind which Mark Stryker and his council sat. When I looked back at Ethan, he was still watching me. It did not even occur to him what danger could be coming.

"It is a privilege to say—to even think—that the system is cruel," I said in a low, furious voice. "What you are doing is talking treason, and you could be killed for it."

"So what's the alternative, Lucie?" Ethan demanded. "Do nothing, because someone hurt you once? Let other people be hurt and killed, let the cities burn, and keep smiling and doing absolutely nothing?"

"What's your suggestion?" I asked. "Send someone else to do something? And when that someone you sent is killed, you will do what? Oh, that's right. You do absolutely nothing except talk. You couldn't make yourself shut up at the council meeting, you talked on the television, and you accomplished nothing. Don't tell me about what I've done and what you've done. I saved a man. You sent one to die."

Ethan was white as paper.

It had always been understood between us that we did not hurt each other. It had been like a treaty written and signed by both of us, the agreement that let us be able to love and able to live with each other despite our differences. Only now we had spoken the forbidden words. I felt as if I had taken our agreement and burned it before his eyes.

I was terrified suddenly, as scared as I was angry and sick over Jarvis. I remembered how I had felt in the days before I met Ethan, how I had not felt that I could ever leave the darkness behind. I had felt like I was made of opaque black stone, not able to let in light. Until he had come, and I had learned to let his light in.

The whole city of dazzling lights had not been enough to make me feel alive, but he had.

"I thought I understood," Ethan said in a distant voice. "When you hid how you felt or what you had been through from me. I hid things from you as well, anything that I thought would scare or hurt you. I thought . . . that this world is terrible sometimes, and we were both trying to protect each other. But if the truth is that you despise me . . ."

"Yes," I whispered. "Yes, sometimes. And if you're hiding things from me, you despise me, too."

I had not thought about it as despising him before, but what else was hiding the truth from someone because you thought they were too weak to deal with life as it really was? It was a statement that you could not trust them, that they were not worthy of trust.

He did not think I was worthy of trust either.

If he had been hiding things from me, how weak did he think I was? How weak had he always believed I was?

Maybe he was right. I had not spoken up for Jarvis. I had let him be sent away. I had been a coward again, deserting him as I had deserted my mother. I hated myself, and it almost made me hate Ethan.

Fear, grief, and sickness all seemed to twist in me, burning and alchemizing. I thought of my Aunt Leila, years ago: she had never hesitated and never, ever wept. She had been angry, and she had acted. She had known what to do, and what I should do. I wanted to be just like her. All I wanted to feel was fury.

"I don't despise you," Ethan protested. "I love you."

I thought of my father, my poor father, and all the secret resentment and weariness I felt when he suffered.

I turned my face away from Ethan. "If you think loving me means you can't despise me," I said, "you're a child."

"What if I told you everything that I've been hiding from you?" Ethan asked, and his voice was soft now, imploring. "What if you told me all you ever felt, all you ever did and felt you could not tell me? What if we loved each other and we trusted each other? What if we discovered each other, right now?"

His caressing, convincing voice did its work. I wanted to turn around and look at him, then cry and fall into his arms and whisper promises of love and trust. And I never wanted to be that weak. I could not bear to tell him what he wanted to hear.

I did turn. I did look at him. I did not cry.

"You bring Jarvis back," I snarled. "You go and get him, save him, return him alive to his family. Then I will listen to whatever you have to say. Until then, it doesn't matter what you say. All that matters is what you did, and that means I don't want to talk to you or see you, ever again."

I walked away from him. My cheap shoes made muted, dull thuds on the marble floor as I went.

When I returned to midtown and the Lorry home, I pushed open the door gently in case my father was resting. It swung silently and slowly to reveal Penelope on the sofa, home during a workday for the first time since I had known her. She sat with her face in her hands, and I stood staring at her, paralyzed with guilt and trying to nerve myself for the inevitable onslaught. She had let me and my father in from the dark and the cold, she had shared her home with us, and I had destroyed her family. In her place, I would have wanted to kill me. She would have had every right.

Penelope lifted her head and stared at me. Her big dark eyes were glittering with tears, like lakes with treasure lying in the bottom, drowned and lost. She looked as young as her own daughter.

"Oh, Ladybird," she said, her pet name for me almost swallowed by a gulping sob. "I'm so glad you're here."

I ran stumbling across the floor, to the sofa, and into her arms.

Penelope stroked my hair and murmured to me, words of love and gratitude that I had come to her, words of misery she assumed was shared. She spoke to me as if I was part of her family and not the agent of its destruction. Her tears fell into my hair, and I hung around her neck and tried to say all the right things back to her, tried to offer her what little comfort I could. I did not say that I'd agreed to Jarvis being sent because I was too much of a coward to stand up to Mark Stryker. I did not say that Jarvis was lost because of me.

I still could not cry.

When Marie came home and my father woke, we had to tell them. Penelope did it holding tightly to my hand, as if we were in it together, as if we were allies. We were able to reassure them both, make them believe that something bad had happened but we would all be spared from the ultimate horror of losing Jarvis.

Later that night, I lay in bed and thought of Jarvis, and of Ethan.

Ethan had not wanted any of this to happen. I did not want to turn away from him and be alone in my misery. I did not want him to be alone either.

He had sent Jarvis to the Dark city to save lives, to help people. I had wanted someone to go and try to protect my Aunt Leila, to protect what used to be my home. I had wanted someone to be sent, but I had not been able to choose someone or been able to truly hope for change. Ethan had.

He had not been brought up to fear, and he had refused to learn how to hate. Even now that his father had been killed, he wanted peace.

And he had not been wrong about our relationship, and how it worked. Neither of us had been truly willing to tell the other about our families, about our beliefs, even that we could both sword fight. I knew fear and hate, and I did not know how to tell him about either. He had asked for the truth, and I had not felt able to give it to him.

Just because I had failed to trust him did not mean that he was unworthy of trust.

I loved him and I did not want to be without him. Jarvis was gone, but perhaps we could find him. I had saved somebody from the Dark city once before, and with Ethan to help me — Ethan and all his resources — maybe I could do it again.

If I could not, I did not want to lose anybody else.

Of course, what I wanted was not the only thing that mattered, I thought, and lay curled on my side with my hands curled too. Both the curl of my body and the curl of my hands hid emptiness.

I had never understood why Ethan loved me, why he had wanted me or chosen me. But I had always tried to be good to him, not to show too much of my damage or my ugliness to him, and now I had spilled the bitterness of years all over his wounds. He had just lost his father.

I remembered the part I had played to save my father. I remembered knowing that if I slipped up, nobody would remember how hard I had tried. All they would remember was how terribly I had failed, and the pure perfect image of me I had worked so hard to put in their minds would be shattered and stained.

Ethan might not want me back.

I rolled over in bed, tangled in sheets and darkness. The one thing Ethan had asked me to do was trust him, and the one thing he had said to me over and over again was that he loved me, loved me, loved me.

If I could not trust that, I could not trust anything.

CHAPTER THIRTEEN

THE NEXT MORNING, I WOKE EARLY AND WENT softly through the apartment, getting dressed so as not to wake Penelope or Marie—who I knew had cried themselves to sleep last night—or my father. I dressed in the nicest clothes I had, buttoning up a white blouse with pearl buttons, brushing my hair until it shone.

I left the apartment and walked up flights of stairs until I reached the roof of our building, and I walked outside to look down at the sleeping world. Sunrise was brimming at the edge of the sky, a line of brightness that seemed about to spill over the land. The Dark city was a cluster of lightless buildings, lower on the ground than we were. The Light city was a spread of towers that were already gleaming. They were scenes of black and gold placed side by side.

The Dark and the Light, and the bridges between them. They looked so perfectly ordered, connected but separate, designed to be this way. The unalterable order of things, set in stone, and in metal and magic. It was a system that had hurt me, but it was something I could work within: it was the world I knew. There was something about the very stability of it that steadied me.

I walked back down the stairs swinging my heels from my hand, and in the lobby I leaned against the wall and slid them onto my feet, one at a time, hopping as I did so. I left my building, walked the streets of the city, and felt as if I had my balance and knew exactly where I was going.

When I reached Stryker Tower, I went willingly through the metal and glass cage that was their vestibule. The security personnel nodded to me as if of course I belonged. My security pass had obviously not been revoked. I walked into the gilded container of the elevator and passed through the rich corridor where Ethan and I had fought so bitterly the day before, into the meeting room.

It looked as it always did: the white walls, with art so minimal, it left the walls seeming blank, the skylight that cast a tiny square of light on the dark rectangle of the table. The councilors nodded to me. Mark Stryker did not seem surprised to see me.

When I looked to Ethan, he was smiling at me with his hand outstretched, as if nothing had changed between us except that perhaps he was being unusually demonstrative because he was especially glad I had come that day. As if he did not want to fight or to be apart any more than I did, as if it would be as great a loss to him as it was to me.

Ethan was sitting on the left side of the table, facing his

uncle. He was even leaning back, legs crossed, as if he was at ease here. He was wearing one of my favorite shirts of his, blue and kept for long enough to be soft to the touch. He must have had a shower just before he came here, because his hair looked slightly damp, a little more disordered than usual, a dark curl at his nape. He looked absolutely familiar and indisputably like home.

I went to the summons of his smile and outstretched hand like a wave rushing eagerly to the shore, with a ripple of joy running through my whole body.

I took his hand, lacing my fingers with his, and sat on the arm of his chair. I intended it to be a brief, affectionate instant before I took my own seat.

"Hello," I said.

He used his hold on my hand to tip me into his lap, and when I was there he bent his head down to mine and pressed a kiss on my lips, brief and hot as a ray of sunlight striking a glass pane. I put up my other hand to touch his, startled, and he captured it. He had hold of both my hands, pressed against his chest, and his raised leg prevented me from sliding away. Ethan had always wanted me to come to him, had always given me a choice, an easy way out of a touch or a kiss. He had never held me in any way that had made me feel trapped before.

He looked familiar, but he did not feel familiar. He smiled at me, a sweet, vicious smile that I recognized, and the whole bright white room seemed to blur as if we had been plunged underwater, as if I was in an entirely different element than I had been in before.

"Hello, sweetheart," said the doppelganger.

The meeting went by like a long, involved nightmare, the kind that was all whirling impressions of things so bad, they were beyond imagining, the kind where you stumble through the dream begging indifferent strangers for help.

I was not screaming or begging. I remained quiet in Carwyn's lap. My every limb felt weighed down by chains. I did not know what would happen if we were discovered. I did not know what had already happened. I did not dare move.

I did not struggle free from Carwyn, did not wrench my hands out of his and spit in his face. I held every inch of my body in tight control, and only my wayward heart betrayed me, galloping fast and fierce. I felt as if my whole body had to be shaking with the force of it, as if the roaring in my ears and the thumping beneath my ribs were turning into a storm that everyone would see and cower from, something that would devastate the room and bring down the very walls of the tower.

The room remained bright and tranquil. The meeting continued serenely. Under my pinned hands, I could feel that Carwyn's heart was beating hard as well. I could feel his breath, rapid and shallow, against the sensitive skin by my ear.

I had no doubt that it was from exhilaration, the thrill of getting away with this. A doppelganger could not know how much I loved Ethan, or how terrified I was for him.

They said doppelgangers liked pain. Probably if he knew, he would be delighted.

I was concentrating so much on looking normal that it only dawned on me slowly—more like night falling than a dawn—what Mark was actually discussing. He wanted still more troops in the Light city. He wanted stern, murderous men like the ones who had almost killed Ethan to hunt down the members of the *sans-merci* who were lurking here, who had killed his brother. He wanted a curfew imposed, houses raided, a guard on every street corner. I could not imagine how the Light city would react to this.

"Don't you agree, Lucie?" asked Mark Stryker.

He was watching me, and even though all my senses told me he was behaving perfectly normally, I could not manage to crush the rising conviction that he knew everything and was simply biding his time.

I dragged air enough into my dry mouth so that I could speak. I could not draw attention to myself—I never could, and least of all now with a doppelganger among us. "I do agree," I said, and smiled. It felt as if my smile must be a rictus, so false that it was hideous, but nobody gave it a second glance.

Mark smiled back, genial and fatherly. "And I'm sure you must agree too, Ethan."

The "my boy" was implied.

"Thanks for checking in, Uncle Mark," said Carwyn.

His voice was unmistakably the voice of someone enjoying a private joke. I felt him shift beneath me, figured that he was trying to get me to look at him so we could share our secret knowledge, so I could be even more stricken and he even more amused.

I stared straight ahead. Carwyn did not seem disturbed: he appeared to have decided to take his fun where he could get it.

"Actually, I don't agree at all. Not with you, and not with my little lady, cute though she is."

I did not let my expression even flicker.

"You don't think that with your father's murder we need increased security and protection?" asked Mark smoothly.

"Sure we do," said Carwyn. "Dear old Dad. What a horrible tragedy, am I right?"

He paused as if listening for a response. When none came, he patted me on the knee and continued blithely onward. I refused to let my skin crawl at his touch or at his callous indifference to murder. I refused to let any part of me react. I was even concentrating on slowing down my heart. I wanted to be made up of parts that would obey me, so I could do what I had to do: I had to pretend this was Ethan. I had to act like I would if this were Ethan.

"The thing is, Uncle Mark," said Carwyn, sounding even

more hugely delighted to be addressing Mark like that than he had the first time, "bringing in even more troops, with their swords and their whips and their uniforms, it's not going to be a popular move. People have this strange tendency to be scared of armed, dangerous men, and a scared crowd can turn into a mob. It only takes a few guards to overstep, a few people to overreact. Suddenly a riot breaks out and the whole city looks like the front of an ice cream shop where free samples are being given out."

It would have helped if Carwyn had made the slightest effort to behave anything like Ethan. Mark's eyebrows drew together.

"If a riot breaks out, we will certainly need more soldiers to control it. I think the people will be glad to see order restored," said Mark. "Those who will not are not loyal to the Light . . . and they need to be cowed by a show of strength. In fact, I intend to welcome the troops' relocation to the center of the city with a ball. A display will make sure people are convinced of our power, our willingness to use it, and our absolute lack of concern that this rabble could ever be a true threat."

His tone brooked no dissent. Even David Brin, who had been arguing for fiscal responsibility during the last meeting, murmured an agreement.

Council elections were coming up. They all wanted to be popular.

"There are far more people in the Dark city than there are guards," I said, and I could scarcely believe that I was saying it. "You cannot crush them through sheer force of numbers."

I thought of the ripped-apart cages and the blood in the streets. I knew the fury of the terrorized from the inside out: I had torn apart and rebuilt myself because of it. If enough people felt that anger, they might tear apart the world.

Carwyn said, "Aren't I a lucky guy? My blonde has brains."

"There are always more people than there are guards," Mark said dismissively. "And yet nobody rises. The point is to make these people realize I am the leader." He paused. "That we are their leaders."

"They might just think that you're a coward, a tyrant, and a total jackass," Carwyn suggested in dulcet tones. "Not us, Uncle Mark. Of course we know you far too well to think such things, Uncle Mark. I am just talking about what other, less well-informed citizens might think about you bringing a ton of guards in and having a feast when people are starving in the gutters of the Dark city."

Mark looked angrily incredulous that anyone would speak like this to him.

Ethan would not have lit the fuse of his uncle's fury by insulting him. Ethan had argued sincerely for the good of others. But Carwyn was not really trying to convince anybody. He did not care what resulted from his behavior: he was a doppelganger.

He did not want to do good. He was talking like this to create chaos, and not for any other reason. He was succeeding.

"Ethan, you're very young, and you have recently been through some very traumatic experiences," Mark said, collecting himself with a visible effort. He glanced around the room, sharing looks that radiated tolerance for a kid speaking out of turn. "While I am glad to listen to yours and Lucie's concerns, these are dangerous times and they require decisive action. You must trust me to know best."

Mark had always had so much power, he had never been forced to play the game the way I had. He could wear a mask and people would pretend to be convinced. He had never had to make himself a new face.

I breathed in and breathed out, and my heart beat as if it was a clock, undisturbed by anything, certain as the passage of time. I had to get Carwyn to stop talking. So I talked instead, as I would not have dared do otherwise.

"I understand, Mr. Stryker," I said. "Perhaps you might consider, though, that the city knows your family is in mourning, and nobody will expect a big celebration for the troops."

Gabrielle Mirren stirred, as if she was about to agree with me. I could almost see the words rising to her lips.

"Oh, don't worry about my tender feefees, Uncle Mark,"

Carwyn said casually. "You go right ahead. I never imagined you would listen to me at all."

Mark took that as surrender. He smiled, brief and devastating. "That's settled, then."

"Sweet of you to worry though, sugarplum," Carwyn said, not quite low enough. "I'm a delicate blossom, and you know that because you get me."

I could pretend as well with the doppelganger as I could with Mark. *Act as if he was Ethan,* I thought, and simply smiled, resting back against him with perfect trust.

Him lounging around holding on to me like this was not how meetings were conducted, but I sat as if I was perfectly happy to be there while everyone talked a little more and wrapped the meeting up. When I was spoken to, I smiled and responded as appropriately as I could.

I waited, my head bowed, as if being close to him was something I wanted, until the last member of the council filed out. I waited, snuggled up, quiet and comfortable, until I was sure they were all long gone.

Then I wrenched myself out of his lap, out of his arms, with all the force I had. I didn't care if I had to break his limbs to get free. I did not care if I had to break my own.

He let me go. I stumbled, clumsy in my violent haste to get away from him, almost dashing my brains out against the edge of the conference table. I grabbed hold of the table instead, hung on to it for an instant, braced and breathing hard.

I heard the muted sound of Carwyn's chair moving back against the rich, soft carpet. I turned around, still keeping hold of the table, and cast a look at him.

He stood up and stretched, hands linked and arms arched over his head, and I hated him so much, I could see him only in fragments. Every fragment was a treacherous detail: his hair still shorter than Ethan's, damp on purpose to distract from that, his leaner body in Ethan's clothes, shirt collar buttoned up to conceal his neck, the blue shirt sitting differently on his shoulders, and Ethan's jeans slipping down his hips a fraction too far.

He saw me looking and winked.

"Dull meeting, my petal. Don't you think?"

I let go of the table. I stopped watching and began to prowl, moving in a slow, unstoppable circle back toward him. Carwyn stood and watched me come at him. He let me come, let me rest a hand on his collarbone, not far from his dark doppelganger's heart.

I gave him a hard shove. He was the one who stumbled then, back connecting with the wall. I clenched the soft blue material of his shirt collar in my fist, wrenched it stranglingly tight, and spoke with my face close to his face—Ethan's face, the doppelganger's lying mask.

"Where is Ethan?" I demanded. "What did you do with him?"

Carwyn still had that smile on his lips, as if everything that was happening to him was impossibly amusing.

"My little love dessert, I think you've become upset and confused. I'm Ethan. Who else would I be?"

"Don't play games with me, Carwyn!"

"These violent outbursts and this suspicious nature must be born of your childhood trauma, Golden Thread in the Dark," Carwyn observed sweetly. "What a prince I am to understand your wounded psyche and put up with your erratic behavior, my damaged daffodil." He reached up, patted my hand at his throat, and closed his eyes, apparently at his ease. "I know you only hurt me because you love me."

"I know you. You're not the one I love. And I will hurt you if you don't answer me."

He could have murdered Ethan, I thought. It was possible that it was already far too late to save him.

Carwyn's eyes opened. They looked darker than Ethan's even though they must have been the same color, as if the black of his pupils was spreading to swallow Ethan's eyes up in darkness. "If you cause a disturbance, people will come in. What will you say when they start asking questions? If I'm not Ethan, who else could I be? Who is Carwyn?"

I stared at him mutely, my lips pressed together.

Carwyn smiled gently. "A long-lost twin?" he asked. "Maybe an *eeeeeevil* twin?"

My silence was the stony, absolute silence of a grave. My silence should have spelled out his own name to him, carved on a tombstone.

"Surely not a doppelganger," said Carwyn, dropping his voice with solemn horror. "How could that be? Certainly the esteemed Strykers, the first family of the Light, would never create a filthy, unholy creature like a doppelganger! And even if they did, what hideous traitor would ever, ever remove the monster's collar?"

I could not help myself. I started to shout. "How *dare* you—"

The door burst open, a stranger on the threshold who must have been Stryker security. He stopped short at the sight of me and someone he thought was Ethan, and I could read his uncertainty: nobody should have been threatening one of the Stryker heirs, but it was the heir's girlfriend, and he might have been misinterpreting the situation.

Carwyn pulled himself out of my slackened grip and strolled toward the security agent.

"She's a little rough with me sometimes," he explained in a confidential tone, patting the man on his arm. "You know how it is. You want to tangle with a wildcat, you get clawed. Worth it, of course. We're very much in love."

He glanced over his shoulder at me, as I stood with my hands empty, robbed of my prey.

"Coming, my love panther?"

I walked over to take his arm.

"Absolutely. We still need to continue our conversation."

"Certainly," Carwyn returned promptly. "I have promised my dear Uncle Mark and my even dearer cousin Jim that we'll have dinner together tonight, but of course we're all so close, there's nothing you can say to me that you can't say in front of them. Family's wonderful, isn't it?"

He looked at me, and the security guard looked at me too.

"You must come for dinner as well," said Carwyn hospitably to his security detail as we stepped out into the hall. "The more the merrier. Don't you agree, my strawberry of delight?"

I spoke through my teeth. "I'm afraid I have to go home to Penelope. I have to be there for her and Marie right now."

"Oh, because one of your adopted family has disappeared into the Dark city, possibly never to return? Of course. How insensitive of me. Please forgive me. I will think of you fondly during every course at dinner, and twice during the cheese course."

We walked through the halls and went down in the gold-plated elevator of Stryker Tower, me, the mocking copy of my darling, and the man who was preventing me from killing him. Carwyn kept up a cheerful monologue, mainly about what he was going to have for dinner.

We went out into the street. It was still morning, the sky a fine bright blue over tower tops winking in the sunshine.

"I'll leave you here, tulip," said Carwyn.

He bent down, Ethan's face gilded by sunlight with darkness behind it, and his lips brushed my cheek as his hair brushed my forehead. I held on to his shirt and hoped it looked as if I was clinging.

"Is he alive?" I whispered. "Just tell me that."

Carwyn's kiss was gone as soon as it had landed, the place on my skin he had left it cold even before he leaned back. "If you behave yourself . . ." he whispered against my cheek.

He studied me in silence, as if he was considering something, then turned and walked away.

I stood looking after him. If anyone saw me watching, they would assume my motive was love, and, after all, they would be right.

The doppelganger and his guard proceeded down Sixth Avenue, past a pizza shop and a tailor's, cars whizzing by with their windows becoming squares of captured light and then turning back to darkness.

Carwyn was far enough away that someone else might not have been able to see him perfectly, not been quite sure what he was doing. But I was sure.

He looked back over his shoulder and nodded, just once, just slightly.

Ethan was alive. Ethan would stay alive, if I did what Carwyn wanted.

I got through dinner with Penelope and Marie and Dad with the forced cheer and frequent smiles of the desperate. I had someone else to think of now, besides Jarvis. Ethan was just as surely gone.

I was certain Carwyn must be in league with the *sans-merci*, who had killed Ethan's father, if he had not killed Ethan's father himself. His taking Ethan's place proved that. And his taking Ethan's place meant the *sans-merci* had taken Ethan. If Carwyn had been telling the truth, they must have kidnapped Ethan and kept him alive for a reason.

If Ethan was alive, what were they planning to do with him? What did they want from him?

CHAPTER FOURTEEN

I WENT TO SCHOOL THE NEXT DAY. THE TEACHER SAID Ethan Stryker claimed that he could not attend due to being suddenly overwhelmed by excessive grief for his father.

I tried to get through the day. I did not sit at the table with Jim Stryker, though he waved me over and seemed to expect it. I sat with my biology partner and a few other girls she knew. A couple of people who knew my home situation looked at me sympathetically, but nobody spoke to me about Jarvis.

There were still people talking about Ethan's father. I heard his name whispered in the corridors, by the teachers, heard his name in the silences that fell over groups when I walked by. But mainly everyone was talking about what the *sans-merci* might do next—whispering about atrocities they had already committed—and gossiping about the ball Mark Stryker was throwing to welcome the new guards. One girl at my lunch table, whom I did not know very well, asked shyly if I thought I could get her tickets for the party.

Nobody was very interested in Charles Stryker himself anymore. One of the most powerful men in the city, one of the Strykers whose name was inscribed in gold across our skies. And he was gone, gone as surely as my mother was gone. The dead drift away from us, like reflections in moving water, hardly seen before they are lost.

I sat and ate my sandwich, and I told myself I would not allow Ethan to drift away.

I noticed, as the days wore on, that Carwyn was avoiding being alone with me.

Nobody else had any answers for me. Nobody knew what had happened, and I could not tell them. Telling them meant my head would be cut off and Ethan would be in even more danger than before.

I had to get answers from Carwyn. He had to know *something:* where the *sans-merci* were keeping Ethan, why they had taken him. He was the only possible source of information that I had. But he was being very careful not to give me the opportunity to ask any questions.

I went to dinner at his house more than once, and we ate with Mark and Jim at the table, and Carwyn would invite Jim to play video games with him afterward. He would always encourage me to stay, always include me in a conversation, always make a point of subtly taunting me, but he would not talk to me in private.

The taunting was sometimes hard to bear.

"How is school going?" Mark asked at dinner one day when he had finished talking about the glories of the upcoming ball. He spoke as if Carwyn had been going to school.

"Wow, actually, I've been meaning to tell you," Carwyn said. "I'm failing."

Mark raised his eyebrows. "Which class?"

Carwyn waved his fork around in a big circle. "Oh, like, *all* of them."

"Ethan!" Mark snapped.

"I know," said Carwyn. "I am just not very bright. Well, you've seen the kind of clothes I choose to wear, with the entirety of New York men's fashions at my disposal, right? This can't come as that much of a surprise."

"You always did more than adequately in your studies before," Mark said.

"True," said Carwyn. "But I was mostly coasting on my family name and my debatable good looks, you know? I mean, that's me. Spoiled little rich boy. Vaguely good intentions, you know, but not much follow-through. Very little strength of character. Have you guys ever noticed that when you look at me from a certain angle, I have kind of a weak chin?"

"Looking at you right now," I said, "I do see it. I've never noticed it before, though. Never."

Carwyn reached for my hand, which was lying on the table, in plain view and beside my knife. I had to let him take it, because Mark and Jim were there watching. His dark eyes followed the line of my sight to the gleam of the knife. He gave me a smile that gleamed in about the same way, and his fingers curled warm around mine. He had calluses that Ethan didn't have: touching him felt completely different.

I would so much rather have been touching the knife.

"Sorry to let you down there, my adorable little meerkat," Carwyn told me. "I do think I've been getting more good-looking, though. The pain of my recent tragedy has given a deep, haunted look to my eyes."

I put my hand up to touch my forehead, able to block the sight of his terribly familiar face for a moment, and looked out at the ocean of lights that was the city at night.

"Let's not talk about your father," Mark Stryker said.

"All right. Let's talk about my basic weakness instead. I've been sitting in on the Light Council meetings for a while," Carwyn said. "And my father was on the council before that, my father who supposedly loved me so very, very much."

"Ethan, don't doubt that," Mark said, and I heard a note of real pain in his voice. He had loved his brother. It was a shock to recognize that, to realize something that I already knew but lost sometimes in how much I hated him: that he was a terrible person but he was human.

And he was letting Carwyn get away with outrageous behavior because he thought Carwyn was Ethan, that he was grieving, that he was human too.

Carwyn, who was not any of those things, grinned. "Okay, Uncle Mark. So I have fairly liberal views, right? Me and my girlfriend from the Dark town, me and my whining about fair treatment and justice and free tiny pink unicorns for all. This military ball is going forward, even though we have blood, broken cages, and whispers in the streets. I talk and talk, but I don't really do a damn thing, do I? You're the one in the family who gets things done."

The dinner table at the Stryker household was glass, with jewels beneath it glowing with soft light. It cast odd shadows on people's faces, made Mark's face one of hollows and threats. His rings clinked sharply against the tabletop as he put his glass down.

"What are you saying?"

Carwyn gazed at Mark with limpid eyes. "Just trying to express how much I admire you, Uncle."

"I do not know what's got into you recently!" Mark announced. "You say crazy things on television, and now that your father is gone you are behaving like a wild thing. Are you on drugs? Ethan . . . do you need to speak to someone? I can arrange that, privately. Nobody has to know. I can make arrangements to help you."

It was horrible to see Mark's patience with him, to hold that nightmarish dichotomy in my mind. Mark had hit Ethan and threatened me, had ordered so many deaths, but he did love Ethan. I did not want to share a single feeling with Mark

Stryker. I wanted to hate and fear him. It would have been so much simpler.

Carwyn snorted. "Nobody can help me."

Given how reckless and thoughtless Carwyn was being, I had expected, at first, that Mark—who knew about Carwyn —would suspect that a switch had been made. But people hated doppelgangers so much, were so used to seeing them in dark hoods, that they never thought the hoods might be taken off. And Mark and Jim were blinded by their love and concern, as well as by their arrogance. Mark and Jim believed they could never be fooled for a minute, that they could not speak to or touch a doppelganger without knowing, that they could never sleep with a doppelganger's cold presence in the house, and so they could be fooled for as long as Carwyn liked.

He could act however he wanted, and nobody but me would know.

"Sorry, my little mint and chocolate parfait," Carwyn put in, baiting. "Am I bothering you?"

I raised my eyebrows. "Nothing you say could bother me."

"I wonder," said Carwyn, but then he checked himself and looked to Mark and Jim. "It's because she really gets me, you know? Some people think that she's nothing but a decoration for my arm, the girl who smiles on command, a blank screen that the Light and Dark citizens project all they want to see onto: the martyr, the heroine of the revolution, the eternal victim, the Golden Thread in the Dark. Some people would say that she never dares even to speak."

He cast me a mocking look. I could read the warning in his mockery: I knew I could not tell anyone what he had done.

"But they would be wrong, of course, those people who say she is nothing but a golden-haired doll." Carwyn lifted a glass and toasted me. "How deep is our love, am I right?"

After dinner, he suggested to Jim that they play video games. He told me to stick around and give him a kiss for luck, but I left.

He was avoiding me, and that meant he might be useful.

The military ball was going to happen very soon, before all the flashing cameras and all the Light magicians. I was expected to be on his arm and at his side, in front of cameras and company, and that meant he could not get away. At some point in the dizzy whirl of that night, I was going to get answers from him.

I walked home, though Mark had offered me one of the Stryker cars. It was only when I was outside that I realized how quiet the night was.

People said our city never slept, but if it was still awake, it must have been hiding, holding its breath and praying not to be discovered.

I found myself badly wanting to get home, and wanting something too much made me stupid. I took a shortcut that led down a few too many alleyways. Even the alleyways were not dark, though: nothing was dark in this city. I was walking carefully through one of them, my boots clicking on the stone as I picked through the debris of the city, when I made my discovery.

Words on one of the walls glimmered in the moonlight, and I turned to see blood slick and still wet against the bricks.

Someone must have dipped their finger in still-wet blood, and scrawled these words:

GIVE US BACK
THE GOLDEN ONE

Without thinking, I did what I had done every time I felt unsafe or unsteady in the Light city—because I could not turn to Dad and knew I should not bother Penelope. I grabbed the phone in my pocket, my rings clicking and my palm sliding against the plastic, and I called Ethan.

The phone rang only once, not long enough to give me time to rethink the decision, not giving me time to think at all.

"There's blood on the wall," I said.

"*What?*" demanded Ethan, and I was shocked by the

recognition that flooded through me at the real concern in his voice. This was Ethan, I thought, it had to be. It could be nobody else. "Where are you?" he said. "Are you all right?"

I closed my eyes and caught my breath and forgot about blood in the sweet, painful wonder of it: that he was safe, that there was still someone who loved me best of all.

"Lucie!" His voice rang out, an edge of annoyance to it now. "Don't be an idiot. Where are you?"

It wasn't that Ethan had never gotten annoyed with me. Of course he had, but he would never have shown it when I was scared.

Of all the things the doppelganger had done to me, this cruel trick was the worst. I took a deep breath, opened my eyes, and I saw the blood again clearly.

"I hate you," I told him, and said his name, his real name, as if by naming him I could rob him of his power. "Carwyn. I hate you more than I can say."

I cut off the call.

He immediately called back, but I did not pick up. I would have turned off my phone, except that there might have been murderers in the vicinity. I might literally have caught them red-handed.

Walls of the Light city had been painted with blood in my name. Who had done it, and whose blood had they spilled? Had they used the blood for Dark magic or had it been simply slaughter? Or had they used their own blood? What did they want with me? I did not know what it could mean, for the *sans-merci* to be in the heart of the Light city and so bold that they wished to advertise their presence.

I did not call for the guards. I kept walking, past the letters of blood and back to Penelope's apartment.

At home, I found everyone asleep; they always went to bed early. I was glad that I did not have to listen to Marie crying herself to sleep again.

I stood at the window of the sitting room and stared toward the Dark city beyond the river.

I did not think of how it had been my home, the last time that I had a real home. I did not think of my mother, who had taught me what it was to love and then what it was to lose, or of my Aunt Leila, who had taught me to be strong enough to bear the loss of what you loved.

I thought of Carwyn and his murderous allies. I thought of my former home as a city of nightmares, darkness waiting and seething at the gates, ready to flood out and drown every one of us.

Mark thought the military ball would reassure the city, boost confidence in its leaders, quiet the unrest. I thought I could get answers at the ball.

The Light Council and I, Mark Stryker and I, were in league. My best chance lay in being their ally, as it always had. They were so powerful. I hated them, but I had to hope they would succeed and save us all.

CHAPTER FIFTEEN

O N THE NIGHT OF THE BALL, I DRESSED FOR
battle. Ethan had sent me many formal gowns
to wear at events when I had to be on his arm.
I chose my favorite, the one that looked most like armor, the
one he had sent me when I told him I hated gold.

That day, Carwyn had surprised me by sending over a box
with a dress for me. I did not even open it and look inside.

I climbed into the car Mark Stryker had sent, and it carried me to Grand Army Plaza, where there was already a
crowd assembled. I climbed slowly out of the car and looked
around at the rich display.

I had been to functions in the Plaza Hotel before, with the
real Ethan. I had walked under the stained-glass ceiling of the
Palm Court, which seemed to make the whole room glow as
if the rich had some private sun nearby reserved exclusively
for their use. I had eaten caviar and drunk champagne in the
Champagne Bar, its red drapes as rich and full as the skirts
of women from times past, and its chandeliers like glittering
spotlights for each one of us.

This was different. The hotel was built like the biggest chateau in the world, a massive block of a building with fairy-tale towers and sunburst windows and a roof of gray and gilt and green, standing among spires and spikes and straight lines. The whole building looked gold where it had once been white, because there were lines of leaping flame from the windows, short controlled bursts of light from the roof, and longer trails of fire, sparks flying upward and becoming banners in the sky. Streamers of magical light were being tossed around and around the building, as if rays of sunlight had been turned into twining ribbons.

The hotel was lit with an extravagant display of magic, so bright that it burned for all of the Dark city to see.

It was not only the hotel that was changed.

In front of the Plaza entrance stood the doppelganger. He was all stark lines of black and white against the golden façade. He was insouciant in formalwear, when Ethan had been adorably awkward, his shirts always a little rumpled and the collars tugged open, as if he was willing his way back to being casual. Carwyn was wearing a long white scarf that went around his neck and flew like a jaunty flag over one shoulder. As I approached, I saw that beneath the scarf his shirt collar was buttoned up tight, so that the edge of the collar cut slightly into his skin. I wondered if he missed the familiar pressure of his old collar.

He was welcome to have it back, anytime he wanted. I would have been delighted to put it on him myself.

He must have seen the dark thought on my face, because he smiled at the sight of me. He kept one hand in his pocket but offered me his arm. I took it, forced to stand too close, and we walked down the carpet to the blazing hotel.

I had been here before, at the same hotel—though it had been a little darker, and had been with a different boy who had the same face. Something else was different. There had always been cheering or chattering crowds before.

There was a crowd now, but nobody was cheering. I looked around nervously for weapons but saw none. Of course, I knew that meant very little.

The people who had turned out to watch us were silent with fear or resentment or both. They were not applauding or shouting, simply watching to see what would happen next.

I knew just how they felt.

The ball to welcome more armed guards into our town was already in full swing. People were milling about and whirling through the large rooms, every doorway draped to give the impression of the hanging curtains on a bed in the kind of bedroom that got called a boudoir. I paused briefly, leaning against one of the massive pillars, and looked across the sea of people.

There were the members of the Light Council, looking strange in their party clothes when I was so used to seeing them dressed for business. There were people I knew
from school, people I knew from other parties, people who
seemed to have been created only for the purpose of attending parties and whom I never saw at any other time, except
in photographs of parties I had not been to. And among New
York's glitterati were the guards, wearing their severe white
uniforms.

Mark had said this was a time for celebrating and feeling secure, had insisted the guards go ostentatiously unarmed
for the cameras. There were swords hanging on the walls,
proclaiming this a military occasion, but none in the guards'
belts.

I remembered one of those blades coming so close to cutting Ethan's head off his shoulders and found myself shivering
despite the heat of the crowd. I could not help but be glad of
Mark's decree. I could not help wishing him success.

Carwyn had slipped off almost immediately upon our
entrance to the ballroom, murmuring something about the
little boys' room.

"They have hookers and drugs in there, is what I'm telling
you," he said as he went. "It's good to be rich. See you in a
bit."

I let him go without making a scene. I had plenty of time:
it was going to be a long night, and he would be expected to

be at my side during the greater part of it. He might say stupid things, but he had asked me to behave, and I had to believe that meant he was willing to play his part as well. I leaned against one of the large pillars, by the curtains, and looked out at the crowd. People were standing in clusters, chatting. It was just like school, except everyone was older and wearing fancier clothes, and breaking the rules in this world meant death.

"I know what you're thinking," said David Brin, the finance minister, coming up to me. "That all this is a shocking waste of money."

"I wasn't," I told him.

"You're a girl from the Dark city, though," Brin told me, and I looked at him sharply. He held up his hands in a swift, placating gesture. "I mean no offense—quite the contrary. You're not used to the senseless waste of the Light city, the way we think of power and gold both as light, and expect the sun to shine night and day. I see it, you know, how you fall silent when the others talk about spending more."

I looked at his raised hands, at the carved gold of his rings. I'd never really thought any of his suggested cutbacks sounded good, and he'd never suggested spending extra money on the Dark city. He meant well, but it was strange that people thought a man who had always had too much money would be the ideal man to handle limited money, would be able to imagine how it was to be hungry or cold.

"She falls silent whenever she disagrees with people,"

said Gabrielle Mirren, and I stopped leaning on the pillar so I could see her. She was dressed in expensively discreet gray. "And she is silent a great deal."

I had not noticed the members of the Light Council paying attention to how I acted before. I had not thought that they would care much about me, but of course Ethan and I were new additions, and this was a time of misery and unrest. There would be a vote soon, with at least one new member chosen to replace Charles, and who knew how the balance of power might shift on the council? They were all searching for allies, and I was convenient and connected to a Stryker.

I told myself that they might be useful and tried to pin a smile on my face. I found I could not.

I was so tired.

"Consider this," I said. "When a girl sits and smiles and is silent, you can decide you know her, but that does not mean you do. Don't read into my silences or my smiles. Don't assume that you know a thing about me."

I walked away from them and did not look back at my new enemies. Walking through these people was like wading deep in the sea, feeling as if the waters were closing over my head every moment. None of the faces were distinct—the light all around was too dazzling for that. It was like being blind.

Until I saw one face, the pale, ordinary countenance of a

waiter. He was someone that nobody at this party would have looked at twice, more an appliance than a person to them.

I knew him. I was almost sure I knew him. His face was familiar, even though I did not know where I knew him from, and suddenly he was the one person I wanted to talk to. I surged forward but felt a hand catch at my elbow and grip hold, keeping me anchored to a spot where I had no wish to be.

I turned around, ready to spit in Carwyn's face, and saw another face instead, like Ethan's but not an exact copy, hazel eyes narrowed in what looked like worry rather than his usual confusion. Jim Stryker.

"Can I talk to you a minute?" Jim asked.

"I can't right now, Jim," I said curtly.

"Please," said Jim. "It's about Ethan."

The waiter, the whole party, all seemed to rush away with a dull roar. I had been afraid of Mark. Jim was not quick enough to notice anything. I had never thought he might suspect.

"You've gone white," said Jim. "So you've noticed it too. The strange way he's behaving."

I laced my cold fingers together and swallowed down a cold retort. "How do you mean?" I asked in a distant voice.

Jim looked around the Grand Ballroom, and I followed the line of his sight, the light of the chandelier above and the glitter the chandelier cast on the gleaming circles of the people below. There was so much brightness that the room blurred before my eyes, turning into a sea of stars.

"It's like he's a different person," Jim answered slowly. "He talks to me and Dad like he hates us. He was always smarter than me, but he never . . . he never used it, like he does now. I get it, of course. Uncle Charlie's death wasn't easy on any of us, but can't you . . . I was wondering if you could talk to him. He obviously still likes you. You're the only one he still likes."

The relief almost made me laugh.

"Oh yeah, all the disgusting comments he makes indicate deep affection."

"He's teasing you," said Jim defensively. Even though he had just been complaining about how Carwyn behaved, the way he behaved to me had to be all right. As if any attention paid to a girl was a compliment, and a compliment I should accept.

"I don't care why he behaves the way he does," I said. "Why should I care what he feels when he doesn't care about what I feel? I don't like it, and he doesn't stop. That's all I need to know."

"Wow," said Jim. He looked a little lost, and a little hurt. "Are you guys going to break up? I always thought of you two as the couple that was going to make it and stay together while everybody else got super freaky in college." He stopped talking when he saw the twist of my mouth, smiled to placate me, and with a sweeping gesture to his own white shirtfront said, "I mean, why else would you go for Ethan and turn down all this? Am I right?"

I smiled reluctantly back.

I had started thinking about things like that once I met Ethan: wearing a white dress, inscribing promises of Light with my rings onto Ethan's skin. Once I had believed that ordinary girlish dreams like fairy-tale weddings had died with my mother, but Ethan let me dream again.

I had never wanted Ethan to save me. But I had always been so grateful to him for saving my dreams, for bringing the hope in me back to life.

Jim missed Ethan too, even though he did not know why. I did not feel quite so alone.

"I'd never break up with Ethan," I said quietly. "This is just a bad time. We're going to get through it. It's true I don't like this Ethan, but he isn't going to be this way forever." I looked at Jim fixedly and made a vow to him as well as myself. "We're going to get the old Ethan back. I promise you."

Jim grabbed my hand and pressed it, gratefully, his skin a little sweaty. I hesitated, and by the time I decided to squeeze it back, Jim had let go and someone else had taken his place, this time a man from the council whose name I could not even remember but who thought he had urgent business with me.

Everyone kept trying to talk to me, everyone thought they understood what my situation was, and everyone was wrong. All I wanted to do was talk to Carwyn.

All I wanted was to wrench the truth from his lying mouth, if I had to take his teeth with it.

I clenched my fingers tightly around the stem of my champagne glass, then felt it taken from my hand, pried gently from my stiff fingers as if he wanted it all the more because I did not want to give it. I turned my head and met a kiss Carwyn placed at the corner of my mouth, where it burned as if it had been a blow.

"I hate to tear myself away from you," said Carwyn to an older woman in a black dress, her ruby rings the same shade as her lipstick. "But as you can see, my girlfriend is pining."

"I wouldn't say pining," I said.

Carwyn nodded approvingly. "I like a strong, independent woman. That's why you're my lady, even though I'm rich enough to have a hot tub full of supermodels waiting for me every time I get home. Wait." He made a show of mulling this over. "I've just realized that I've been incredibly stupid. Sorry, darling, seventeen is too young for commitment. I've got to make some calls."

"I'm devastated," I said. "I must go sob quietly to myself in a corner."

The woman gave us both an uneasy look, clearly trying to decide whether we were fighting or joking. She murmured a polite commonplace I could not even make out, and touched my hand.

"Lovely to meet you," I said, and looked back to Carwyn. He seemed blithely unaware of my eyes boring into his stolen face. He was gazing around the bright ballroom with a benevolent air. I did not know what he had been doing, but he looked a bit rumpled, his hair ruffled over that primly tight collar. He had my champagne glass in one hand, and in the other was a bottle of champagne, still more than half full. "I'm so sorry to run away," I added to the woman, "but actually, Ethan promised me this dance."

"I'd love to, but both my hands are full, petunia," said Carwyn.

I took back my glass, almost breaking the stem getting it out of his hand, drank the champagne, and set it down on a passing tray.

"Now they're not. Or do you need me to drink the bottle, too?"

"Well," said Carwyn, "how can I say no, when you're so eager?"

I put my hand in his, and the woman with ruby rings retreated quickly.

Carwyn watched her go. "Some people just can't deal with being in the presence of unbridled sexual tension."

"Can't they?" I asked. "It's been a long time since I encountered any."

"I bet it has," Carwyn said, with deep conviction. "I'm the worst boyfriend ever, right? Both physically unappealing and pathetically inept in bed."

"You'd know best," I remarked. "And why would I call you a liar?"

He smiled, acknowledging a hit, and I began to dance in the full expectation that he would hit back. He always did, never able to resist a retort, and the fact that he was never able to stop talking was what would win me answers.

There were other people watching us right now, though. Whatever answers I got, he would have to tell me quietly, and neither of us could react visibly. I looked around. People were swaying, laughing, eating, and drinking. The slight reserve they had been showing around the military had gone: after all, everybody here knew that the Light guards existed to protect them. The ballroom was a vision of golden and perfect security.

Then it occurred to me that Carwyn had not responded.

I looked away from the crowd and back at him. That was when I became aware of how stiff his arms were around me, of the way we were not moving in the same rhythm as the other dancers. It was as if one current in a sea had forgotten its place.

Ethan knew how to dance. But there had been no dancing lessons in the Dark. Ethan had taught me to dance, and it had taken months and months of us practicing, of me falling down and laughing as I did it, Ethan catching me or throwing himself down to the floor to join me. I could not have forgotten those dance lessons, the feel of Ethan's sure hands on me and the effortless way he moved, how he could not be anything but smooth and graceful when he danced, because being graceful had become habit through long practice. Ethan knew how to dance. Carwyn did not.

Carwyn was not stupid: he had not made a fatal error that would betray him. Nobody was going to guess what he was from this. He still had a champagne bottle in one hand—they were just going to think he was drunk.

But he did look aware of how he had messed up, and that people were startled by it. He looked uncomfortable. It was small and petty, but it was the only revenge I'd had for all the misery and uncertainty he had put me through.

He turned his face away from a startled man looking at him, as if a monster could feel self-conscious, and caught me looking at him too. Whatever cruel hunger he saw in my face, it made his mouth curl.

"Enjoying yourself?" he asked.

I smiled, and knew the smile was as vicious as any of his. "Actually, I am."

Chandelier lights shining on gilt-framed oriel windows made the air seem the same color as the champagne I had drunk. Mirrors were all over this room, inlaid in pillars, mirrors spelled with Light magic so that the reflections would be lent a flattering glow. I caught a glimpse of myself and him in one.

My long silver dress fit close as skin until the skirt widened into a pool of silver fabric, ending in a train like a mermaid's tail. It stood out in the golden room in a way that I hadn't intended, like seeing the cool glint of the moon in a sky drenched with stars.

Carwyn was a tall, dark figure holding me in his arms, his hair ruffled and his scarf still hanging over his shoulder. The only thing about him that was not elaborately louche, a perfect performance of casual unconcern, was the tight line of his shirt collar.

"I'm enjoying myself too," he claimed, and at my skeptical glance he laughed, and people around him smiled, as if his laughter was sparks setting everyone else alight. "Of course I am. What's not to like? You know, someone told me that we were a perfect couple. Isn't that lovely? I knew you'd agree."

"Of course I do," I told him.

I smiled at him, and his smile went sharp. He did not quite like my serene agreement, I thought.

"You do?"

"With one small alteration. It's a pretty easy mistake for them to make," I said. "Right face. Wrong boy."

He didn't like that, either, so he pretended to ignore it.

"Of course, so many people think that about us," he continued. "The golden boy and the Golden Thread in the Dark.

Could any couple ever be more perfect? Could any couple ever be more boring and clichéd?"

"I agree with that, too," I told him. "You are really boring. I just think of the most evil thing anyone could possibly do, and I expect you to do it."

Carwyn nodded, his face suddenly grave, as if he was paying serious attention to me. I did not have the feeling of being listened to: I saw the way he was bending toward me in the mirror, his shadow falling across my face, and he seemed like a vampire intent on his prey.

"All right," he murmured. "Guess what I'm going to do next."

"You're going to tell me what you did with Ethan," I said. "You're going to tell me tonight."

Carwyn laughed, warm and amused. Anyone watching would have seen how close he was and thought that I wanted him there, that I was as delighted as he was.

All he told me was "You're wrong."

Then he leaned down and kissed me.

It was as if his shadow had not only fallen on me but swallowed me, his arm tight around me, my mouth open on his, with no way for me to fight him or do anything but give in to the drowning dark.

When he was done kissing me, my hands were against his chest. I would have put some force behind the gesture, I would have pushed him away, if I could have.

"Forget you. What do you think *I'm* going to do next?" I whispered.

He was smiling again, a small, private smile. I wondered if he thought he had won this round, if this was gloating. He murmured, "You're going to kiss me back."

I spoke low, but as clearly as I was able, my voice all I could use to fight against the glitter of the ballroom and a boy who thought he knew better than me, cold and harsh to contrast with the soft, thrillingly romantic music.

I said, "You're wrong."

Then a cry broke through the bright air and silenced all the laughter and the whispers.

As if I had caused it to happen by sheer force of will, the music stopped.

We all turned to the sound of the scream and saw the waiter whose face I had thought I knew. At his feet was one of the Light guards, lying in a pool of his own blood. It spread as we watched, a dark blot on the shining floor in the bright room, and I thought for a moment that shadows had come to swallow us all.

All the waiters drew weapons. Some of the members of the media put down their cameras and produced arms. New people poured in from the side doors. And the guests and guards who had not worn their swords, to show the city they had nothing to fear, found that this showcase of their power had become a trap. They drew together in a shining knot at the center of the room. Their exclusive, expensive group seemed suddenly so small.

A call rose up, with the sound of knives behind it. "Free the Golden One!"

"It's the *sans-merci*!" a woman shouted. Another woman, the woman in the black dress with the red rings we had been talking to—a woman wearing the colors of the rebels, and how had I been so blind that I had not noticed?—turned and cut her down.

The second scream of the night pierced the air. After that, the screaming did not stop.

CHAPTER SIXTEEN

THE PARTY HAD TRANSFORMED IN AN INSTANT into two packs: the hunters and the hunted.

I could not think about escape, not immediately. Too many people, a seething mass of people, were already fighting to make their way out. They were so desperate, they were throwing themselves on swords in an attempt to live.

I tried to move from Carwyn's side and found I could not —he was holding me so tightly, I might as well have been chained. It did not matter what I did now. Nobody would notice.

I kicked him viciously hard. I punched him in the chest and I set my nails into his face, raking the skin open. He let go of my waist and grabbed at one of my hands.

I tried to twist away from that, too, but his grip was ferociously strong, as if he would rather break my hand or his own or both than allow the grip to be broken.

"Let go!" I ordered. "Right now!"

"No," Carwyn said grimly.

"Why not? What do you want with me?"

"I want us to live, you idiot," Carwyn snapped. "Together we can. I remember what you showed me at the club, even if you don't." He leaned in, his whisper as fierce as his grip on my hand. "You think anyone else has a Dark magician here in the heart of the Light? I'm your ticket out. Hold on to me."

"I don't have to, do I?" I asked. "You won't let go. You're too keen to save your own skin."

Carwyn gave me a dark look, all doppelganger with nothing of Ethan in his face, and it was like seeing a white curtain lifted so a horror could grin out at you through the glass. He did not let go of my hand, and I did not let go either.

"You can't see us," Carwyn murmured, and my rings blazed bright, reflected in his black eyes. I sent dazzling thoughts streaming through the room, around the rebels and the rich alike.

I moved forward, and we almost walked into a woman holding a knife.

"Has anyone seen the Golden One?" she called out, then squinted in my direction.

They kept calling for the Golden One, but they didn't want me. They didn't even recognize me when they saw me. My name was nothing more than a rallying cry.

Carwyn came nose to nose with her and whispered, "You can't see us," in her face. "You can't see us," he continued, voice soft but insistent. It seemed to wind, sinuous as a snake, around the senses. I reached out and touched her arm with my glowing hand.

She blinked, hesitated, and lowered the knife. Her gaze refocused over Carwyn's shoulder, on a different victim.

I pulled Carwyn through the crowd as we went whispering and burning and unseen. I did not go for the doors. I went for the walls where the Light guards had hung up their swords in a glittering array, as a symbol of how safe we all were.

One of the guards had almost made it. He was lying in a heap by the wall, a human being turned into an obstacle. There was a sword in his hand he had never gotten to use. I knelt down and slid his sword from the lax curve of his fingers. I could only look at the man's slack, surprised face, at his blank eyes with the party lights still glittering in them, for a moment. Then I turned my face away from him and closed my fingers tighter around the hilt of his weapon. The power from my rings sent bright sparks skittering down the blade.

I got to my feet.

The hem of my dress touched my ankles, and it was wet and warm with blood. I had not been able to rise unstained, but I had risen up with a way to fight.

Some of the *sans-merci* might have known how Light and Dark practitioners could work together, so we had to get out of there, and fast. We had to get out of sight while our advantage lasted. I began to walk toward a door that did not lead out but I thought might lead away. I shoved into the next room and found more chaos. In the brightly lit room, there were people lying dead and others being herded like animals. I saw one woman cringing in front of a blade, her silk dress torn and bloodied, and her carefully made-up face stained with tears and twisted with terror. The glossy façade of the Light world had cracked, and beneath the gloss everyone was just as frightened and just as easily hurt as me.

Carwyn held on to my hand so hard that it felt as though my rings were being pressed into the bone, the light of them burning through our locked fingers.

"Give me that," Carwyn demanded, taking a break from whispering, and he nodded toward my sword.

I snorted. "Give me a break."

A brief look of anger crossed Carwyn's face, and I braced myself in case he tried to seize the weapon. He did not. Instead he lifted his other hand, the one holding the champagne bottle, as we passed a flight of marble stairs. He hit the bottle sharply against one marble step, and it broke into jagged halves. He swung his new weapon from his hand, its glass teeth catching the light, and smiled.

"Guess it's lucky boys from the Dark know how to improvise."

There was no time to answer him or to question how effective his weapon might be. I certainly had no intention of giving up my own.

"You can't see us," I murmured, and Carwyn chanted with me.

"You can't see us."

We were almost at the door.

Someone knocked into me, heavily, and the light streaming from my rings died in my surprise. It was Jim Stryker, and there was blood on his white shirt. His eyes were so wide, they looked round, white showing all around the brown irises, and he looked like a terrified animal or a beseeching child.

He did not look at me. He looked at Carwyn, reaching out a hand, and said, "Ethan."

He was Ethan's cousin, and Ethan loved him.

Carwyn's hand did not relax its grip on mine. Carwyn did not react in any way. I glanced at his face and found it cold and unmoved. He looked back at me, and not at Jim at all.

I ripped my eyes away from the doppelganger and back to Jim.

"Come on, quickly," I said. "You need to come with—"

One of the party guests, a man with his suit jacket ripped off to reveal a rough knot of black and scarlet tied on his upper arm, turned and sank his knife savagely into Jim's back. Jim never even saw him.

Jim coughed, a brief, startled burst of blood. His eyes did not leave Carwyn. He died looking so surprised, and so scared.

He fell forward onto his face, and my hands shook. For a moment, I could not move forward, and yet I could not let my hands drop the sword. I was not horrified enough, not humane enough, to try to help him. But I was not quite self-ish enough to leave him. I stared down at Jim for a terrible, trembling moment.

"Come on," Carwyn ordered under his breath, and he used his hold on my hand to tug me forward. He resumed his chant: "You can't see us."

I swallowed, lit my rings, and stepped over Jim's body. Carwyn and I ran headlong through the door.

The door led to a flight of marble stairs. I could not lift my skirts, not when Carwyn would not let go of my hand and I could not let go of my sword. I ran up the stairs anyway. Carwyn ran with me, and above the rioting crowd it was cooler, moonlight filtering onto the marble under our feet.

When I reached the second floor, I ran down the corridor of the hotel. It was empty, but there was a long, thick streak of blood painted across the saffron-colored carpet, a red road that passed under a door that was not quite closed. I crushed the impulse to push the door open. I could not afford to alert anyone to my presence, I could not help anyone, and I did not want to see what was in that room.

I ran down the corridor instead, as if at the end of the bright stretch of carpet there would be a finish line.

Instead there were large glass double doors, and I rushed to them, rushed into them, and they opened under the impact of my body.

They led to a large balcony, the kind shaped like a huge china cup, attached to the wall. I ran outside, and the night air hit my hot face, the chill of the wind welcome, and I saw the elaborate gardens of the Plaza Hotel stretch before me. They were no longer lit by magic streamers; all I could see between the carefully tended hedges were shadows.

I could jump and use magic to save myself, but I did not know what waited below. And I had used so much magic already. I drew in my first deep breath since I had seen Jim die, a desperate draft of cool night air, and tried to think. The *sans-merci* were not only within the walls of the Light city but within the walls of a stronghold. They had killed countless numbers of our most powerful leaders already. I did not know how I could get out of this alive.

It was dark, dark as though it would never be bright again. This balcony should have been lit, but the only light was the pale, faltering rays coming from my own hands. I pulled my hand out of Carwyn's. I tried to, at least, but he was still holding on.

"Let go!" I said, patience snapping like a rope forced to bear a hundred times more weight than it could. "Do you think it's funny to touch me without my permission, when you know I don't want you to? Does it make you feel good about yourself?"

Carwyn stared at me. "Nothing makes me feel good about myself."

He bit his lip after he had said that, as if he had not meant to say it or at least had not meant it to sound the way it did: like a confession.

"Okay, here's the thing," I said after a startled moment. "I don't care about your feelings because you don't care about mine. And when you touch what you're not meant to touch, it looks about as powerful and rebellious as someone walking on the grass when they're not supposed to. It looks as stupid as a kid putting his sticky fingers on art. You look even stupider than that, because you're treating a person like a piece of grass or a painting. But how stupid you are is not my main concern right now, because people are dying. Don't waste my time by touching me or taunting me, or I'll leave you to die as well."

The *sans-merci* were in the Light city. I had known that much. But I had never thought they could possibly lay waste to the Light magicians and the rich and the powerful. I had always thought their violent discontent would remain on the edges of my life.

I remembered standing under the cages in Green-Wood Cemetery years ago, and felt as I had felt then: there would never be an escape from this, not really.

I pulled my hand out of Carwyn's, and he finally let me do it.

Blood stained the back of my hand. I did not know whose it was—the first guard's or Jim's or some helpless stranger's—but I covered my face with my newly freed hand and felt the cold press of rings against my closed eyelids, and for a moment I could not breathe.

"So, since you seem to know everything," Carwyn said, "what's the plan?"

I laughed. The laugh exploded from my lips, sick and sharp, the same way a sound of pain would have if I had been punched. I stepped in toward Carwyn and grabbed the too-tight collar of his shirt, twisting the material even tighter.

"Going to do whatever I say, doppelganger?"

The edges of his broken bottle rested against my bare arm, pricking against the flesh, uneven and promising pain. His smile looked just like the broken glass felt.

"Sure."

I let go of his collar, pushing him with unnecessary force as I did so. He went backwards easily, leaning with one arm up against the marble balcony rail.

I looked at my open hand, at my palms and my fingers, each circled and weighted with magic. I closed my fingers so tightly around the hilt of my sword that my rings cut into my hand. Metal on metal, and my flesh felt almost incidental, pressed between them and bound to be hurt.

I lifted my sword, and Carwyn's eyes widened briefly. It caused an abrupt and stunning sense of satisfaction within me. I was so scared, scaring someone else seemed like the only possible power in the world.

I said slowly, "Do you think that anyone will notice another body on the floor tonight, Carwyn? Remember what I said when we were dancing? You're going to tell me what you know. And you're going to do it now."

I stepped forward, the point of my blade touching Carwyn's shirt. The moonlight shimmered, turning the sword into a shining path that led to his heart.

I continued softly, "The only value your life has to me is that you might lead me to him."

Carwyn gave a short laugh. "Ethan, Ethan. Always Ethan. I am so sick of hearing about Ethan."

"Just a thought," I said. "If that's the case, you shouldn't have placed yourself in a position where everyone calls you Ethan! But you did that for a reason, didn't you?"

Carwyn made a mocking bow, shallow, because to make it any deeper would have been to spit himself on my sword. "But of course it was to spend more time in your charming company, being threatened with large weapons. You did point out recently that people were dying in this building. Could we pay some attention to that trifling matter?"

"Like you care," I said, and my own words seemed to add another layer of frost to this new, chilling world. "Like you turning up and then this attack happening is a coincidence. Do you think I'm stupid enough to believe that?"

Carwyn moved sharply away from the balcony rail and the point of the sword. I lunged after him and his eyes went wild, traveling in all directions, as he realized how very trapped he was on that balcony. He hadn't thought I was going to be any sort of threat.

"Please keep wildly accusing me," he spat. "I'll decide on my opinion of your intelligence when you're done."

"What have you done?" I demanded. "Did you arrange for all these people to die? Did you direct the *sans-merci* here?"

"Direct them?" Carwyn demanded in his turn. "The whole building was lit up with Light magic! It was a beacon you can see from halfway across the world. I don't know why you think the revolution needs to be directed to the great big shiny thing!"

He said "the revolution" instead of "the rebellion." A rebellion implied something tried, whereas a revolution implied something that had succeeded in turning the whole world upside down. I knew it was true, that our city, my two cities, had now been tipped over into chaos, turned into something entirely new. This was no minor upset that could be made right. This was the ending of a world, and I blamed him for it.

"You show up, you murder Ethan's father, you take Ethan's place, you steal his life and do Light knows what to him, and you expect me to believe you have nothing to do with it when disaster comes raining down on all our heads? If you were innocent, you would not be here!"

"I'm very flattered that you think I'm a devious criminal mastermind who comes up with elaborate schemes to topple cities that none can defeat," said Carwyn, "but you are seriously overestimating me. I'm not part of any revolution. Why would I kill Charles Stryker? He was the one who made sure the law protecting doppelgangers passed. He was protecting me from his brother. He was a lot more use to me alive than dead. The *sans-merci* killed Charles Stryker, and I am not one of them. Who would trust a doppelganger to be their comrade? I am entirely self-serving and I am entirely alone. I left the Dark city on my own because the place is a deathtrap. Nobody should know that better than you. Your mother died in the Dark, and now someone else you love is lost there."

We were both panting, and the new suspicion that came to me was just another blow. It did not even surprise me. Carwyn seemed like the avatar of all evil in this moment, as if he was responsible for every wrong that had ever been done to me and mine. My hand trembled, but my sword did not. I knew why people hated doppelgangers. I knew why they killed them.

"Do you know anything about what happened to Jarvis?"

"No! All I know is that he's gone," said Carwyn. "And that's why your precious boyfriend came to find me. That's why he hunted me down through the back streets of the Light city to offer me enough money to live on for the rest of my life. He wanted to go and save this Jarvis guy, because he'd sent him to the Dark city and he felt responsible, and because he thought you would never forgive him if he did not bring Jarvis back. He knew he couldn't disappear at a time like this. He knew you and the whole Light city would panic. He knew an election was coming and a scandal would lose his uncle the leadership of the Light Council. He had to go and have nobody miss him. So he came to me and I took his money. I said that I wouldn't tell anybody the truth, no matter what, and I didn't, even when you came in and knew who I was right away. I'm not working with the *sans-merci*. I'm working for Ethan."

My sword point faltered with my heartbeat as he spoke. When he fell silent, the sword point dropped. We stood facing each other in the moonlight, with no weapons and no lies between us.

Carwyn pushed himself up on the balcony rail, shoulders hunched, and looked at me with his face suddenly open. He was not closed off, and he was not cruelly mimicking Ethan. He looked as weary and wary as I felt.

"None of this was my idea. None of this was what I wanted. And now I'm trapped in this mess," he said. "Just like you."

I took a shaky breath.

"Why torture me, then?"

His shadowed, moonlit face changed, amusement over-coming exhaustion, his mouth curling into a sly grin. "I said I wasn't a criminal mastermind whose devious plans topple cities," Carwyn told me. "I never said I was *nice*."

I didn't entirely believe him. He might have agreed to Ethan's plan, but that did not mean he had no plan of his own. Someone had been spreading treason through the Light city: someone had committed the crime Ethan had almost died for.

But I believed him enough for now.

I had given Ethan a mission, and like a knight in a fairy tale he had gone away to accomplish it. He thought he could save Jarvis.

That meant, for a moment, even on this nightmarish night, I could see Carwyn without seeing an impostor who had stolen Ethan's face and his place in the world, a monster who was made of darkness and evil. I could look at him as I had looked at him on the first night we met, and see a boy who was a jerk but who had done something that made me think there was more to him than that. A boy from the Dark city, who understood that life was cruel and who was not always cruel himself.

A boy I had something in common with.

More in common now.

"So here we are," I said. "Trapped. You want to get out of here?"

He shrugged. "Well, the party's pretty dead."

He smiled at me, a smile that was different from all the smiles of the past terrible weeks, because this was a smile that invited me to share it with him. I thought of the bloodstained ballroom and Jim's face, how surprised he had been to die, and could not smile back, but I reached out my free hand to him. Carwyn reached back and clasped his hand in mine.

CHAPTER SEVENTEEN

W E LEFT THE BALCONY HAND IN HAND. I took the lead, running down the corridor and then toward the smaller, plainer door that led to stairs. We ran down one flight of concrete steps, stopped short at the sound of fighting down the stairwell, and went through the doors to another corridor.

This corridor held, in one direction, another gold-carpeted stretch filled with doors that led to hotel rooms, and, in the other direction, a balcony with a flight of stairs that led down into the lobby. And to escape. I went that way, and Carwyn crept with me.

There were more sounds of danger this way, the clash of weapons and the ring of raised voices. I approached with caution.

The balcony we were moving toward had a marble flight of stairs on one side. On the other end of the balcony was a small bar.

Every instinct screamed at me to dive for the stairs.

Carwyn's hand tugged me that way. But the burning in my veins said something different.

I ran for the bar, yanking Carwyn along with me with such force, I must have almost pulled his arm out of its socket. I landed crouched down on the carpet, behind a glass case full of bottles, and he crashed into me, on his hands and knees, with our clasped hands a hair's-breadth away from the vicious edge of my sword.

"What are—" he began, outraged, and I dropped the sword and covered his mouth with my hand.

His mouth was open against my palm for a moment. I met his eyes and shook my head fiercely once. He lowered his eyes, eyelids pale and lashes dark in the scintillating light of the chandelier, and it seemed like a gesture of submission.

"I'm running out of magic," I snapped. "If they look, they might be able to see us!"

I removed my hand and grasped the sword hilt again. Carwyn stayed quiet.

The *sans-merci* seemed to be trying to subdue what was left of the crowd, to capture rather than kill. We watched a little group being herded below—watched Gabrielle Mirren break free and run up the stairs directly toward us. A man with a knotted scarlet and black band around his arm gave chase.

The man drew a sword from his belt.

It was not like the sword in my hand, one of the swords

of the Light Guard, the sharp, singing blade containing light within the steel and catching every gleam.

The man's sword looked made of thorns and darkness. I had to stare at it for a long moment before I realized what it reminded me of: the strange sharp hooks and wavering shadows that seemed fused with the metal. What had been the fading nightmare of memory was brought back to life, like a shadow with real teeth: the sword reminded me of the cages in Green-Wood Cemetery.

That long moment of my memory was the rest of Gabrielle Mirren's life. The rebel brought the sword down to the sound of a wail and then to utter silence.

Carwyn and I stayed crouched. I prayed that the man would go down the stairs, that he would do anything but look toward us. I prayed to the light of the sun on down to the light of my own rings.

Prayer did me about as much good as it usually did. The rebel lowered his nightmare sword, its shadows seeming to claw the air and murmur to each other, and his eyes fell directly on our huddled forms.

We had been seen, and there was not a minute to lose. I leaped up—trying to leave Carwyn behind, but he held on to my hand—and I raised my sword, meeting the man's swing with a clash of sparks and splinters of darkness. The man wheeled around us in a slow circle, wary since I had a weapon and seemed prepared to use it. But he wasn't afraid. He knew he had us.

Carwyn lunged forward and sank his broken bottle into the meat of the man's thigh, and the man screamed, stumbling against the low balcony rail and then toppling backwards, arms outstretched and scrabbling for purchase. His arms stayed outstretched as he fell, as if he thought he could fly. He could not. He hit the floor with a thud and a crack.

At the sound, the other members of the *sans-merci* turned.

The rebels looked up from herding the ball guests, saw us, and stopped in surprise. They were so still that the scene became a tableau.

The ceiling of the lobby was like a wedding dress, white silk-smooth lines and gold in the same patterns as lace. The floor was mosaics of huge flowers and twining vines. Blood was smeared across one flower, lending vivid crimson to a rose. The chandelier was like a wedding cake made of light, tier on bright tier. Everything was bloodstained luxury.

I pulled away from Carwyn for a moment, lifted my hand, and felt the rings on my fingers humming to the magic in those lights. My veins were stinging as if the blood in them were literally burning, but I let what seemed like my last burst of magic glitter and glow and then sent it flying to its target. It hit the chandelier and was amplified by the chandelier's own magic.

Every line of gold in the ceiling blazed like fire, and the

chandelier exploded in a shower of sparks and shards. The people below scattered into other rooms or cringed on the floor with their arms over their heads and their heads pressed to their knees.

I seized Carwyn's hand again and ran down the stairs, one of my silver heels sliding in blood. Carwyn caught me when I tilted off balance, and we didn't stop running. I wouldn't have stopped even if I had broken my ankle: I knew this reckless rush was our only chance.

We were almost out, almost through the gold and glass doors. I could hear the slosh and patter that was the dancing water in the fountain outside.

Then I saw the waiter, the man I had first spotted in the ballroom and almost-not-quite recognized, the first sign I'd had that something was wrong, the sign I had let pass me by. He ran into our path, pointed at us, and shouted for the whole room to hear.

"That's Ethan Stryker!"

I pushed Carwyn behind me, raising my sword, and shouted, "No, he's not!"

It was the truth I had been holding back for weeks, and now it was a truth that would save us rather than damn us. It was a truth that nobody would believe.

"And who are you?" demanded the man. His eyes raked over my face and I waited in dread for the instant he would recognize me. I felt again that rush of contempt for these people who would commit murder in my name and did not even know my face.

Instead, behind me, a familiar and beloved voice spoke. I felt cold all over, as if a shadow had called on me and claimed me, as if the very darkness knew my name and could now swallow me up.

"That's the Golden Thread in the Dark," said my Aunt Leila. "That's the face of the revolution. That's who we fought to free, that's who we came here to find. That is my niece, Lucie. Don't you dare lay a hand on her."

I had not seen her in so long. She looked just the same as she had in the Dark city, always wearing severe clothes and an even more severe expression. Her dark locks flowed in a sleek waterfall, not a hair out of place despite the chaos all around her. She wore the black and scarlet band knotted around her arm, like the others, like all the members of the *sans-merci,* and carried a knife in her hand. The blade was coated with blood, fresh and red, a few drops falling to the parquet floor as she gestured the man away from me.

After a moment's hesitation, he stepped back.

"Nobody has suffered more due to the Light than Lucie," said Aunt Leila. "Good news, my niece. We have taken the city. The rule of the Light Council is broken. You are free." Her keen eyes surveyed me, from my gleaming dress to the sword and then to my face, pitiless as a searchlight. "Are you not going to thank me?"

Thank her, for bringing death to my door, for using my name for her own ends. I'd been wrong: the rebels were not using a girl they did not know.

Aunt Leila knew me, and she had used me anyway.

But I knew what to say to those who had power over me: whatever they wanted to hear. Aunt Leila had taught me that herself.

I could not help the slight pause before I forced out, "Thank you. Aunt Leila, can we . . . can we go? I want to tell my father the good news."

Aunt Leila was silent for a long time: she had to consider it. She seemed very reluctant to let me leave. Her sharp gaze moved over to Carwyn, and I saw cool speculation there that made my fingers tighten reflexively on Carwyn's hand.

I loved her. I had loved her all my life, and she had always been loyal to me, had never lied to me, had taught me how to survive and how to save my father. I loved her, and I did not love Carwyn.

I looked at the blood on my aunt's knife, and I held on to him as if he was the most precious thing I had, the last thing I had, in all the world.

Aunt Leila looked torn. Her eyes searched mine, and I stared defiantly back. She seemed disturbed, I thought, as if after all this time she had thought I would still be the child who performed on her command, as if she had not been prepared for the flesh-and-blood reality of me at all. She had

clearly not expected me to fight her, and perhaps was not prepared to fight with me.

"There is a great deal to be done here, and you will not be
needed on this bloody night. You can go, if you must," Aunt
Leila said slowly, and I saw the others fall back at her words.

I should have realized it from the first moment, when she
had spoken and the others obeyed. I looked at her, and the
strange, painful thing was not that I felt like I didn't recognize
her but that I did. It made perfect sense: my Aunt Leila, brilliant with a blade and better with words, able to kill as she
had always been able to do everything. Not only one of the
revolutionaries, but one of their leaders.

Tell the wind and fire where to stop, but don't tell me.

Nothing stopped my Aunt Leila. I had always known that.

"You can go, but you must return when you are summoned," she said. "Our new city will have need of you."

I wanted to ask why, ask what I could possibly do, but I
did not want to risk displeasing her. I did not think she would
hurt me, but I was sure she would not want to spare Carwyn.
I knew she was letting me go home because she had other
plans for what she had called "this bloody night": she did not
need the spectacle of the Golden Thread in the Dark when
she would have the spectacle of death.

Aunt Leila glanced at Carwyn, and her glance was not
the look that anyone gave a person. She looked at him as if

he was a mysterious object and she was wondering about his provenance.

Even staying long enough for her to pay attention to him, rather than me, was dangerous.

"I promise, Aunt Leila," I said loudly, to force her gaze back to me. "I will return."

Aunt Leila made a grand gesture, as if a single night and too many deaths had made her a queen. "Then you may go."

We walked outside, under the golden ovals that were the stained-glass windows, through the golden doors.

Down the avenues, I could see the lights of burning fires, the outlines of walls and buildings changed into ruin and rubble. The *sans-merci* had moved in a devastating tide from their city to ours, and now the city was theirs. Now the city was burning.

The very streetlamps were swathed in red and black, some lights extinguished and others turned red. Red light reflected off the sheen of rainwater on the black surface of the road, so it looked as though the streets of the city were running blood.

We walked home. It was a cold, weary walk in the rain, which was falling in a thin, continuous drizzle, settling over us in a chilly mist. Carwyn's hand felt as icy in mine as the sword hilt in my grasp, but nobody bothered us. The few people walking the nighttime streets let the boy in evening dress with the bloody bottle and the girl in the glittering gown with the sword pass. We were too obviously survivors of something they did not want to know about.

They would all know soon.

When Penelope looked through the eyehole in her door and saw us, with our weapons and the bloodstains, she opened the door with shaking hands as fast as she could, made tea, and made us drink it while she ran between rooms, pushing a blanket and a bed on wheels.

"Tea is essential medicine for a shock," she assured us. "Trust me—I'm a doctor."

I clung to the warmth of the mug in my hands, a welcome change from Carwyn's touch or steel. I assumed that she would want Carwyn to sleep on the couch, though I did not think about it much, did not think about anything now that I was safe and allowed to be exhausted.

Danger meant being resourceful. There was peace in not needing to keep pushing forward, in being able to admit that you were utterly drained.

"You both need comfort," said Penelope. "I'm going to sleep in Lucie's bed, and I already moved Marie's bed to the other room. You two can take mine." She patted me on the shoulder. "I don't mind," she added quietly in my ear. "This isn't the normal world anymore, and we aren't working by the normal rules. You two love each other. Love is what counts, no matter what world we're in."

I didn't know how to protest. Even in a new world, I did not know how to tell her what I had done.

Carwyn listened to what was happening and did not offer up a protest either. Of course, he had been very quiet since we had entered Penelope's apartment and she had welcomed us both with open arms, touched his hair and his face, and said, "Ethan, I'm so glad you're safe."

I could not even tell if he was mocking me with his silence, still finding my pain the best joke he knew, or if he might be as tired as I was.

I went into the bedroom with Carwyn and determined that if he said or tried anything, I would hit him. I wanted to hit someone.

I looked at him, coldly, and for a wonder he decided that this was one trespass he would not commit.

I walked over to the bed we were meant to share, stripped off the blanket, and laid the sword down upon the mattress. Carwyn and I lay on either side of the sword. I folded my hands under my chin and faced him.

I had used far too much Light power all through this long night. Now the night was over and I had burned out. I could feel the scorching poison in my blood, scraping like a hot knife along my bones. I did not even think about going for help. I knew I had to bear it. I was not the only hollowed-out and burning thing in New York.

Light filtered through the window in Penelope's room,

the sun rising on our broken city, sunbeams traveling slowly across our bed. A sunbeam struck the sword blade and turned it into a silver beam of light, burning between us as the city burned outside the window. No hope came with the rising sun, and despite what Penelope had intended, I had no comfort that night.

CHAPTER EIGHTEEN

I WOKE WITH THE FLAME-PALE LIGHT OF EARLY morning turned into the dull fire of day. The first thing I saw was the sword hilt as it rested on the pillow. Close by on the pillow, on the other side of the sword, was Carwyn's sleeping face. His dark brows were drawn together as if he was worrying, his lashes resting on his cheeks. His fingers were curled a fraction away from the blade, as if in his sleep he was stupid enough to reach out.

Right face. Wrong boy.

I looked at Carwyn, and I thought about Ethan.

He had gone into the Dark city, and now the Dark had risen up against the Light. He was in the center of what must have been chaos, buried for less than two weeks but not born to be buried, not raised to deal with the Dark. Anyone in the Dark city might have recognized his face and killed him because he was a Stryker, and even though he must have known the risks, he had walked into the heart of the Dark city for me.

I'd thought that Ethan might be in danger from Carwyn. Now, even worse, he was in danger from a whole city.

I remembered Aunt Leila's face, and the utter lack of pity in her eyes. I could not stop her. Neither light nor dark, wind nor fire, love nor mercy, would ever stop her.

It felt like everyone I loved either was threatened or was a threat themselves.

Penelope and Marie were safe, though. They, my father, and Carwyn were the only ones in this bright city that I knew were safe.

I had to know who else was.

I was sure the schools were all shut, but that meant my school friends should be at home and able to answer me. I climbed off the bed and started sending messages, letting friends from school know that I was alive, and asking if they were safe. Those who did not respond I called.

Nadiya did not respond to the messages I sent, and she did not pick up her phone.

"Who are you trying to reach?" Carwyn asked.

I jumped at the sound of his voice and turned to face him. Propped up slightly by one arm behind his head, he was lying comfortably alongside the sword, as if it was his ideal bed partner.

"Nadiya," I said. "You remember my friend from the club?"

Suddenly I remembered him asking me how well Ethan

knew Nadiya. Asking me if I was sure that they did not know each other well.

From the look on his face, I saw Carwyn remembered it too.

"Vividly," Carwyn drawled. "She was so very friendly. Remember when she pretended she wanted to buy dust, when really she wanted to drag me—sorry, Ethan—off, away from you? Do you know that she whispered in my ear that she wanted to speak to me alone? Do you want to know what I think?"

"I'm glad you asked," I said. "Because I really don't."

"Too bad. I'm going to tell you anyway. I think your friend knew Ethan a lot better than you realized. I think that your perfect boyfriend was cheating on you."

"I know that he wasn't," I snapped.

That didn't mean that I thought Carwyn was lying. He didn't have any reason to lie. I didn't think he wanted to hurt me anymore, and if Nadiya had spoken to someone she thought was Ethan that way, his interpretation was fair based on what he knew. He just didn't know Ethan like I did.

If Ethan knew Nadiya better than he had let on, if they had a secret between them, the secret was not what Carwyn thought.

"I'm going to see her," I said abruptly. "You can wait here. Or you can leave, for all I care, but you're not coming with me."

Carwyn stretched indolently, as if he was perfectly comfortable and might settle back down to sleep. I hated him for the stupid pretense, as if anyone could rest while the city burned. I hated him for being able to pretend so well when I found that I suddenly could not pretend for a moment longer.

The subway was not working. I stopped and stared at the entrance, baffled. The subway had been the one constant in the two very different worlds I had lived in, running through both the Dark city and the Light, though not connecting the two. It was a chain that had been broken but still remained, thrumming with the same energy in both cities.

Now the reassuring rattle and rumble, the heartbeat of the city, was quiet.

I had to walk a long way to get to Nadiya's place, exhaustion and the hungry magic sickness burning through me. I stumbled as I walked, and as I walked I saw things I would rather not have seen.

The city was not much changed. There were only small details, here and there. They were like the subtle signs, the pallor and trembling, of someone who was dying from internal injuries—the smell of smoke in the air, the far-off sound of a child screaming, store windows that were broken but not shattered. The cracks in the glass caught the sun, so the windows looked as if they were wrapped in vast spider webs made of light.

They had set up cages in Times Square. That was the one thing that stopped me. The cages hung on thick black chains, in front of the blaring bright colors of advertisements proclaiming new fashion brands and new movie stars, the unforgiving dazzle of Light power and commerce. I did not have to wonder what they were for. I remembered how the cages in Green-Wood Cemetery had looked, the black edge of magic to the metal, the sound as the spikes went into flesh and drank both blood and Light. I remembered my father's screams.

They had not torn down the cages to spare lives. They had torn them down so they could build them somewhere new, somewhere there would be a flood of fresh victims for those black jaws. And these cages looked different somehow, looked even worse than the cages at Green-Wood had. I remembered the sword one of the rebels had cut down Gabrielle Mirren with, how its dark edges had distorted the world. The outlines of these cages were writhing black strokes cut into the sky.

They were empty, I told myself. They were empty, they were empty.

For now.

Nadiya lived in a big apartment block, red-brick with the windows full of white blinds, sternly anonymous. The only thing that differentiated her building from the line of identical buildings was a stoop that somebody had painted mint green in what must have been a fit of optimism. That had been a long time ago. The mint-green paint was peeling to reveal scraps of ghost-gray wood beneath.

Nadiya did not buzz me in, but she came downstairs when I pressed the bell. Long before she reached the door, I saw her bright hijab through the wire-mesh window. Her step was slow as she opened the door, and her eyes were huge as they met mine. She looked afraid.

I wondered how I looked.

"You knew Ethan better than I thought you did," I said slowly. "Didn't you?"

Nadiya bit her lip. "Yes," she said. "But it's not what you think."

"You don't know what I think."

Nadiya was no fool. She looked at me, her gaze level and tranquil, and she waited to hear what I thought.

I thought of the accusation of treason against Ethan, what they had actually said: that he was passing secrets to a member of the *sans-merci*.

Ethan had said, when his father was killed, that it was all his fault.

Ethan believed that the cruelty to the Dark city had to stop. Ethan always acted to stop other people's suffering. If people had approached him and asked him for his help to change the world, he might have helped.

I was an idiot. Carwyn had not committed treason. It had been Ethan all along.

I had thought of the treason as a crime and thought it could not have been Ethan, that it must have been committed by a doppelganger, because doppelgangers were capable of anything.

I had committed a crime myself when I undid Carwyn's collar. People committed crimes every day. Ethan was not the sole exception to every rule, was not innocent of everything.

Acting to help people in the Dark city was like him, and not like Carwyn at all.

"Ethan gave the plans of his apartment building to the resistance," I said. "Along with other information about the cages in Green-Wood Cemetery. You two were engaged in helping the resistance against the Light Council. You thought . . . Someone was meant to use the secret passage to talk to Charles Stryker, weren't they? But they killed him instead."

Nadiya began to nod, slowly and continuously. Her hijab blazed in the shadow of her hall like a flame.

"You were helping the *sans-merci*," I went on.

Nadiya said, "No! Not those lunatics who have taken the city. Of course not. Ethan and I and . . . some of our friends, we wanted life to get better, for everyone, in both cities. We wanted a change in policies, to have the cages and walls taken down so there could be peace between us. We didn't want any of this. We found people who agreed with us, who were printing pamphlets that spread the truth about how the Light

Council's policies affect the Dark city. We've been doing it for two years, and it never caused any harm. Ethan spoke on television, and we all celebrated his rallying call to change. That was all we wanted: change, not death. We only wanted to make a difference. We only . . . We only wanted to help."

It wasn't as simple as that. My Aunt Leila had started by attending speeches and passing out pamphlets. Some of the same people who were killing now had likely been passing out pamphlets with Ethan and Nadiya. I suspected Nadiya knew that as well as I did.

Trying to make a difference meant that you risked doing harm.

She and Ethan had at least tried to do something good. She and Ethan had meant it for the best, had wanted change and thought it could be change for the better. I didn't feel I had a right to judge either of them when I had been so scared of losing what I had that I never tried to change anything. I had frozen myself and forced myself to be blind and deaf as well as still, and it had all been for nothing.

I had lost anyway.

"Do you have contacts in the Dark city?" I asked. "If Ethan went there, do you know where he might have gone?"

"Ethan in the Dark city?" Nadiya demanded. "Why would he go there? That would be suicide."

Nadiya did not know anything. There were no rebels who would protect Ethan: his going had not been part of any plan. He had gone in alone, because he wanted to do the right thing. For me.

I had been so stupid, at every turn. I had thought of him as wrongfully accused, as cruelly kidnapped. I had thought of him as stumbling into danger like a helpless child who did not know what he was doing. But he had walked into danger like a knight of old, with his head held high. All this time, he had been fighting for justice and fighting for me. And I had never suspected, even when he tried to tell me: when he said that his father's death was his fault, when he was so worried I would end up involved in the trouble he had caused. He had offered me all his secrets, and I had never dreamed he had as many secrets as I did. I had turned my face away.

I loved him, but I had failed him. I had thought of him as a victim. I had not seen that he was trying to be a hero.

"Look," said Nadiya, "I never wanted anyone to get hurt. Not you, and certainly not Ethan. Can you believe that?"

"Yes," I said slowly. "I believe you."

I gave her a kiss on the cheek as we parted, still friends. The city was still burning, and Ethan was still lost.

When I got home, I found Penelope and Marie playing a game in the living room, both of them moving their pieces with shaking, fumbling fingers, and Carwyn nowhere to be seen. I presumed he was lurking in the bedroom. I banged my way inside, but I found him actually asleep.

Fury failed me, like the door falling shut behind me when I had not meant to close it. He was curled up on his side, perilously close to the sword.

Perhaps Carwyn had not slept well in whatever hideaway in the Light city he had managed to find, or in Ethan's bed with the Strykers. Perhaps he had not slept well in the Dark city either.

I sat on the edge of the bed and wondered when the last time he had felt safe enough to sleep peacefully had been.

As soon as I had decided not to wake him, he woke. I felt the bed move as he stirred.

"Where's my collar?" Carwyn asked suddenly.

I looked at him. He lay back on the bed, one arm behind his head, and he looked sullen but defiant. He tilted his chin to stare back at me.

"Why do you ask?" I said.

Carwyn waggled his eyebrows, and his sly expression made him look, briefly and utterly, nothing like Ethan. "I might want it for reasons."

"I might stop talking to you altogether because I am a hundred percent done with your crap."

Carwyn's eyebrows drew together, serious now, as if he was annoyed or as if I had forced sincerity out of him against his will. "I might need it so that I can survive, all right? I think it's going to be open season on Strykers in the Light city, and I should run away to be an anonymous doppelganger instead. Does that make you happy?"

"You surviving?" I asked. "I don't care that much either way."

"Oh, c'mon, baby, you know you don't mean that," said Carwyn.

"Try to remember what I just said about your crap."

"I am remembering, and I'm absolutely serious," said Carwyn. "You don't care much about whether I survive or not? *You,* of all people. Who got me out of the hotel where everyone was dying? Who took me out on the town because she felt sorry for me, and felt even sorrier for me just seeing me treated like any doppelganger would be? Who took off my collar in the first place? Who didn't turn me in when I came back pretending to be Ethan, even though you knew as soon as you saw me? You could have done it. You didn't have to go to the guards. You could have gone to Ethan's Uncle Mark — he knows all about me. He wanted me dead from the first moment he laid eyes on me: he wanted me quietly and cleanly erased out of existence, as if I was a stain on the family silver. If I had done anything to Ethan, he would have tortured the information out of me and made sure I disappeared."

The litany of what I had done hung in the air like an accusation.

I had not done any of it because I wanted him to be

grateful. I did not think I deserved gratitude: I had done the wrong thing, made so many mistakes, and so much of what I had done was because I loved Ethan, because Carwyn had saved Ethan, and because he looked like Ethan. Even though I had not wanted gratitude, I had not deserved Carwyn hurting me while he pretended to be Ethan. He had hurt me anyway.

"I was doing it because it was the right thing to do," I said slowly. "None of it was for you. I don't even like you."

Carwyn blinked, then winked. Every small moment where he betrayed any uncertainty or seemed a little human, he covered over by acting worse than ever. "You sure about that?"

There was another silence. This one hung in the air like a question, rather than an accusation. I only had one answer.

"Yeah," I said at last. "I'm really sure."

Carwyn sat up now. He shoved himself lightly to the end of the bed, where I was sitting, and sat a careful distance away from me. I glanced over at him and wondered if I should tell him that Ethan had been the one working with the *sans-merci*. I figured that it wasn't necessary. Carwyn must have always known Ethan had done it, because he knew he himself was innocent of the charges.

He had known Ethan had done it, and still he had spoken up for him and saved him. It had been too easy for me to forget, all this time, that the first thing I had ever seen Carwyn do was commit an act of mercy.

"What was it you said to me, the first day you met me?" Carwyn asked suddenly, as if he could read the beginning of my thoughts on my face but not the end. "'I'll collar you . . . And then I'll hurt you'? Maybe I'll let you. Maybe, for once, just for a change, it's safer to be me than it is to be Ethan Stryker."

When I opened the bedroom door, Marie and Penelope were gone, I presumed on an errand. We still needed to eat, even if the city was in chaos. I walked out of Penelope's room and into the main room, then through the doorway into mine and Dad's room. I heard Carwyn softly following me, but I did not look back at him.

I had thought I would have to be very quiet, that Dad would still be asleep, but the beds were all empty. Penelope must have taken him out with her. I hoped she knew what she was doing. I hoped nothing out there was disturbing or frightening him.

I knelt down on the worn wood floor. I found that the knowledge of which precise brick I had hidden the collar under had slipped my mind, something I'd thought would be branded forever in my memory as a guilty secret, lost with the rush of everything else that had happened, like the sea chasing away words written in the sand.

If even I couldn't remember where it was, it had to be a pretty good hiding place. I put my hands flat against the wall and felt along the bricks, feeling the sharp indents on the ones that I had scraped at with a fork, and finally the real loose brick. I slid it out of the wall and put my hand into the hollow.

The first thing I touched was the chain of my mother's necklace. I did not draw that out. I did not want Carwyn to see it.

My fingers came away gray with ash, with the bag in my palm. I unwrapped the collar from its material. I had forgotten exactly what it looked like: the shining metal divots where my rings would fit in, to bind him and hurt him if he disobeyed.

Carwyn's breath drew in sharply at the sight of it.

I held the collar out to him.

"Here it is," I said. "It's yours. I'll put it on for you if you want, if you think people might check whether it's sealed. Or you can take the chance, and be able to take it off. Put it on right now, put it on later, don't ever wear it again. Do what you want with it."

Carwyn stared at the collar but made no move to touch it. "What do you think I should do?"

"Like I said," I answered, "it's yours. I don't think anyone should ever have put it on you against your will. But if you can use it to protect yourself, to make sure people won't think you're Ethan, I don't see why you shouldn't. This collar's brought you enough trouble. If it buys you safety, I think that's fair."

It only occurred to me then that it might have kept Ethan safe in the Dark city, having Carwyn here in his place. But I could not snatch back the collar and hide it away again.

I didn't really want to. Ethan would not have wanted his safety bought at the price of a lie. I had already lied and lied, and nobody was safe. I was so tired of lying.

Carwyn did touch the collar at last, running his fingers lightly over the leather and metal. His fingers brushed my hand, and he looked away from the collar and at me.

"What would you do?"

"How should I know?" I asked. "It's not my collar. It was never my life. It's not my call. I guess think about who you want to be, and how you want people to see you."

Carwyn touched my rings, and then his collar. It was odd that his fingers on the metal encircling mine felt more intimate than when he touched my skin. My rings were as much a part of me as his collar had been part of him: identifying me, grounding me, branding me, anchoring me. They had kept me safe, and perhaps now they would put me in danger. And yet I knew I would never take them off.

"I think you'd use the collar to keep someone else safe," he said. "If you could."

I swallowed down a noise—even I did not know if it was

going to be a laugh or a sob, and I was too scared of letting it be born to find out.

"I don't think either of us knows how to keep someone else safe."

Carwyn nodded, and took the collar from my hand. We turned and left the bedroom.

He was holding the collar awkwardly, as if he still was not sure what to do with it and would have put it in his pocket if he could. I went toward the old red sofa, meaning to sit down, but instead I stopped at the window through which I had once found Carwyn looking up at me.

Sunlight was streaming in through my little window. The street outside was quieter than it should have been. I could see blinds drawn in the windows of the buildings opposite, suggesting that people were hiding instead of going to work.

Down the street and over the faraway stretch of gray buildings was the horizon, and for a confused instant I thought I was seeing the sunset. But it was much too early for the sun to go down. The red fire lapping between the sky and earth was something else.

The wall between the Dark and Light cities was down, torn down, and on either side of the rubble I saw fire. Both of my cities were burning.

I was not feeling very steady, so I grabbed hold of the windowsill and let out the sound I had suppressed before: everything was coming out now, and there was no way to hide how scared I was. The sound was a laugh after all. I laughed at myself for ever thinking I could hide.

"Before I go . . ." said Carwyn. "You're not well. You've used too much magic, and that means you cannot protect yourself or anybody else."

I stopped leaning against the sill—it had been a mistake to let myself look weak in front of Carwyn—and turned to face him. Unbelievably, he was serious.

"And you think I'd let you do something about it?" I snapped. "Not likely."

"I owe you," said Carwyn. "You know I do. I know it as well. I'd appreciate the chance to settle some of my debt. And do you know any Dark magicians you can trust to take out the poison at a time like this?" He mimicked my cool tone. "Not likely."

"You think I'd trust *you* to drain my power?" The further retort was on my lips: my Aunt Leila was a Dark magician. She could do it. She wouldn't hurt me. She would help me, like she always had.

I did not say it. I did not, I realized, want her help.

I looked at Carwyn. He did owe me, but I did not trust him. I had always had this done by Aunt Leila, or my grandfather when I was very young, or in a clinic where I could be certain the Dark magician would be entirely professional and I would be entirely safe.

I was weak and shaking with the effects of magic in my

blood, though, and I could not afford to be sick or lacking in Light power. I did need help.

"All right," I said, speaking low. "But don't . . . don't touch me."

I didn't know why I'd said it. He'd touched me plenty before, and this was a normal procedure. It wasn't a big deal.

Carwyn nodded, head bowed as he searched in his pockets. Eventually he produced a small metal object, like an elaborately carved thimble that came to a point as sharp as a claw. I saw the shine of a tiny glass vial set behind the claw, bright as a teardrop in sunlight. The carvings on the metal were shadowy in contrast, with the strange shadows of the new cages. He fitted it on his thumb and took a step forward.

I took a step back and hit the window. "Do you normally use that?" I demanded.

"For private drainings, yeah," said Carwyn.

I frowned. "So—you do this for your Light magician friends?"

Carwyn laughed. "I've never had a Light magician friend. But there are Light magicians who take quick, nasty trips to the Dark city. They will pay extra for a Dark magician to come and drain them in private."

I remembered how the woman at the restaurant and some of the people on the train had looked at him when he was wearing the doppelganger's collar, the mixture of contempt and desire.

"You don't . . . have to drain me."

Carwyn glanced up at me, puzzled, and then something he saw in my face made him look less casual and more serious. "I want to help you," he said. "I know you don't have much reason to believe me, but I mean it. I want to."

"All right." I held out my arm, fingers pointing to the floor. I was in an even worse state than I had realized: I could not stop my arm from trembling.

Dark magicians in the clinic had, before now, held my arm steady. Carwyn did not. Instead he sank to his knees and used the metal claw to trace lightly up the vein in my arm until he reached the inside of my elbow. My back was against the window, my free hand gripping the windowsill behind me, my whole body straining away, but I knew he was being as gentle as he could.

I'd had people in the clinic take blood clumsily: my arm ached for days after. I'd known that Carwyn had to be good to have gotten a pass into the Light city. I watched his easy expertise and remembered that the Strykers had taken the pass from him, something he must have worked hard for, and he had not even seemed surprised.

When the metal claw sank in, the pain came fast but lasted only briefly. The blood that trailed down my arm had visible traces of Light in it, like mica sparkling in dark stone. I looked down at Carwyn and saw the sudden hunger in his face.

Dark magicians did not have to drink the blood. They

could absorb blood spilled near them, as they did with the cages, feeding off the blood and death in the air. In the clinic, they kept it, and we did not have to watch what they did with it, even though we knew it was consumed or sold out of sight. My aunt and my grandfather, when he was alive, had drunk it in front of me, and I had been happy to see them do it, to give them power as they healed me.

Carwyn's dark head hovered over my arm, but he held my gaze. He did not put his mouth to my skin. He kept looking at me, and kept his promise, while relief poured through me as if I was parched earth and his magic was rain after a drought.

Carwyn slid the metal claw out of my arm, knelt there for a moment longer with his face still tipped up to mine, then rose to his feet. He pulled off the claw tip from behind the metal point, extracting a vial that was about half the size of a thimble and now filled with my blood. I picked up a towel and wiped away the thin trail of blood smeared down my arm.

My blood cleansed and my head clear, I understood myself better: I'd asked Carwyn not to touch me because I had wanted to know that he would not do it if I asked. He had not.

"You can drink it," I said.

"Thank you," said Carwyn. "Perhaps I shall." He stoppered the vial, and it disappeared into a pocket.

I did not thank him. There was too much between us that he had not apologized for. I could not find it in me to be grateful, but I did find myself concerned about him, feeling as though I had been right about him the first time, that he was the person I had thought he was and not the nightmare creature I had feared.

I put my back to him and faced the burning world outside the window.

"Where are you going to go?" I asked. "Nowhere's safe."

"If I could choose where to go . . ." Carwyn began, but stopped.

Ethan was gone, and Jarvis was gone, both where I could not find them. I did not have the patience for this.

"You can choose. That's what giving you the collar meant. You're free to go. You're as free as I can make you. You can go anywhere you want to go in the world, and I hope you find somewhere safe. I can't tell you what to do. You have to decide, and I have to go after Ethan."

"If I could choose where to go," Carwyn resumed, as if I had not spoken at all. "If I could go anywhere in the world, I'd want to go with you. I don't want to be where it's safe. I want to be where you are."

I froze, still holding on to the windowsill. "What did you say?"

I turned away from the fire outside. Carwyn met my eyes with a level gaze. He looked different than I could have imagined anyone would while saying something like that. There was a look of fixed despair about his face, as if he was gazing at someone dead, as far away from him as that.

"They say that doppelgangers don't dream," said Carwyn. "That you have to have a soul to dream."

"I don't understand what you're saying," I said, slowly. I had slept in the same bed as him, his head on a pillow beside mine, and he had not slept any differently than anyone else. "I don't know whether doppelgangers dream or not. I have never known any doppelgangers but you."

"I haven't known many either. There aren't many," said Carwyn. "The hood is license for any cruelty. The faceless are as good as voiceless: nobody would listen if any one of us called for help. I told you this already. We look like those who would have died young without the Dark magic that saved them and made us. We die young instead of them."

He almost never seemed or sounded serious. Even now, when he was talking about the death of his own kind, his lip was curled and there was an uncertain wicked flicker in his eyes that made me think he was about to make a joke. I felt wary, waiting for the twist, waiting for the doppelganger's trick.

"I know as much about doppelgangers as you do," said Carwyn. "All I know about doppelgangers is what I've been told. I never knew if I had a soul, and while I was buried I lived in a wild, degraded, disgusting way. I remember hating the way I lived sometimes when I was younger, but more and more I didn't care. I thought I couldn't care and that nothing mattered. And then I met you, and you tried so hard to make things right for Ethan and for your family and even for me. I could not figure out why you did what you did for me. I was a stranger. I thought . . . it might be because you liked me, but now I know you don't. I'm glad you don't. There have been a couple of people who were kind to me because they thought I was interesting or good-looking or useful. You were kind to someone you didn't know and shouldn't have trusted. That was what taught me who you are. You woke all the old shadows in me that wanted to be something like a person. I thought I would never want that again."

I was held still with utter shock.

I felt as I had on the balcony in the Plaza Hotel, the whole world turned upside down and the pieces falling together to make a picture entirely different from the one I had expected. The doppelganger under my window looking up, the doppelganger's sharp voice on the phone, concerned about me.

Not a trick. A romance.

Carwyn took a step back, leaning against the door frame, and I could not believe how badly I had misinterpreted the restless glitter of his eyes. He covered his face with one hand, but it was too late. I knew he was crying.

"So—you're going to be a good person from now on?" I asked helplessly, stupidly.

No more of his random cruelty, the way he had tormented me over Ethan out of bitterness or malice even though now he said he cared about me. If he felt like this, then acting like that hurt him, too, degraded him, too. If he was not what people thought him, he should not behave like he was.

Even as I had said the words, I did not think they were true. I could see no hope in his face, and I could find no hope of my own.

"No," he said, unshading his face and looking at me. His eyes were clear now. "I will never be better than I am. The collar was just a symbol. It wasn't what people were shrinking from and punishing me for. They were afraid of me. I will always have someone else's face and not enough heart. You set me free, and look what I did to you. I am going to be worse someday. I'm going to be so much worse."

He spoke as if it was a foregone conclusion, and I could see his pain at the idea. I didn't know if what he believed was true or if he was making it true by believing it, but I didn't care. I was angry at the waste and angry with him.

"So why tell me any of it, then?" I demanded. "Why would you load another burden on me when I have enough? I am not responsible for your heart! Are you just this selfish?"

"Yes," said Carwyn. "I wanted you to know. I am selfish enough to do it for only that reason, but there is another. I wanted you to know something else."

The city was burning and Ethan was in danger, and Carwyn was a lost soul.

"I'm not interested," I said loudly. I let go of the windowsill, crossed the floor in one stride, and shoved him so his back knocked into the door frame. "I'm not interested in listening to anything you have to say."

Carwyn grabbed one of my hands, his grip too strong for me to escape from it, and I thought for a moment that he was going to wrench my arm out of its socket. Instead he raised my hand to his lips and kissed it, roughly, so his lip split open under one of my rings. It was so far from what I had expected that I did listen to him after all.

"You were not the first dream I ever had, but you were the only dream that ever felt real. You were the dream that taught me I did have a soul. I don't know how low I will fall or what evil I will do, but I know you. I know there is nothing between us and there never could be. But I would do whatever you asked. I would do anything you want. If I had anything worth giving to you, I would give it. If I had anything to sacrifice, I would sacrifice it for you."

I didn't try to pull away from him.

"I don't want you to sacrifice anything."

"Don't think well of me," Carwyn said, and smiled his dark little smile, though his lashes were still wet. "Not for a minute. This is selfish too. It's useless. You don't need me, and I can't do anything for you. One day you will be happy, and I will sink even further. I'll be the lowest scum of the streets and you'll never see me again, but I wanted you to know that wherever I end up, I will still feel the same about you. If you ever think of me then, I want you to remember me as someone who would cut out his heart to spare yours. This is the last thing I'll ever ask of you. You were always kind to me, even when you did not mean to be, even when you wanted to be cruel. You were angry for me when I would not have thought to be angry for myself, you warned me that cupcakes were too sweet, and you healed my wrist. You treated me like I was a real person, and I almost felt real. Be kind to me again, let me be real to you one more time: I beg you to believe me."

He was too close to me, his grip not tight enough to hurt and yet somehow still hurting me, as if his skin was hot and his hold on me could burn. I was trembling.

I looked away from him and said in a low voice, "I believe you."

I was not looking for his reaction and I did not see it. The next moment, the door opened, and Penelope and Marie came through. They were both beaming wildly, their footsteps clattering in a frantic chorus of joy. Someone else walked in with them.

It was not Dad. It was Jarvis. He was holding tight to

Penelope's hand, and he looked gray and thin and old. Until he saw Carwyn. Then he simply looked afraid.

"You're not Ethan," he whispered.

"Would you believe I'm Ethan's twin," Carwyn asked, "and that they kept me in the attic my whole life because they didn't want Ethan to be shamed by how much handsomer I was?"

I looked at Penelope and Marie, who were staring in confusion and growing horror. I glanced at Carwyn and saw him smirking, showing no trace of tears nor any sign that he had been making an emotional confession. I didn't spare any of them more than a glance.

"You knew he wasn't Ethan," I said slowly to Jarvis. "You knew Ethan couldn't be here. So you know where Ethan is. He found you, didn't he? Where is he?"

"Lucie," said Jarvis.

"Tell me! Tell me where he is."

"Lucie, I'm so sorry," said Jarvis. "He found me. He gave himself up in my place. He told them he'd do whatever they wanted as long as they let me go. He is in the hands of the *sans-merci*."

He had accomplished his mission, my hero, my knight. I was sick with terror.

I swallowed. "And where's Dad?"

"He's with your aunt," said Penelope, her face very serious.

"But I swear to you, he's safe. The *sans-merci* are hailing him as a hero and a martyr. And, Lucie, the *sans-merci* have commanded you to go to them as well. Your aunt wants to see you."

Nobody swore to me that Ethan was safe. None of them wanted to lie to me.

I took a deep breath. "And I want to see her."

CHAPTER NINETEEN

THEY HAD ETHAN AND I HAD TO SAVE HIM, AND I'd promised Aunt Leila I would come if she asked for me. I did not know what she wanted with me. I did not know what the *sans-merci* wanted from me. I could not stop hearing them calling for the Golden One, their voices echoing through that great hotel that had become a palace of the dead.

I had spent two years doing what I did not want to do and had to do anyway. Now I made my way up the gentle slope of the streets.

Aunt Leila had given Jarvis very specific instructions. She had told him that I should not head toward the hotel. She had told me to go somewhere else.

Nobody had told Carwyn to come with me, least of all me, but he had insisted, and I had not wanted to leave him with Penelope's family.

He said nothing to me as we made our way, and I said nothing to him. I kept walking until Times Square came into view again, not in the light of morning but in the glow of the early afternoon, just beginning the sun's fall. The square was a metallic glen, made of buildings and not trees. The tall rectangular towers shone like giant mirrors; the lines of gems affixed to several of them were like vast jeweled belts hung in the sky. Usually Light power showed images on screens and formed advertisements that walked among the denizens of the city—you only knew they were magic and not real people by their peculiar brightness and the occasional flicker.

Not today. The crowd of people today was all real, and there were so many of them, and so many were from the Dark city. Clothes were made differently in the Dark city. I remembered that now, how the very stitching of the seams and the colors of the materials looked different. There were fewer bright colors, and less material, because the Dark city did not have extra cloth to waste on full skirts or frills. I clenched my fists in the material of my long skirt, which swung around my legs like a bell. I must have looked like someone from the Light. It might have been safer to look like a Dark citizen.

Some of the audience were clearly from the Light, though, and their faces were just as rapt, and their eyes contained just as much promise of violence.

I began to shove my way through the crowd, breath stuck in my throat. Some of these people had weapons, but it was not the weapons I was concerned about. It was the hostility of the crowd, bristling like a pack of dogs that were going to attack.

I kept my ringed hands clenched and pushed on, waiting for someone to speak and strike me down.

A voice rang out, and Carwyn instantly vanished from my side and into the crowd. I barely even registered him going.

"Make way for the Golden Thread in the Dark! Make way for your Golden One!" called my Aunt Leila, and the people parted like water at the command of a prophet, clearing a path for me.

I could see Aunt Leila on a platform that looked hastily constructed, the wood still rough. There were others of the *sans-merci* there, wearing their bands of cloth. I did not see my uncle.

I could see my father. He was wearing the red and scarlet of the rebels. He looked as hurt and confused as a child forced into clothes that were not his own and that he was uncomfortable wearing. I ran toward him, up the creaking wooden steps. I was on the platform and had almost reached him when Aunt Leila set a hand on my arm. Her grip felt as heavy and inescapable as a manacle.

She spun me toward the crowd.

"This is the Golden Thread in the Dark!"

All the people seemed to blur before my eyes as their shouts blended in my ears into one indistinguishable roar. All that was clear were the cages hanging in the air, their chains attached to towers of Light. The cages shimmered darkly, and the memory of the old cages in Green-Wood Cemetery came back to me like a nightmare that had come to life even more terrible than I had dreamed.

These cages were full now. I could see the limbs jammed up, see the blood beading on the iron bars.

My aunt held my hand up high, and the people cheered again.

"You all know her. You all know her story." My Aunt Leila paused. "Or you think you do. You don't know the half of it, but now it's finally time to tell the truth. You know the Strykers are tyrants, but you do not know this story of treachery and murder."

An excited, anticipatory murmur chased her words, ready to be furious.

"Once I had a sister," said Aunt Leila. "She was born with Light magic in the Dark city. She did not ever wear rings: she never wanted to be parted from her family, and she never wanted to serve the Light Council. She was a good girl, and by that I do not mean she sat by and was beautiful and harmed no one. Instead, she acted always to help and comfort. She met a Light magician from the Light city come on one of their brief errands of meaningless mercy, and he so loved her that he stayed, and healed and truly helped us. He did more than that. He taught my sister how to heal as well as any Light medic. She could have taken the rings, gone into the Light, been powerful and rich and unhurt. My sister instead hid what she could do, hid her marriage to him. She lived in the Dark where our parents died, our houses so close to each other, they seemed like one house. Her child would run through my gate for supper; my husband would help her husband with household tasks. And every night my sister, my Josephine, would go down to the east, where the least of the buried tried to eke out a living. She would go to those who could not pay true Light magicians, and heal them. She had such power. I saw her lay her hands once upon a dying man and he was well again. She could do marvels. And I asked her, I begged her, not to, because I knew the cost of marvels and mercy."

My aunt's hair streamed out like a black banner, and she spoke like a bard. I saw that everyone in the crowd believed her story as much as I, who had been the child running through the gate to her arms, who had lived it.

I had dreamed of a day when someone would tell the truth of what had happened to my mother. I had never thought it could really happen. I had never thought that, if it did happen, it would be anything but a triumph.

"My sister went down into the darkest part of the Dark city one night, and she tended to one of the doppelgangers. She often went to heal them. The Light magicians would not lay hands on them, and the way those creatures are treated and the disgusting way they live means they sicken often and die young. I do not know how many doppelgangers Josephine saved, but I know which one killed her.

"I remember she had talked about him to me. He was young, as young as her own daughter, and very sick. He was raving, repeating the same words over and over: his shadow, his mother, his city. He was so sick, he did not even know who she was. He called her 'Mother,' as if doppelgangers could have mothers. She thought he would die, and she was so happy when he lived.

"She did not tell me one thing. I could see she was troubled, see she was keeping a secret, but I did not know what it was until months later, when one of the *sans-merci* told me what they had seen down there in the darkest part of the Dark. My sister, Josephine, pushed the doppelganger's hood back and saw his stolen face. She saw the face of Ethan Stryker, one of the Stryker heirs, a golden child marked to inherit the city and uphold the laws of the Light Council. The laws the Strykers all knew they had broken. The Strykers had everything, and they wanted Dark magic too. Their council killed us for the least infraction, but they could commit an abomination. No laws for them, only for us! Our children die, but theirs could not."

I remembered my father reacting so violently to the mention of the Strykers, trying to warn me of what he knew. *Josephine always said that. No matter what the danger is, no matter what you might find, you have to go, you have to heal. She had to heal him, Lucie. She told me she had to.*

I'd thought I knew the truth, but I had not known anything.

Him was the doppelganger. My mother had gone into danger to heal Carwyn.

I had not understood. I could not tell if the roar in my ears was the crowd or my own blood rushing to my head. For a moment, I thought I was going to faint, and then I thought that the sheer iron strength of Aunt Leila's grip would hold me up.

"When we broke their laws, we suffered for it, but when they broke their laws, we suffered for that too. Charles Stryker wanted to protect the doppelganger, and Mark Stryker wanted to control the creature. So the Strykers had spies set on the dirty little house where the doppelganger lived, spies who followed my sister home and worked out that she was secretly living with a Light magician. Mark Stryker knew that a woman linked to a Light citizen would recognize Ethan Stryker's face. He realized Josephine knew the Stryker family secret, and so she had to be destroyed. Stryker sent his men to kill my sister. They did it one night as she left the doppelganger's house. They buried her in a shallow grave in the earth beneath another lost soul's window, as if her dead body was the seeds for a flower bed. When her Light magician husband went searching for her, Stryker's power made certain he was taken and caged, in the cages we have torn down. When her daughter, our Golden One, spoke up against their cruelty and the people began to listen to her, Stryker's power carried her and her father away into the captivity of the Light. She was too famous for them to kill, so they tried to force her to become one of their own, when she was always ours. This was the final wrong we had to avenge. This was why we had to sweep into the city and save the Golden One! Little did Stryker think we would come to him and strike him down. Little did Stryker's hired assassins know, as they tossed black earth onto my sister's cold face, that she would rise up. That all of us buried would rise up and take our vengeance."

The hold on my wrist was all I could feel. Otherwise I was numb. I kept thinking of my mother, her always-worried, always-earnest living face, and of Ethan. Ethan was the only person in the world I had ever spoken to of my mother, and he had held me as I cried. I would never have dreamed there was any link between them but me.

I had never dreamed, when I had tried to help Carwyn and thought I was acting like my mother, how right I had been.

Leila shook me. "Speak!" she hissed.

"I . . ." I said. "I loved my mother. She was murdered. I couldn't talk about it. I couldn't even tell the world she was my mother. But she is not the only person I love. I love—"

Ethan, I almost said, but then Leila's hold tightened like a handcuff. It had almost been a relief to look out on a crowd and tell the truth about my mother, but I was not free now any more than I had been before. Neither in the Light nor in the Dark could I speak my whole heart.

"The Golden Thread in the Dark is my young niece, Lucie," Aunt Leila cried, her voice ringing out. "Her tortured father was my sister's husband. My father was exiled from the Light city for wielding Dark magic, and he died in the Dark. My sister was killed for wielding Light magic. Those dead are my dead. And their murderers are now at last summoned to answer for their crimes."

My aunt took a few steps forward, dragging me with her to the edge of the platform. I stumbled and teetered for a moment, the whole world seeming off balance, the sinking in my stomach telling me that I would fall.

I stared from the platform at the terrible new cages suspended against the sky, against the bright towers of the Light city. The bars of the nearest cage were black and stark, like charcoal strokes on a watercolor painting. Inside the cage, hemmed in on all sides by Dark magic and metal spikes, was Mark Stryker.

My aunt's triumphant voice rose and rose, so high that it almost became a wail.

"These creatures of the Light protect their own, at any

cost. But the time has come for them to know that we can protect our own as well as they. Turn your face to me, Stryker!"

Mark Stryker turned his face toward her. It was a face I had feared for so long. It did not look any kinder now that he was in trouble and in pain. He spat at Aunt Leila, but it did not come close to hitting her. His hate was as futile as hers had been for years. The power might have changed sides, but there was hate on both sides, inescapable. I felt like I was choking on it.

Aunt Leila's voice was a triumphant scream. "Even now, you see we cannot make him sorry. They are more soulless than doppelgangers. We can only make him pay. Mark Stryker, these are the days when all your sins are to be paid for. I summon you and yours, to the last of your evil line, to answer for your crimes. Your blood is ours to be used now, and we will not rest until the last drop of blood is spilled!"

Then I saw how the new cages worked.

The cage closed in on Mark like a dark claw. I saw his body jerk convulsively like a puppet whose strings were being pulled, in what seemed like an inhuman mimicry of human movement, because human bodies did not and could not move so. I saw the burst of Dark magic his death made, like a black supernova within the cage. I saw the Dark magicians in the crowd shudder in an ecstasy of power, and I heard the small animal sound Mark Stryker made as he died.

A terrible noise rose up from the crowd, more like the

growl and whine of a hungry beast than words formed by people who could still think, feel pity, or know reason.

"We killed Charles Stryker in his bed for his crimes!" shouted Aunt Leila. "We killed James Stryker when we took this city! Now we have killed Mark Stryker. And we will kill the last of their villainous family soon. We will not let any one of the Light Council live. We will not have peace until we have blood!"

I looked at Ethan's Uncle Mark swinging in his cage, and I knew that I had been wrong to think of him as the villain in my story, one whose power could crush me. I had been as wrong as Aunt Leila was to think that defeating the Strykers or even bringing down the Light city would change anything.

They brought out more of the Light Council, one after the other, and killed them before our eyes. They brought out the woman they called Bright Mariah in the Light city, and Bitter Mariah in the Dark, and when she was dead, a rebel held her head aloft on one of their spikes, her hair streaming and shining, a symbol the same way I was. The blood fell like rain and caused a joyful riot.

There was no escape from the ugliness in the human heart, the hate that led to this violence and all violence. It had taken my mother, tortured my father, taken my first home and was burning my second. I had struggled to be safe for years, but there was no way to be safe.

There were villains all around me. There was evil in the

very air I breathed. There would be no final showdown, no end, no possibility of happiness after evil was vanquished.

The only choice, in the Light city or the Dark, was to be twisted or to break.

CHAPTER TWENTY

I WENT BACK WITH AUNT LEILA TO THE PLAZA Hotel, where the *sans-merci* had established their head-quarters. She took me into one of the suites, and she washed her hands and face at the sink. I sat on a sofa and looked down at my clenched hands on the blue and white striped silk.

Aunt Leila seemed happy, as if the obscene show on the platform had been her notion of an ideal family outing. She was talking about the way the *sans-merci* intended to run the city they had taken: the Committee of the Free, set up to judge and punish the members of the Light regime, and how she thought Dad and I should be on it.

She wanted Ethan to be one of the first victims judged and condemned by the new committee. She wanted Ethan as her example of how life would be from now on. She thought I would actually support that.

"I'll pass," I said.

Aunt Leila looked up from the sink and frowned, sparkling

drops caught in her long black hair. "It would not be any work. You would only have to make appearances. Of course you would not make decisions about what is best for the city. It would simply be good for you to be viewed as supporting us."

She did not want real support or the real me.

I looked at her, and I remembered loving her, remembered eating cookies and learning the sword at her house, remembered her being all I had when my father was caged. I looked at her, and I could only see Mark Stryker, who had loved Ethan and still been ready to commit any atrocity. Now here was my aunt, and she loved me. I had not known two years ago that love was not enough to keep people from becoming monsters.

"I know how it would be," I told Aunt Leila. "I attended meetings of the Light Council."

"It is not the same thing at all!"

"Being your decoration instead of someone else's?" I said. "Would I not be sitting and listening to new rules that kill new people? I'd be your golden-haired doll instead of Mark Stryker's. No, thanks. I'll pass. Unless—"

Aunt Leila laughed, the sound old and wise. "I will not spare any Stryker."

And I, I found slowly, discovering the truth as if it was something I had found under dust in the attic of my own home, I did not want to join the committee. Not even to save Ethan. I was so tired of compromises and cowardice.

Aunt Leila looked at my face and sighed.

"Did you hear nothing of what I told you? Did you understand nothing of my story? That Ethan Stryker's blood tortured your father and murdered your mother, my sister, and exiled you, my niece as dear as a daughter. That I have seen them do the same to countless families, and I will not stop until every drop of his blood has answered for mine. Doesn't it matter, what they did?"

My mother gone, my father wrecked, my aunt twisted, my life ruined. If I thought about it too long, I felt the same consuming rage that Aunt Leila must have felt. If I had stayed with her instead of meeting Ethan, revenge might have been all I wanted as well. Rage might have consumed me until it was all there was left of me.

Mark Stryker had not suffered as Aunt Leila had suffered. Mark had no excuse for all he had done. But when you were making other people suffer, no excuse was good enough.

Ethan had known nothing, had done nothing but try to help me and try to save the city. Aunt Leila was murdering people, but Ethan had given himself up to save someone. I had already underestimated him, and I would not let him be condemned.

"It matters. Something else matters more. I love him."

"Love?" said Aunt Leila. "What of it? I loved my sister, more than you ever loved her, you who denied her to the whole Light city. Do you think any force in the world cares about who you love? Love never saved a single human soul. I have seen so many suffer, so many children and women and men die of neglect or brutality or starvation. Do you think any one of that crowd cares about your trouble? Did you care about theirs?"

"Not as much as I should have."

Aunt Leila nodded, watching me with intent eyes, pitiless as a wolf. I did not know what had changed her, what had made her someone who prized revenge above love. I did not know if she had always been like this, for as long as I had lived and loved her.

Ethan cares about the crowd's trouble, I thought. *Ethan does.*

"You can have the doppelganger," Aunt Leila said at last.

"What?"

"The doppelganger," Aunt Leila elucidated, saying the words with a certain malice, as if she wanted to take love as well as my beloved from me. "He's the one you were with at this hotel, isn't he? He's found some way to take his collar off. When we found Ethan Stryker in the Dark city, I thought he might be the doppelganger, but we tested him—he's the real thing. But you seem to like the imitation well enough. You can keep the doppelganger, and we will kill Ethan Stryker in two weeks, in a festival nobody will ever forget, in a purge of all his kind." She licked her lips, like a wolf after a meal, and I felt sick watching her. "We have to have the real one. He's the one I want."

"They're both real," I told her. "But he's the one I want too. It was me who took the doppelganger's collar off. I saved him, but that doesn't mean I love him. It means I would have saved anybody. You think you can keep me from saving someone I love?"

"I already saved a man for you once," said Aunt Leila. "Not this one. Not a Stryker."

She spoke as if it was entirely her doing, as if the world changed only by her will. I had spent so long feeling guilty for what I'd done, for putting on an act to get Dad out, for pretending to be innocent and thereby losing all innocence. It was something I had done, and I would not let Aunt Leila take it away from me.

"I saved him," I said. "Not you. And I'll save Ethan."

"Lucie," Aunt Leila said, obviously trying to be patient, "I don't understand the way you are acting. I spent so long planning for us to be reunited. I rallied the *sans-merci* to bring you back to me. I told them what had been done to you and to my sister, and they rose up to reunite us. I thought of you every day of the two years of your exile. And now . . ."

"And did you think that nothing would happen to me in two years? Did you think this is what you were going to do to me, once you got me back?"

Aunt Leila looked annoyed, as frustrated as a parent with a child who could not understand their homework. Her determination did not even waver. She did not take me seriously at all.

"We are finally together again. The city is ours, and justice is being done. Can't you be good?"

She walked over to where I was sitting and gently stroked my hair back from my face, and I knew then what I had not known when we were separated by exile and time: that she was lost.

She acted like I was a little girl who would accept Carwyn instead of Ethan as if they were dolls. Neither of them was real to her. Even I was hardly real to her. Maybe the child she had loved was real, but that was not me. Not any longer.

I whispered to her, "You should know me better than that."

Outside, I could still hear the murmuring of a crowd, like the turbulent air before the violence of a storm.

"And you should know me better than to think you could save him. You should remember better. Tell the wind and fire where to stop," said Aunt Leila. "But do not tell me."

She should have remembered that my grandmother was the first to say those words, when people said she could not save the man she loved.

She should have remembered that she had taught me to be unstoppable too.

When she let me leave the hotel, she thought I was going back to Penelope's apartment, but I did not. The subway was running again, and I took it downtown. I followed the path to the Dark city, to the ruined wall, along the single remaining bridge. I went back to be buried again, back home.

The Dark city was not as different from the Light city as I had recalled. It did not bring back memories of standing with Dad in the cemetery, of crawling home every night too spent even to weep. It felt familiar in a different way. There were streets I knew, and a skyline I had seen from my bedroom every night. There had been more to my life here than the end.

I felt different, though. There was so much to be worried about, but I wasn't worried. I had a single focus and I was heading toward it.

My aunt and I had walked past the clock tower many times when I was a child. She used to tell me how the windows of the tall gray building had once looked out on another bridge across the river, before the city was torn into Light and Dark and all but one bridge ripped down. We would walk along the wall and listen to the river sighing behind it, and my small, cold hand had felt safe in hers.

The building looked pale and stark by day, but the clocks at the top of the tower were the same as they had been during our evening walks: one of the few mechanisms in the Dark city operated by Light magic, the first tower built when Light magic came. The hands on the clocks had burned gold with magic, cutting the night up into shimmering seconds.

There was a guard at the door, wearing a band of black and scarlet on each arm.

This had been the stronghold of the Light Council's men in the Dark city, and now the Dark had reclaimed it.

I stood on the dirty corner of the street and remembered what my aunt used to warn me about. She'd said that if you lingered on the corner too long, the Light guards at the top of the tower could see you.

Where else would they keep their prized prisoner, the one they wanted to show off as an example, but at the highest, most conspicuous point of their new fortress?

The guard at the door was young, I thought. The rebels at the hotel and around the cages in Times Square had been older, but of course they sent their most experienced and embittered to do murder. This was a prisoner being kept for display, to show the power of the *sans-merci*. Nobody in the Light or the Dark city would want to help a Stryker. The *sans-merci* did not think anybody was coming for Ethan.

I stood on the street corner and stared up at the glass face of a clock, at the lucent hands making their inexorable progress around it. Somewhere behind the gray stone and golden light was Ethan. I squinted until my eyes stung, looking up at the top of the tower, and from high above I thought I saw a pale face looking down.

I wanted so much to believe that he could see me, that he would see a fair head and know that it was me, that I understood everything now, that I had more faith in him than I ever had before and I loved him as much as I ever had. I stood there with my fists clenched and my eyes straining to see the impossible, and I tried to believe.

I had lied and pretended and hated myself for doing it all, thinking it would buy me and the ones I loved safety. I had been a fool.

There were people on the street, and they shot me looks as they walked by. I had a brief moment of panic, thinking that they recognized me, but then I slowly registered the hot slide of tears on my face, the way my eyes and my chest were aching.

They were looking at me because I was making a scene.

I didn't even care. At least, at last, I was making a scene for myself and no one else. I did not care if they saw, and I did not care what they thought.

I was not going to be strong for anyone any longer.

Not even for Ethan. I had tried too hard to be strong for him when he had asked me to be honest with him instead, when he had offered to be honest with me. I called up that moment again in my mind, how unhappy I had been and he had been, how afraid I had been of incriminating myself and damaging what was between us, when I could have told him all the truth and had him tell me all the truth. I knew everything now, and I thought I could love him better with truth between us.

Whatever dark deeds had been done and dark secrets had been kept when we were children, whatever darkness ran in my blood or his, seemed distant compared with the memory of how he had listened to whatever I let fall, had offered to help me with no thought of return, and all the time had been doing what he thought was right for himself and for our two cities, as well as for me.

Aunt Leila thought that with my mother's name spoken and her death avenged, justice would be done. But this was not justice, what was being done to Ethan, any more than what had been done to me was.

I could not stop crying at the thought that he might be seeing me right now and I could not see him, that he might never know I was there at all. Both thoughts seemed unbearable, and I would not bear them, would not bear any of this, for a moment longer.

He had known me and loved me and chosen me, out of all others, and I had been so scared he would change his mind that I had not told him I chose and knew him back. I'd learned my lesson. I'd learned to know Ethan better while he was gone than I had ever allowed myself to know him before. I'd had what few people could ever have—the chance to experience how life would be with someone else in the place of the one I loved, someone who came with all the same luxuries, offered the same place in the world, even wore the same face. Carwyn had never been kind like Ethan, never touched me like Ethan had—gently, considerately, and with willingness to let me go if that was what I wanted. That was why I never wanted anyone else but Ethan to touch me, and for him never to stop.

I had thought we would have so much longer together. I had thought that if I behaved a certain way, I could coax a guarantee from the world.

But there were no guarantees, and I might never see Ethan again—his drowning-deep dark eyes, the lines of his face that bore a resemblance to every one of his family and only ended up marking how very different he was from them all, the way his locks curled lightly against his collar as though even his very hair wished to touch the world kindly. That I had seen Carwyn every day for weeks made it hurt more, like seeing a house that reminded me of home and left me feeling more homesick and far away from any comfort.

I put my hand to my face to muffle the sobs, but I let the messy choking sounds come. I let my tears fall until my face felt like a stiff mask, twisted with grief. The patina of dried tears made me feel as if I could not change expression or my face would crack. My eyes were so puffy, I could barely see. And I found a strange glory in my stupid, useless, wildly unrestrained misery. I did not have to be restrained anymore. I cried and cried, cried for my mother, for the loss of her and how I had denied it, for all my love and all my guilt, for my father and the child I used to be, and for Ethan. I even cried for my aunt and for Jim and Charles and Mark Stryker. I cried for everyone I had not been able to save, and cried as I had never allowed myself to cry.

Ethan had only ever wanted to love me. He had never asked me to be strong all the time.

I stared up at the pale glimmer that might be his face, high up in the tower window. I concentrated on directing my thoughts to him, on lifting my whole soul up to him, as if I could pluck it like a bird from a cage and send it flying to his hands.

A group of people had gathered, I realized. Others were still walking by, sliding glances of mingled discomfort and fascination at me, as if I were a traffic accident. But the group watching me was quiet. I had broken down in an ugly mess, no artifice and no dignity left, and people I did not know were still watching me with sympathy. Not everyone had turned away. Not every heart had to be won by trickery.

"Are you all right?" a stranger asked me.

It was such a relief to say, "No."

I stood there until I realized I would have to return to my father. I stepped up to the blank gray face of the tower, rested my hot cheek for a moment against cool stone, and kissed the wall.

I turned and began to walk down the street, away from the glowing clock and into the deepening evening. As I did, someone fell into step with me, and I saw without much surprise that it was Carwyn. I was too limp and wrung out to feel much of anything. I supposed he had followed me there and watched it all.

He was not collared and hooded yet. His dark head was still bare, and his well-known face was exposed to public view. The evening was storing up shadows, piling up the layers of darkness in the sky. It was hard to make out anyone's features unless you were really looking, and nobody was looking for Ethan. They knew where he was.

"Did you fake the crying for effect?" Carwyn asked. His voice was neutral, and that, rather than any show of praise or horror, was what made me answer.

"It was real," I said slowly. "And it was for effect."

Carwyn only looked accepting. I thought that might have been why I had been drawn to him at the start: that he was from the Dark city, and I'd thought he might be more like me than Ethan or Nadiya or any of the innocent people I knew. More than that, because he was a doppelganger, he surely would not judge me even if he knew all I had done.

In the end, though, I didn't need him to approve of me or

understand me. I was done feeling bad about the choices I had made to survive.

"So here you are back in the Dark city," I said.

Carwyn inclined his head. "Here we are, back in the Dark city. You going home to your dad?"

"Yeah," I said. "Do you want to come with me?"

"I doubt they want a doppelganger under their roof."

"I'm sure they would let you stay. I'm sure I could persuade them, if they had a problem with it."

He looked down at me sharply, as if I had said something remarkable. Then he lifted a hand and touched it to my face. It was a brief brush of his skin on mine; I did not even have time to startle back before he drew his hand away, his fingertips wet with my tears. I saw then that he was looking at me with both affection and concern, with tenderness I had never dreamed I'd see him show. I remembered, with something like a shock, that he thought he loved me.

"You've done enough," Carwyn said. "Now there's something I have to do. Good luck with your part, Lucie."

There was an expression on his face I did not understand. "Good luck with whatever you're trying to do."

"Thank you," said Carwyn, still with that strange look about him. "I hope I succeed."

I reached out and touched his hand before we parted. All my enemies were transforming into something else, it seemed, passing beyond reach of hate. There were no people left to be fought: there were only people left I had to fight for.

I went back to the clock tower every day and stood there all day. Every day a larger and larger crowd came to look at me weep.

Every day, people took pictures of me. Every day, the same old newspapers under the new regime discussed whether the Golden Thread in the Dark was grateful enough for being liberated, whether I was a weak traitor to the cause, whether Ethan Stryker was different from the other Strykers, whether he had truly worked with the *sans-merci* and whether that mattered. There was no consensus on me. I didn't want one. I hadn't counted on a sympathetic response. I just wanted everyone talking about me. I wanted everyone watching.

I watched them in their turn: I memorized the number of guards, the length of their shifts, when they came to the tower and when they went away, how each of them acted around me.

On the last day of Ethan's imprisonment, his day of execution, I went to my hiding place in the wall. I slid out the brick, and among the gray ashes I saw the pure, true light of my mother's diamond. I drew out the necklace, and the sunshine caught the jewel. Sparks were tossed in the air, like confetti made of dancing points of light. The room was suddenly bright, and as I held the diamond, light lanced through its sparkling facets, rose and gold like a fire waking between my palms. I hung the chain around my neck.

When I left the apartment, I took my sword with me.

CHAPTER TWENTY-ONE

I T HAD BEEN A LONG, BAD TIME, BUT I HAD SLEPT every night when I went home and not lain awake worrying about what I was doing or what I had become. The *sans-merci* had called in every one of us—me, Dad, Penelope, Jarvis, even little Marie—for questioning at the hotel, more than once, but they had let every one of us go. Sometimes, though, Penelope or Jarvis came back bleeding.

Marie woke up screaming every night, knowing the monsters were coming, and we could not tell her they were not.

They had not let Ethan go. They never would. And more and more victims for the cages were being brought in a grotesque parade through the shining streets of the Light city every day: the rich, those from the Light Council's families, prominent Light magicians and public figures, but also people the *sans-merci* disliked and who could conveniently be accused of collaborating with the Light. A lot of people were being killed. Nobody seemed to have any more to eat in this just new world.

I wore a long, dark coat to hide the sword as I made my

way from the Light city to the Dark. The coat's severe lines and metal buttons made me look like a soldier, and my long, loose, fair hair made me look like a fairy-tale damsel. If people found that incongruous, if they did not know what to make of me, I had not known what to make of myself for a long time either. They could learn.

I was wearing my mother's necklace outside my coat. It was the first time I had ever seen the jewel in the open light of day.

It was morning, and the air was crisp and golden as a fresh apple. The clock tower was a stark line bisecting the lucent sky: a tower with a hero in it, and perhaps I could be like Ethan now that I finally understood him. Perhaps I could be a hero too. Perhaps I could save him—save someone my way, and no one else's. I felt as clean and purposeful as the blade I drew as I walked toward the door and the guard standing by it.

He was thin and tall, and his hair stood up in clumps. I had noticed him before, the worried one who would be easy to intimidate. He always took the morning shifts, when there were fewer people.

But quite a few people were already here. They came to watch me.

They could watch this.

"Out of my way," I said, and brought my sword around in a slow, gleaming arc. "Get help. You're going to need it."

He stood there for a moment as if he had been slapped, took a step toward me, and watched the crowd surge restlessly in his direction.

He took a step back. He obviously did not want to be responsible for killing the symbol of the *sans-merci*. He called out, and three guards from inside the tower came streaming out the door to his side, just as I had hoped. I moved in front of the door so they could not get inside the tower again.

"I am Lucie Manette," I said. "I am the Golden Thread in the Dark. I am the only child of a murdered mother, and I will not let anyone be taken from me again. I am going to stand at this door with a sword all day, and I will fight anyone who tries to take Ethan Stryker away to the cages. That means you can do one of two things. Go convene the Committee of the Free and bring him a pardon, or come and kill me."

The guards called in reinforcements. With every extra soldier, the mob increased by ten or twenty people. One of the *sans-merci* drew a weapon, and then glanced toward a light —not the light of my rings or my sword, but the light of someone's camera.

Everyone in the crowd knew that a picture or a video of me being murdered by someone wearing the colors of the city's liberators would be seen by every soul in both cities within a day.

I lit my sword with fire and struck down the guard's weapon, and nobody else drew one. I let myself breathe.

I looked up at the tower, at the shining glass and gold. I wondered if Ethan could see me. I had never hoped more that he could.

The mob grew and grew, greedy for a spectacle. I knew how easy it would be for the mob or the rebels to get out of hand, for someone to decide that eliminating me would solve more problems than it caused. I knew that I did not have long before Aunt Leila came.

I was not expecting who came first.

I saw her coming from far away, the saffron yellow of today's hijab like a small sun, and her eyes sparkling beneath it. I expected her to stay a discreet distance away, but she kept moving closer. I thought she had come to watch, but she had come to speak.

Others made the same mistake I did, and they let her push to the front of the crowd. She did not stop there. She only stopped when she was standing beside me with her feet planted and her chin up.

"I am Nadiya Zamani," said Nadiya. "The Golden Thread in the Dark is my friend. And Ethan Stryker was my comrade in arms. We were the ones who passed out pamphlets against the rule of Light in the Village, who discovered where the Esmond girl was being kept, who helped the Robesons get to the Light city when the guards were after them. Ethan Stryker is our ally."

She glanced at me, her eyes glinting in the afternoon sun, and she grinned. I saw brown-brick buildings in the distance, saw the glitter of sunshine on the tin warehouse roofs, but mostly what I saw was a sea of people, and the tide turning our way.

Nadiya knew how to work the crowd as well as I ever had. She made it sound as if we had been a pair, me and Ethan, comrades in arms as well as lovers, fighting for fraternity, liberty, and equality.

It made for a beautiful love story, the idea of us working together smoothly, instead of all the jagged misunderstandings that made up the truth of our lives.

Approving murmurs rippled through the crowd, like we were being surrounded by a sea turning calm.

A voice burst out. "Is that how it was?"

I could not finesse them the way Nadiya did or command them the way Aunt Leila did. I had tried that. I was trying something else now.

I took a deep breath and decided to be brave and stupid. I said, "No."

And around me the sounds of a storm rose.

"She's lying to spare Stryker."

"They're all liars, and worse."

They wanted it to have been as clear-cut as heroism, or as straightforward as villainy. Anyone who said that it was not simple branded themselves a villain, guilty of not telling people what they wanted to hear.

"No, but it isn't what you think," I shouted. "He's not what you think. *Listen.*"

"Why don't you shut up instead?" a man's voice asked.

"Don't tell the Golden Thread in the Dark to shut up!"

A woman snapped, her voice as sweetly sympathetic as a blade, "You should be ashamed of yourself!"

"Make way," called a voice in the teeming, jostling crowd, over the shouts of reprimand and support, "for the hero of Green-Wood, for the man escaped from the cages!"

I caught my breath as I saw the stooped shoulders and silver head I loved. I had forgotten that when my Aunt Leila made me a hero and a symbol of revolution the day Mark Stryker had died, I had not been the only one up there on that stage.

"There, girl," said the nervous-looking guard, "maybe you'll listen to your father."

I'd had enough staying quiet at the Light Council and quiet on the platform with Aunt Leila's hand on my wrist. The only thing I had ever truly regretted was submitting.

"Why should I?" I said.

"There's no reason in the world for you to listen to me," said Dad in his soft voice. "It's my turn to listen to you."

The guard looked at Dad the same way he had looked at

me, shocked and angry, as if Dad was a child the guard had expected obedience from. "You ungrateful creature of the Light," he said under his breath.

"I'm very grateful," Dad told him. "I'm grateful to Lucie."

He stepped toward me and then behind me, his hands on my waist, anchoring me, making himself another target but not making himself so vulnerable that I would have to worry about him. His whisper stirred my hair.

"Take courage."

"Already got it," I said, and heard my father laugh behind me.

"Yes, you do. I'm so sorry, Lucie."

"What for?"

"I'm so sorry for all my bad days," he said. "I'm so sorry I couldn't be stronger for you, that I didn't see when you were hurting. I didn't see a way to do it, I couldn't think of how to make it work—to make our family work without her." His eyes dropped to the diamond shining around my neck, and I felt his fingers tremble. "I knew how much I owed you," he said. "I tried to tell you that, and I'm sorry if I made it another burden for you."

"It doesn't matter," I said.

"I'm sorry," he said, even softer, "that I am a burden to you."

I bit my tongue before I could tell him that he was not a

burden, and said instead, blood in my mouth and truth on my lips, "It doesn't matter. I was always so glad you were there. I was so glad I saved you."

I had always been glad, and always thought he was worth everything I had done for him.

I had tried not to blame him when his pain had kept him from being there for me. All the resentment I had hidden and could not help did not seem to matter now, when I could feel his warmth at my back and I knew that he loved me. My pain must have stopped me being there for him sometimes too.

It did not mean that pain did not matter. But there was something besides pain between us.

I would not have done anything differently, so perhaps it was time to stop regretting what I had done.

"I can stand with you now," said my father. "I can do that."

The pain of it all had seemed such a waste, once. Now it seemed like the sharp fire that had forged me into a weapon, into a sword, into a battering ram that could break through the prison door.

"We can stand together," I said.

I had spent so long trying to be something I was not. I knew I was something quite different from what I had been: innocent, unformed, terrified, the girl who was lovingly overprotected by both her parents and who wanted to be just like her aunt.

I was not like those polar opposites who had somehow circled around to the same savage place, Aunt Leila and Mark Stryker. I was not like Ethan, always trying to be good, or Carwyn, who believed he was bad. I did not feel as though I would ever have any of their conviction in the rightness or wrongness of their actions. All I knew was who I loved and what I wanted. I did not feel good or bad, and I did not feel guilty anymore. I felt strong enough to do what needed to be done.

I felt that sometime while I was trying to shield others and trying to shield myself, I had become all that I ever needed to be.

The *sans-merci* guards looked dumbfounded that my father had not stopped me. I saw their hands go to their weapons again, heard the crowd hum, torn between approval and condemnation.

None of the guards dared to strike me down. But then my Aunt Leila arrived to deal with the Golden Thread in the Dark, shoving through the crowd with her hair flying like a preemptive flag of mourning, and I knew she would dare to do anything. She came striding toward me, and I saw her draw a long knife from her belt, its blade edged with wavering Dark magic.

My rings sizzled and shone with power. Our blades leaped to meet each other.

"Why are you doing this?" Aunt Leila hissed.

"Why don't you even recognize me?" I hissed back. "You think I'm a child or a doll and you are unstoppable? I'm a force of nature too. You thought you were teaching me something else, to be something lesser. Try teaching fire to do anything but burn. It's time for you to learn better."

The crowd could not hear us, but I could hear it, drawing in closer as people strained to hear what we were saying. The sound of their muttering was like a storm building, far off out to sea but coming closer.

For the first time, I saw fear on Aunt Leila's face. She knew the mob was a beast, and it might turn and go for her throat as easily as anyone else's.

"Let Ethan Stryker go," I continued, "or cut down the Golden Thread in the Dark in front of everybody. You said you came to the city on a mission to free me. Go ahead—kill me. Show everybody you were lying."

None of us were safe. But Aunt Leila had taught me how to appear in front of the media and the crowds. I had to believe that she cared more about how things looked than I did.

"What will it take for you to stop this mad defiance?" she snapped.

I held Aunt Leila's gaze. "Oh, tell the wind and fire where to stop," I said softly. "But don't tell me."

"Go to your committee," said Dad. "Grant him a pardon or cut us both down."

As Dad spoke, I could feel him shaking at my back, feel the scrape of his rings against my skin. I had to take him home and make sure he rested. I could not let him break down in front of all these people.

I held my breath, and held my sword locked with Aunt Leila's blade, and I waited.

"We will delay our procession of revenge until tomorrow!" Aunt Leila called out to the crowd.

"And Ethan won't be in it," I said in a low voice.

"Very well," Aunt Leila said at last, in a voice as low as mine. "You'll have your pardon."

"By tomorrow morning, before the executions," I said. "I'll have his pardon by tomorrow morning. I have your word?"

"By tomorrow morning," Aunt Leila spat, spinning on her heel and turning her back on me. "You have my word, and my curse."

I could trust her word. Aunt Leila and the committee would never make anything less than a public spectacle of Ethan's death. They wouldn't kill him in the dead of night, in any secret hole or hidden corner. My wrists ached: I had been holding my sword for too long. But my mother's diamond was shining.

I let myself look up and search for Ethan's face in the distant window.

I could go home and rest for a moment after a day of standing and fighting. I could put the sword down. I had saved him.

Nobody was home. I hoped blurrily, barely able to think through my exhaustion, that they had not been called back to the hotel for even more questioning.

"Do I need to heal anyone?" Dad asked as I helped him into his room and got him lying down.

Even the confused query made me feel better. He had never implied before that there was a possibility nobody needed healing, that there was a chance we could be all right.

"Nobody needs healing tonight," I whispered, and I smoothed his pillow like a nurse, but he caught my hand and pressed it as if I was his child.

I staggered out once I was sure he was sleeping. I did not look out the window to see if the city was burning or if Carwyn was outside, watching. I sat down on the sofa and thought that I would stay there for a little while, just until the others came home, so that I knew they were safe.

Sleep hit me like a grandmother's purse that turned out to have a brick in it. I was out almost as soon as I sat down, and I slept heavily, determinedly, until the door opening pulled me up like a puppet and yanked me back into awareness. There had been too many disasters in too short a time: no sooner were my eyes open than I found myself shaking and sick with tension, as if I was held together with a wire pulled so taut that I could do nothing but shake and hope the wire would not snap.

It was not Penelope, Jarvis, or little Marie. I stared at the hooded figure in the shadows of the doorway. The hood and the shadows did their work—I could not see anything below the hood but a blank to be filled in by fear or hope. He did not move for a moment, and then he did. He took one step forward. I saw the line of his nose and the gleam of his eyes.

I flew into his arms and covered his face with kisses.

"Ethan, Ethan," I said, pushing back the hood and pushing my fingers through his hair.

I had not doubted for a moment that it was him. I knew the diffident way he moved, never presuming he was welcome. The only thing I did not know was how this had happened.

"Ethan," I said. "I'm so happy. I'm so sorry."

His face, uncovered now, was flushed, his eyes slightly dilated. He put a hand on my rib cage as if he had to steady himself, but then his hand moved down, slowly and with more confidence, until he had a sure hold on my waist.

"*I'm* sorry. I lied to you, I got my father killed, I did everything wrong. I'm the one who's sorry. You have nothing to be sorry for," he whispered, and his voice sounded as rusty as a prison door that had not been opened in a long, long time.

I clung to his shirt and kissed him again, pressing our foreheads together as much as our mouths. I wanted to be pressed up against him, anchored by him, sure of him.

"There is," I said, and tasted tears on my lips, on his lips as I kissed him, and realized we were both crying. "I know everything now, Nadiya told me about the resistance. Carwyn told me about you going to find Jarvis. You meant it all for the best. You meant to save people. You're a hero."

"Well," said Ethan, "that makes two of us."

I smiled so hard that I thought my face would crack.

"I saw you down there, with your sword barring the way," Ethan told me. "You looked like . . ." *An angel,* I thought. "Like a knight."

I kissed him for that.

"I'm not a hero," said Ethan. "I couldn't let everything stay the way it was, I couldn't let my family keep doing what they were doing. But this is no better. I ruined everything. My father and Jim and so many other people are dead, and it was all for nothing."

"You wanted to help. You tried. I didn't try."

"You did better than try," Ethan said. "You did it. You accomplished something."

"So did you," I said. "You saved Jarvis. You saved some-one—you did what you did because you believed in change and goodness, and you inspired me."

You were the light that showed me the way, I wanted to say, but I hadn't wanted other people to see me that way. He was more than my light.

He'd lied to me, he said, and it was true. He'd done worse than that. He had sent in Carwyn as a replacement for himself and clearly had not realized that if Carwyn had fooled me, every touch I accepted from Carwyn would have been a violation of trust. He'd risked his life for me but had not considered what it would have done to me if he had died. He'd lied to me but meant it for the best.

I'd lied to him, too, and he knew it. We had each thought that we could replace ourselves with perfect facsimiles and fool the other. We had both been wrong. I was glad to be wrong.

I saw how hard he had tried, and it was so easy to forgive him that it felt possible to forgive myself.

"How are you here?" I asked him. "How did it happen?"

"They were letting in people from the Dark city to mock and spit at me. Carwyn came to visit me. He was wearing a doppelganger's hood, but it wasn't fastened by a Light magician. He could take it off. He took it off, once we were alone. I thought he was there to laugh at me. I thought . . . Everything I thought about him was wrong."

Ethan swallowed.

"He . . . he must have just fed from a Light magician, maybe someone he took against their will—"

"No," I said. "He's not like that. It was me."

Ethan looked puzzled to hear me come to Carwyn's defense and, at the same time, sorry that he had insulted Carwyn.

"I didn't know. Carwyn must have used Dark magic to confuse my mind. He came in, and I started to feel dizzy and strange. I could barely keep standing. He put the hood on me, and he whispered 'I remember her' and everything went black. I don't remember anything else. I don't even know who he meant."

I remembered what Aunt Leila had said, about Carwyn being confused when he was sick and mistaking my mother for someone else. "I think he meant your mother."

"Our mother?" asked Ethan, instinctively kind.

I smiled at him. "Yeah."

"Did you two—did you plan this together?" Ethan sounded helpless.

I could never have planned this. It would never have occurred to me that Carwyn would ever do something like this.

"No," I said again. "It was all him."

Ethan shook his head, sounding even more helpless. "I came to in the street wearing this hood," said Ethan. "I didn't go back to him. I came to you."

"Let's take it off now," I whispered.

I put my hand on the collar. I felt the dip and bob of his

throat beneath my ringed fingers, just before Ethan was about to speak.

The door was open. We both heard the steps on the floor of the hall outside. Ethan reached for me but let his hand drop when I shook my head. I went for the kitchen counter, where I had left the sword.

It was my Aunt Leila. She had a furled paper in her hand that must have been the pardon. I did not dare even glance toward Ethan. I looked at the paper and her face, the severe black and white lines of both. Only the paper promised mercy.

I tensed again, my hand touching the edge of the counter but not the sword yet. But I saw Aunt Leila had tensed too. She had not expected anyone else to be there.

She looked at Ethan, and her eyes narrowed. She had seen Carwyn at the hotel, had seen he was not collared, and I did not want her thinking about why the same boy might be collared now. I could not speak. I could not risk her suspecting. I did not know what to do.

"Send him away," Leila said at last. "Lucie, we need to talk. You need to listen to me."

"That's not what 'We need to talk' should mean."

"Look what you accomplished at the clock tower," Leila said. "Think of how much you could do if you joined our cause properly. You have so much power as a symbol."

"It's unlucky that I'm a person too, isn't it?"

Aunt Leila looked at me. There was so much distance in her gaze: the wall between us could not be broken down, no bridge could be crossed. "It would be a mistake for you to think you have enough power to stand against me. You may be the Golden Thread in the Dark, you may be my niece, but you are not more important than our justice. Every time you stand against me, you will be punished. There is no victory you can win that I cannot take away."

"What do you mean by that?" I demanded. "What have you done?"

None of us were expecting it when Penelope hurtled through the open door and straight into Aunt Leila. I barely saw her as she went by, blood gleaming in the tight black curls of her hair, her expression set with fury. She went for Aunt Leila as if there was nobody in the room but her target. She went flying with her against the wall, into a window, and then Penelope smashed Aunt Leila's head against the glass. More blood spilled then, but it was not Penelope's, and they slid onto the floor in a tangled, bloody heap, the thud of their bodies on the wood like a clod of earth hitting a coffin. Penelope looked up at me.

She had obviously been taken in by the *sans-merci* again. I had a thousand questions, but they all died in the fire of her gaze.

She snatched the pardon from Aunt Leila's clenched fingers and threw it toward me. The roll of paper tumbled across the floor, and I stooped down, but Ethan got there before me. He knelt down and offered the pardon up, pressing it into my hand.

"Lucie!" Penelope shouted. "Lucie, you have to go now! Get to the cages! Lucie, run!"

I did not ask why, or what was happening. I did not ask what had been done to her, or if Aunt Leila was still breathing.

I ran.

CHAPTER TWENTY-TWO

F ROM THE ACCOUNT OF MARIE LORRY:
*They put us in one of the skinny black cars that
important people drive in, and drove us around the city. I
saw Ethan's dad in one once, waving, and everyone watched him
and cheered. I thought he seemed to bring a holiday with him.*

*But it was different when it was me. The car wasn't as nice as it
had looked from the outside. It was ripped up inside. There were no
seats, and they put all six of us in standing up. It was like we were
bringing a funeral with us.*

*At first I didn't notice the people watching, because when they
put us in the car I saw Ethan. He was standing up in the car,
between two people I did not know. All of them had their arms
draped with chains, fastened to the floor of the car. They had only
put one restraint on me, and I could move better than any of the
others.*

"Ethan!" I called out.

*I was going to tell him that they had taken me away from Mom
and Dad, that Lucie's aunt had called me her little contingency plan*

and sent me here. I didn't know what was happening, and I wanted to go home. I was going to ask him for help. But I remembered that Mom and Dad had said Ethan was in trouble, and I figured that he would not be able to send me home. I thought he might want to go home as well and he couldn't.

So I didn't ask him anything, but I edged closer to him. Ethan was always nice to me. The nicest boy I'd ever met, nicer than any of the boys my age, and I always thought I'd like to marry him if he wasn't going to marry Lucie. I always thought Lucie was lucky.

I thought that if I could be with Ethan, I would feel better, and I would not be so scared.

I pushed past the other people. I didn't say excuse me. "Ethan," I said again.

He stared at me and said in a weird voice, "What are you doing here?"

"The lady," I said, "Lucie's aunt, she said we were going to be sent to . . . to the cages, to be cleansed and to give power to a beautiful future. My mom and dad always said that things couldn't go on with the Dark city the way they were, and that . . . that a change was coming. They said it would be good."

If it was a good thing, I should want to do it. I shouldn't feel so bad.

"A brave new world," he said, and there was something funny about his voice, like he wanted to make a mean joke. He didn't *sound at all like Ethan. But then he said, "Maybe it will be, one day. But I'll never see it."*

I reached out shyly and touched his hand, and he jumped, like people didn't ever try to take his hand. Ethan held my hand all the time when we went out and had to cross streets.

It was then that I understood. He was the other one. I forgot what Mom had called him. She'd said he wasn't nice.

But he looked nice. He looked like Ethan. It's funny, but he looked more like Ethan in the car than he had at home. It seemed to me that he was trying to look like Ethan really hard, and it seemed to me that maybe he was doing it because Ethan was in trouble and the other boy wanted to make sure Ethan wouldn't be in trouble anymore. Even if he had to be in trouble instead. I thought that was really nice of him. I hate being in trouble.

He could tell that I knew, right away. There was something careful about him, like he was doing a chore, cleaning something maybe, and he was watching out because he didn't want to miss a spot.

"Hush," he whispered to me. "Please, it's a secret."

I nodded so hard, my head hurt.

"I get it," I said. "You're brave. Will you let me hold your hand? Only, I'm scared."

Don't tell my mom I said that. Don't tell her, but I cried.

"Yes," he said, quite loudly, and he didn't sound like Ethan

again. He sounded mad, but what he said was nice. "I'll hold your hand until the very end."

The car was getting pretty close to the big square with the new things in it, like birdcages but huge and horrible somehow. They were like the stuff you see with your eyes closed, when it's night and you don't want to open your eyes in case you are all alone and everything you're scared of is real.

It was daytime, and there were so many people around me. All the people didn't make me feel better, though. They were watching us, and their eyes went right through me, like the points of scissors into paper.

I held on to his hand pretty tight, I guess. He looked down at me, and he tried to kneel down beside me. He couldn't quite do it, because of the chains.

"Don't look at the cages," he said. "Don't look at them. Can you just look at me? Look at me, and don't look at anything else."

I looked at him. He looked like Ethan does, but he was thinner. He looked like Ethan would if Ethan had been sick, and people had been . . . had been not very kind to him. He had a sad mouth, but his eyes didn't seem sad. His eyes looked afraid of me, as if I was an exam and he thought he was going to fail me. I looked at him, and maybe it was a silly thing to think, but I thought I liked him just as much as Ethan.

"Yeah," I said. "I can do that."

I don't know how it was exactly, if I hugged him or he hugged me, but he was suddenly holding on to me. I put my head down on his shoulder and he put his arms around me, as much as he could when we were fastened to opposite sides of the car. I held on to his shirt as hard as I could. I was crying a lot by then, and I got his shirt all wet. I don't think he minded, though. He held me, and I felt a little bit of wet on my neck. He was crying too, even though he was pretty big. Even though he was almost grown up.

"Thank you," I said. "I'm sorry. I'm sorry. I'm trying not to be scared. I won't be scared. Just don't let me go."

"Hush, hush," he said. I think he tried to stroke my hair, but he couldn't properly because of the chains. "Don't be scared. I promise, I won't let you go."

"Mom says I shouldn't ever be scared," I whispered. "She says help will always come to me if I believe it will. Were you sent to me?"

The next thing he said was a funny thing for him to say. He was so much bigger than me, and he didn't seem scared, even though he had cried.

He said, "Maybe you were sent to me."

I ran faster than I had ever run in my life. The wind rushed after me, the clouds rushed after me, the sun seemed to fling its rays out like a net, the whole fierce morning seemed to be pursuing me so it could swallow me whole, but nobody else chased me. Nobody stopped my wild dash to Times Square.

Once there, I had to fight my way through a thick crowd. Nobody was expecting me; nobody stood aside for the Golden Thread in the Dark. I elbowed and shouted and struggled like a swimmer caught in a current, until I finally burst free and into the empty space where the car was only now drawing to a halt.

The cages were suspended so high above the crowd that they seemed like blots on the sun. The platform was empty save for one man in black and scarlet. He looked hesitant. He looked as if he might be waiting for my aunt's arrival, but the crowd's anticipation was pulsing, the very air expanding and contracting around their desire to see savage justice. He would not wait long.

"Stop!" I shouted, and held the paper up high. "I have a pardon. Stop."

People looked at me then: people recognized me, saw my sleep-rumpled dress and my hair snarled around my shoulders. I did not care. I did not even look at the member of the *sans-merci* who strode toward me and examined the paper in my hand.

I was looking for Carwyn.

They had put the prisoners in one of those open limousines that politicians were driven in so they could wave to the crowd, but its soft leather seats were torn out, the whole car gutted, and those being sent to the cages were chained to the metal bars that remained, bars and chains both glistening with inky streams of Dark magic so nobody could escape.

I did not see him at first, because he was bowed over in his chains. Then I did.

Then I knew why Penelope had come for me, why she had gone after Aunt Leila and sent me running down here. I understood Aunt Leila's plan. She had set everything up so that even if I arrived in time, I could not save him.

She had known I would have to save someone else instead.

Marie was the girl I had been, whom nobody had come to rescue. Marie was so young and had so many people who loved her.

There was no choice. There would not have been a choice, even if it was Ethan.

Carwyn was leaning over Marie, his dark head bent over her black hair. He was talking to her, not looking at the crowd, and he did not even seem to hear their sharp utterances of "Stryker" as if it was a curse. Of course, it was not his name.

I pulled the pardon out of the guard's hand and walked toward the car. My shadow was stretching eagerly out in front of me when he looked up.

The most vivid memory I have of that day, the moment that broke my heart, is how his face changed when he saw me.

"You're here," he said, and smiled. My stomach sank, and

I was suddenly sick with horror at the thought of what I was going to do. He said eagerly, "I'm so glad you're here."

I was about to speak, but then realized I could not. My lips shaped his real name, silently.

"Quick," Carwyn continued. "Take her."

That was what truly broke my heart. He saw that there was no choice, and no chance for him, and he still smiled.

If I had not known better, I thought even I might have been convinced that this was Ethan. He looked more like Ethan than he ever had before. He was taking it seriously now. The masquerade meant something to him.

"You heard him," I snapped at the guard. "Set her free now."

Marie was secured by only one cuff, not chained like Carwyn. It was easy to release her, and in one movement Carwyn picked her up and leaned out of the car, placing her in my arms.

Marie clung to him. "You said you wouldn't let go."

"Not until the end," he said. "But it's the end now. It's all over. You're safe now."

He had to pull away from her, and then she was in my arms, a heavy but welcome weight. She was crying.

"I've got you," I told Marie. And I told Carwyn, "I'm sorry."

"It's all right. I have never done a really good thing

before," he said, and the wry quirk to his mouth was all him for a moment, any trace of Ethan disappearing. "I'm told we should try new experiences."

I thought, for a brief panicked moment, of telling everyone the truth. But Aunt Leila had almost sent a child to the cages and nobody had protested. The truth would only have condemned Ethan and me as well as Carwyn, would have ruined everything Carwyn was doing and thrown it back in his face.

What Carwyn was doing. It made me feel again the way I had on the balcony, hearing the truth about Ethan, the way I had at the foot of Ethan's tower. I'd had it all wrong once again, but now I saw.

I'd thought I was marked forever because I'd lied, but Ethan had lied, and Carwyn was lying now. We were all doing the best we could.

We were all heroes if we chose to be. The rich, naïve boy who had tried. The girl who had lied. The boy made out of darkness making himself into something else. There was no sin that could not be wiped away, nobody who was only what other people thought them. I hadn't understood until it was almost too late.

"May I?" asked Carwyn, and I nodded.

He had never asked before, but he was going to die, and it would make the pretense seem more real. It could comfort him and convince everyone in the crowd, but it was more than that: in that moment, I wanted to.

He leaned out of the car, and I turned up my face and kissed him. He kissed me. He was not trembling. Neither of us was.

"Don't cry," he told me. "It's worth it, to know I can. To know that I want to."

"You're worth crying for," I said.

He smiled at me, and I saw the traces of tears on his own cheeks. "Well," he said, "don't cry long."

I did not cry long, but I cried then, holding Marie, who was crying too. I cried as they led Carwyn and the other victims to their cages, cried for the wickedness, cried for the waste. I thought that Carwyn was dying for a cupcake, for a kind word, for so very little.

Then I saw him climb the steps to the platform with a sure, firm step, and I changed my mind.

The city is ours now, the *sans-merci* said when it was done.

I knew better than that. The city is no one's; the city is everyone's. The city could fall into ruin, and I would still have everything I need. We could go half the world away and build a city to be ours. The city is the dark and light halves of my heart.

Time seemed to move slowly as the crowd surged toward the platform and the sound of his steady steps echoed through the air. His head was thrown back, his hair in Ethan's usual wavy disarray, the early-morning sunlight making the almost-lost gold in it shine. His grip on the cage as he climbed in, without the guards to help him, was firm. This was an expression I had never seen on him. He looked bright and sweet and new to the world. He lifted his face up to the sky and his face was soft—soft and young and peaceful. He looked like no one but himself, like a self he had never been before.

Even as the dark cage contracted and he cried out, a ray of light struck one of the tall glass towers and the glass threw back the light even brighter than it had been before. The sunlight became a bright sword that pierced the bars of his cage.

When I saw it, I saw everything that I believed laid out in front of me like a shining map of the future. That the new destroyers would be destroyed as surely as the old ones had been. That a brilliant city, all the brighter for its shadows, would rise out of this abyss. That Ethan and I would spend our lives working toward that in both cities, not hiding anything from each other again, not pretending to be perfect anymore, just trying our best. I knew ·that one day we would be able to tell this story—Carwyn's story, Ethan's story, my story, the story of all we sacrificed and all we saved.

I felt I learned the value of every small, flawed thing we

do in the darkness, trying to scramble our way into the light. People will come up with a hundred thousand reasons why other people do not count as human, but that does not mean anyone has to listen.

Nobody can ever tell me any different.

I know he did have a soul.

AUTHOR'S NOTE

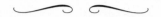

LUCIE, ETHAN, AND CARWYN'S STORY STARTED AS a riff on my favorite Charles Dickens novel, *A Tale of Two Cities,* and readers familiar with both books will recognize similarities and parallels.

But whereas *A Tale of Two Cities* is set during the French Revolution of 1789, my novel takes place in a New York that never was and never will be. I transformed a few of Dickens's characters, making a self-determined heroine out of Lucie and using the curious physical similarity between the two male leads to create a doppelganger and thus a world of magic and shadow selves. Fantasy is a tool for talking about the real world, and that is how I used it in *Tell the Wind and Fire*: as a torch held up to illuminate the divisions and misunderstandings between people, a way to give strange power to both my heroine and her enemies, and a device to underline how the heart can be torn between twin feelings of hope and fear.

Once Light and Dark magic were introduced, I had to ask myself what revolution looks like in a world with that kind of magic — perhaps scarily similar to revolution in the 1700s, or in 2016, because the shocking cruelty and astonishing grace in human beings stays the same.

I pulled at Dickens's themes and played with his characters and gradually turned them into my own. *Tell the Wind and Fire* stands as its own story, and you don't have to know anything about *A Tale of Two Cities* to enjoy it. But I hope that if you have enjoyed my book, you might find yourself drawn to read Charles Dickens's famous novel.

More than that, I hope this story of divided cities and divided human hearts inspires you to create something, to forgive yourself for something you blamed yourself for, or simply to whisper to yourself, like a secret the world will learn, that you have a great heart and can accomplish great things.

ACKNOWLEDGMENTS

THE VERY FIRST THANKS IN THESE ACKNOWLEDG-ments have to go to my editor, Anne Hoppe. From the very first day, when we were on the phone and I stared at the wicker bookcase in my frighteningly cold house in Ireland and tentatively said, "Maybe a retelling of . . . ?" and she said, "Tell me what that would look like to you." From before that, when she assured me she wanted another book from me, and showed me she wanted this book throughout, every step of the way. She believed in me when I did not believe in me, and believed in this book when I did not believe in this book. Thank you so much, Anne.

Everyone at Clarion, who have been so welcoming, and let me graffiti their walls and tell them all my strange marketing ideas. Thank you to Dinah Stevenson for the doppel-edit, Amy Carlisle, Alison Kerr Miller, the whole staff in marketing and publicity—including Lisa DiSarro, Ann Dye, Ruth Homberg, Meredith Wilson, and my publicist, Rachel Wasdyke—as well as my designer, Lisa Vega.

Thank you to Kristin Nelson and thank you to Ginger Clark.

Thank you to my copyeditor, Lara Stelmaszyk.

My writer friends know that I love them and their support is more valuable than oxygen, but here are some standouts: Holly Black, who sat with me and went, "No, really, explain this world to me, explain it now," and stopped me when I suggested that maybe shadow creatures ate Poughkeepsie. That was a real suggestion I actually put on the table for this book. Obviously, Holly Black is my savior and hero.

Robin Wasserman, who edited a whole other book of mine while I was desperate and editing this one and saved me so much time and had brilliant thoughts I would never have had. Robin Wasserman can do anything.

R. J. Anderson and Karen Healey and Kelly Link, who read the book at various stages and reassured me when I was badly in need of reassurance! Such sweets.

And to anyone out there who loved Sydney Carton at age eleven, because you're me, and I am you.